STARFISHERS

Other books by Glen Cook

STARFISHERS

THE STARFISHERS TRILOGY
VOLUME TWO

WITHDRAWN

GLEN COOK

NIGHT SHADE BOOKS
SAN FRANCISCO

Printed In Canada

First Edition

ISBN: 978-1-59780-168-3

Night Shade Books
Please visit us on the web at
http://www.nightshadebooks.com

This one is for Robin Scott Wilson, one-time spook and erstwhile comrade/teacher.

ONE: 3048 AD
Operation Dragon, Carson's

In that frenetic, quick-shift, go, drop-your-friends-possessions-roots-loyalties like throw-away containers age, heroes, legends, archetypal figures, and values as well, were disposable. They were as brilliant and ephemeral as the butterflies of Old Earth. One day someone on the marches of science might burst the pale and wrest from Nature a golden, universe-rocking secret. A bold naval officer might shatter the moment's enemy. Either could be a hero, a legend for a fleeting hour. And then he would become one with the dust of Sumer and Akkad.

Who remembered on the seventh day?

Who remembered Jupp von Drachau's raid in the Hell Stars? Mention his name. Blank stares would turn your way. Or someone would say, assuming memory, "He's too old," meaning too long gone. Von Drachau had been relegated to the historical toy box with the Caesars, Bonapartes, and Hitlers. Half a year, Confederation standard, had passed. The Now People had abandoned him. The yesterday people, the Archaicists, would not pick him up for a hundred years.

Luckily, benRabi thought, Jupp did not need the adulation.

The Now People, the down-planet people, who rode the screaming rockets of technological and social change, bought

1

their values plastic-packed, to be disposed when their usefulness was done. BenRabi found no satisfaction in that. He could hold on to nothing long enough to wear the rough edges off, to make it comfortable with time, like an old couch after years of use.

He thought those things as, toolcase in hand, he wandered toward the gate of Carson's Blake City spaceport. The name he wore felt a size too small, yet it could become a burden heavier than the cross the Christian god had borne.

He was going to hate this. He loathed pipes and plumbing.

He wore a union-prescribed commercial spacer Liquids Transfer Systems Technician's uniform. It consisted of tight, dull grey coveralls with green and yellow piping. His sleeves boasted three red hashmarks where Servicemen wore chevrons. They indicated that his union rated him a Master.

He did have the training, though his acquisition of it lay nearly forgotten amid that of countless exotic skills.

His teaching-couch days seemed part of another age. Still in his thirties, he felt the weight of a thousand years. Lifetimes worth of knowledge had been pressure-injected into his skull. And the education would never end.

The Bureau was his surrogate mother, father, and wife. It insisted he be ready for anything. Just in case.

The Bureau was a family without love. It left him with dissatisfactions that could easily grow into hatreds. The things they did to him…

They never justified. They never explained.

But lately he had been dissatisfied with everything. The image of the gun had become merciless. He had developed a crying socket of soul-need into which nothing seemed to fit.

And there were the aches and pains.

He *hurt*.

Within him he bore a second set of nerves. *They* had implanted a complete instel radio powered by bio-electricity. A small, dying pain surrounded a knot behind his left ear. That was the largest lump of the radio.

He had other pains. His ulcer. A little finger he had bruised playing handball. A hint of the headache that had been with him most of his life.

Each slow step drove spikes of agony up the bones of his legs. They had been lengthened six centimeters, hastily. His arm bones felt no better. The skin on his stomach itched where they had trimmed off twenty pounds.

His fingers, toes, and eyes itched too. His fingerprints, toeprints, and retinal patterns had been too quickly changed.

Carson's was as back of beyond a world as he had ever seen.

The damned ulcer… The fast-push to Carson's had reawakened it. It was a hurry-up job from the go.

But, then, they all were. How long had it been since he had had time to catch his breath, to relax, play with his collections, or just loaf around that house he owned, unshared, on the quiet government retirement planet called Refuge? Or to tinker with his literary opus, *All Who Were Before Me in Jerusalem*?

There was no time to loaf. Nor to plan operations in advance. In a rush of maddening changes, civilization seemed to be hurtling toward an apocalyptic crisis. Nothing was permanent. There were no fixed points on which to anchor.

Moyshe benRabi's life had become like the flash floods of Sierran rivers in Thaw Time, roaring and cascading past too swiftly, too liquidly, for any part to be seized and intimately known.

But wait! In the river of life apassing there *were* a few solid rocks. They were the long-lived legends lying heavy on his mind. Like the boulders in the turbulence, they had endured a forever compared to anything else of his age.

Something was missing: fixtures, solids, foundations for his life. There had to be something for him, something real… *I want*, he cried to the corners of his soul. And here came the image of the gun, that sprang to mind at the oddest time. Bow, howitzer, rifle, pistol, whatever, always unmanned, usually in profile and firing. What did it mean? A goal? Some sexual symbol? An expression of his sometime want for heroism? A sign of a secret urge to kill?

Memories returned, of the day he had entered Academy. He had been nervous and polished and proud to be part of Navy, proud to be one of the rare Old Earth appointees, and scared they would hold that against him. A bee of uncertainty had buzzed his butter soul even then. He had taken his oath with private reservations. He had devoted a quarter of his short life to winning the appointment, and success had left him with the feeling that something was missing. But Navy had seemed to promise what his *want* demanded.

The Academy years had not been bad. Hard work, hard play, not much time for introspection. But the first few months of line service had brought the hurt back stronger than ever. Casting about desperately, he had put in for intelligence training without understanding his own motivation. He had told his wardroom acquaintances that he wanted more adventure.

Even then his words had rung false. There was adventure enough in the line hunting Sangaree and McGraws.

All of which had come to a head in the now, with Moyshe benRabi, a flying knight, being sent to find a dragon hiding behind the eyes of the night.

Ahead, he spotted his small, brown, Oriental, Manchu-mustached partner, Mouse. Making no sign, he entered the gate behind the man.

He slowed momentarily, staring across the field. The lighter from the raggedy-assed Freehauler that had brought them in from Blackworld was still on the ground. It should have lifted last night. They had caught the Freehauler at the end of a fast-shuffle through a procession of ships designed to cover their backtrail.

Mouse saw it too. Nothing escaped Mouse's little devil eyes. He shrugged, lengthened his stride so benRabi would not overtake him.

They were not supposed to be acquainted this time. That left Moyshe without any anchor at all. He did not need lots of people, but he felt desolate when he had no one.

He daydreamed about Stars' End and the High Seiners, the unchanging boulders that had ghosted across his mind before he had become distracted by his own past.

Sheer mystery was Stars' End, a fortress planet beyond the galactic rim, bristling with automatic, invincible weapons that slaughtered everyone fool enough to come in range. Not one of a dozen expeditions had produced a shred of why.

In the lulls, the deep, fearful lulls when there was nothing to say and nothing being said, people seized on Stars' End as strange country to explore, in litanies meant to exorcise the dreadful silence. They were intrigued by the godlike power there. Theirs were the eyes of the godless seeking gods in a majestically powerful unknown, a technological equivalent of an Old Testament Jehovah.

Or, if Stars' End was momentarily passé, they turned to the High Seiners. The Starfishers.

The Starfishers should have been no mystery. They were human. Stars' End was just a dead metal machine voice babbling insanities in non-human tongues, the toy of gun-toting pyramid builders so long gone no extant race remembered them. But, because of their humanness, the Seiners had become the greater, more frightening puzzle.

Landsmen did not comprehend the quiet, fixed culture of the Starfishers at all. They yearned for the Starfishers' obvious peace, yet hated them for their blissful stasis. The Seiner trail was a perilous one, wending tortuously among yin-yang pitfalls of envy and jealousy.

His thoughtful mood departed. Work came first. He had to be alert. Lives could hinge on his slightest misstep, and the life at the head of the list was his own.

He entered the Blake Port terminal. It was a massive plastic, glass, and steel cavern. Its vast floor was a crossroads of color and movements, its entrances and exits the mouths of tunnels opening on other worlds.

Moyshe had wanted to be a poet once, a spacefaring Homer like Czyzewski. A child's dream, that had been. Like the one about having secret powers if only he could find their handle.

An instructor had made him read Czyzewski critically, then had forced him to examine his own secret images of space and night and the womb. That had been a broomstick fly. Strictly from hunger. The backs of beyond in the shadowy reaches of his mind were lands of corruption and horror he would never journey again. His muse had abandoned him for brighter skies. Now he played with prose, *All Who Were Before Me in Jerusalem*.

This mission should give him time to polish it.

Light surrounded him. Human scent hung heavy around him. People rushed hither and thither like swarming bees who had lost track of their queen. Their effluvia was too much for the air fresheners. It was the same in every terminal he had ever visited.

The citizens were there in their multitudes, dancing atoms pursuing the rituals of terminals. The costumes of a dozen worlds mixed in a kaleidoscopic choreography.

A small, subdued crowd occupied one backwater of the waiting room floor. A long table had been set up there. Behind it a half-dozen men in off-white, undecorated jumpsuits fiddled with forms and questionnaires. A girl at table's end, armed with an arsenal of secretarial gizmos, reduced the forms for microstorage. She was pale, had blondish hair that hung to her shoulders. He noticed her because her hair was unusually long for a spacegoer.

The men, though, conformed to the spacer stereotype. Their hair was cropped to a centimeter's length. "Like induction day at boot camp," Moyshe muttered.

These people would be his new employers. The ones he had been sent to betray.

Mouse passed, small and brown, with a wink. Why he had that name benRabi did not know. He had carried it for years, and seemed to like it, though for lookalikes *Weasel* would have done better.

A weird one, my partner, benRabi thought. *But we get along. Because of commensality of obsession. In some areas.*

Mouse was a mad collector too: postage stamps from the days when they had been used, coins, bottles, mugs, wrought-iron, almost anything old. But the ends they were after varied.

BenRabi collected for escape, for relaxation, as a means of learning. Mouse had gone mad Archaicist during his recent stay in Luna Command. His collecting had become a means of slipping into the gestalt of departed life styles. He had fallen in love with the twentieth century, the last with a real spectrum of class, ethnic, and cultural differentiations.

BenRabi did not comprehend Archaicists at all. His opinion of them was, to use Mouse's words, lower than a snake's butt.

The old distinctions had changed. Race, sex, wealth, style, and manner of speech no longer set a person apart. Prejudices pivoted round origins and profession, with Old Earthers the niggers of the age, and Service personnel the aristocracy.

BenRabi, under his other names, had known Mouse a long time. But he just did not know the man. Professional acquaintance and even a budding friendship had done nothing to break down Mouse's defenses. BenRabi was Old Earther. Mouse was Outworlds and third generation Service. That was a barrier across which little could trickle.

BenRabi studied other faces, saw bewilderment, determination, malaise. A lot of these people were not sure why they were here. But he was looking for the nonchalant ones, the ones who did know. They would be the competition and beekies.

The Bureau was far from unique in its interest in Starfish. Half these people, probably, were spies... "Uhn!"

"Excuse me, please?"

He turned. A small blue nun had paused beside him, startled by his grunt. "Pardon, Sister. Just thinking out loud."

The Ulantonid woman wobbled off wearing a perplexed frown, perhaps wondering what sort of mind thought in dull monosyllables. BenRabi frowned himself. What had become of the human need for faith? The Christians he encountered were almost always conquered aliens.

His curiosity faded. He returned to that disturbing face.

Yes, it was Marya, though she had changed as much as he. Her hair, skin, and eyes had all been darkened. She had put on twenty pounds. There were other changes, too. They were subtler, but did not prevent his recognizing her. She had not disguised her ways of moving, speaking, listening.

She never was much of an actress, he reflected.

She did have a talent essential to their profession. She survived despite the odds.

She noticed him looking. Her eyebrows rose a millimeter, then puckered in consternation. Then she smiled a wicked iron smile. She had recognized him, too.

How big a demotion had she earned for failing on The Broken Wings? How much had it cost, beyond the cruel, slow deaths of her children?...

Frost mites danced between his shoulder blades. She would be doing score-evening calculations already.

She nodded ever so slightly, politely.

It was a vast universe. There was no way he should have run into her again, ever. He was too stunned for rational thought.

Nothing could have shaken him more than her presence.

He did not fear her. Not in a cold sweat way. She would see Mouse. She would know she had to let be, or die, or make damned sure she got them both with the same hit.

Several other faces teased his memory. Trace recognitions trickled back from his studies of Bureau files. None of them were outright enemies. They were competitors, beekies from the Corporations. Or possibly McGraws.

He tried to view the crowd as an organism, to judge its composition and temper. It was smaller than he had expected. Not more than two hundred. The Seiners had advertised for a thousand, offering bonuses and pay scales that approached the outrageous.

They would be disappointed.

He supposed there weren't many techs romantic enough, or hungry enough, to plunge into an alien society for a year. That might mean returning to a home changed beyond recognition. After the lighters lifted there would be no turning back. No one would be able to quit because he did not like his job.

Moyshe shuffled into the check-in line four places behind his partner. Mouse was shaking.

Moyshe never ceased to be amazed. Glacial. Glassteel. Conscienceless. Stonedeath. He had thought Mouse many cold, hard things. Yet there were unpredictable moments when the man let slip the humanity behind the facade of adamant. BenRabi watched as if witnessing a miracle.

This might be the only time during the operation that Mouse would let the hardness fall. And that only because he was poised on the brink of a shuttle fly.

Liftoffs terrified him.

"Dr. Niven." A whisper. Warmth caressed benRabi's arm. He looked down into eyes as hard and dark as Sangaree gunmetal coins.

"Pardon, ma'am?" He put on his disarming smile. "Name's benRabi. Moyshe benRabi."

"How quaint." She smiled a gunmetal smile. "Candy, even."

She must be more widely read than he had suspected.

Moyshe benRabi was the protagonist of Czyzewski's sole and almost unknown trial of the novel, a cartoon caricature painted in broad strokes of Gargantua and Don Quixote. The critics had said too much so, stopping only on the edge of accusations of plagiarism.

Strange that a Sangaree should be familiar with *His Banners Bright and Golden...*

Sangaree. He had to remind himself. He had shared her bed. There had been feeling in it during those hungry days on The Broken Wings.

She might willingly share beds again, but...

In the end she would drink his blood. Sangaree nursed their hatreds forever. For generations, if rumor was true.

"And the Rat, too, eh?" Meaning Mouse. She would have a special hell set aside for him. But the feeling was mutual. BenRabi knew Mouse would plain love a date with her in a medieval torture chamber. "All you Confies and beekies and McGraws pretending you need Seiner money... Orbit in an hour, Gun. See you upstairs."

More gunmetal smiles as she took her gunmetal-hard body toward the Ladies.

She would see him upstairs.

No doubt. He wondered if he could conjure up a Mark XIV Combat Suit real quick. Or spider's eyes so he could watch his back. This mission was going to be Roman candle all the way.

And he had hoped for a vacation operation. For nothing to do but loaf and work on *Jerusalem*.

TWO: 3047 AD
The Olden Days, Angel City

A whisper swifted on lightning feet through Angel City's underworld. It said the Starduster was on The Broken Wings.

A private yacht had slipped into Angel Port after making a surreptitious worldfall. It was registered to a Dr. Gundaker Niven. The cognoscenti in the outfit remembered that name in connection with a blow-up on Borroway that had set the Sangaree back a billion stellars.

Port workers with connections started the excitement. The bounty on Gundaker Niven was immense. The Sangaree would not sit still for a billion-stellar burn from God Himself.

The dock workers passed the word that the *Lady of Merit* boasted just two passengers. One was Caucasian, the other a small Oriental.

That got their attention downtown. Niven had something to do with the Starduster. He might even be the Starduster under an alias. And the Starduster's number-one man was an Oriental, one John Li Piao.

These men, though, looked like Old Earth shooters, not the masters of a shadow empire rivaling that managed by the Sangaree.

Nevertheless, heads nodded in the board rooms of crime.

Orders went out to the soldiers.

The Starduster was a unique creature. He was a man in limbo. A crime czar who had built a kingdom independent of the established syndicates. He preyed on his own kind rather than pay a single credit for Sangaree-produced stardust.

His was the most feared name on the Sangaree hate list.

Sentences of death had been pronounced on a dozen worlds. Open, often redundant contracts approaching a hundred million stellars existed.

Time and success had made of him an almost mythic devil.

He had been claimed killed a half dozen times. But he kept coming back, like a thing undead, like a dying wizard's curse. Hardly would the jubilation end before his invisible hand would again strike swiftly and viciously, ripping the guts from another syndicate pipeline of profit.

Was there more than one Starduster?

The Sangaree Heads, to whom most organized crime could be traced, sometimes suspected that he was not a man at all, but a role. Perhaps Piao was the real Starduster. The handful of men who had been pinned with the Starduster name were as diverse a group as could be selected from a good-sized crowd. Short, tall, thin, fat, white, black.

The Sangaree family dictators knew only one thing for certain. The Starduster was human. Sangaree might be contentious, piratical, greedy, and short on conscience, but only a human who hated would slash at them as bloodily as the Starduster did.

Even his motives were obscure. The narcotic he stole did not always find its way back into trade channels. Greed had no obvious hold on him.

The yachtsmen rented a groundcar and vanished into Angel City's warehouse district. Gundaker Niven was a chunky man of medium height. He had hard, dark eyes of the sort that intimidated civilians. He had thick, heavy hands. He jabbed with forefingers for emphasis whenever he spoke. A wide scar poured from his right ear down over his cheekbone to the corner of his mouth.

"Take it out with a kilo of D-14," he growled, punching a finger at a dilapidated warehouse. His words came out slurred. The right side of his mouth did not move. "Burn them and run."

His driver was a small man with Fu Manchu mustaches. He had the same cold eyes. "But this ain't no shatter run. All that would do is show us how good they die."

"Working for Beckhart is getting a meter too tall for me, Mouse. This underworld stuff isn't my specialty. It's too rough. Too complicated. Suppose the real Starduster has people here?"

The smaller man laughed. "He does. You can count on it."

"Oh, Christ!"

"Hey! Working for the Old Man is an honor. When he asks for you, it means you've made it. Didn't you get sick of that military attaché dodge?"

"No. I was drafted into this."

"Come on! Engineering coups in the outbacks. How dull can you get? There's no rise to give it spice. When things go broomstick you go hide in the embassy."

"You think it's all champagne and ballroom conspiracy? I got my spleen burned out on Shakedowns. Inside the embassy."

"Still ain't the same. Yeah. The Starduster has people here. But by the time the word floats up and the shit comes down we'll be long gone."

"That's what you told me on Gorki. And New Earth was supposed to be a piece of cake."

This was their third mission teamed. Admiral Beckhart's specialized, secretive division of the Bureau of Naval Intelligence had found that they complemented one another well.

"So you should be used to it."

"Maybe. Gundaker Niven. What the hell kind of name is that?"

"You take what they give you. This ain't the diplomatic service. You're in the big time now."

"You keep telling me. But they don't job you. You stay Mouse every go. They never crank you through the Medical mill. They don't have the Psychs scramble your brain."

"They don't need to. I'm not the front man. I'm just around to drag your ass out of the fire when it gets hot."

"I don't like the feel of this one, Mouse. Something's wrong. There's going to be trouble."

"Man is born to trouble as the sparks fly upward."

"Holy shit! I'm looking for toilet paper and he throws the Bible at me. It's sour, Mouse."

"Because we got no backup? Hang tight, Doc. We don't need it. The Sangaree outfit here wouldn't make a pimple on the ass of a Family like the Norbon. They've only got five or six people on the whole damned planet. They get the work done with local talent."

"Stickers can burn you just as dead as any Homeworld shooter. Beyond-the-resurrection. What's out here, anyway?"

"Got to go with you there, Doc. Not a million people on this rat hole. Three lousy domes, and enough swamp to supply the rest of Confederation."

"It even stinks in here."

"It's in your head. Going to circle the block."

They idled on, learning the warehouse district's tight, twisty out-of-the-ways first hand. Street maps and eidetic holo-memories had been given them, but only exploration made a place real. Every city had its feel, its color, its smell, its *style*. Psych's familiarization tapes could not capture the intangibles of reality.

Knowledge and preparation were the corner- and keystones of their trade.

"I need a bath," Niven complained. "I can smell swamp muck on me."

"Let's head back to the Marcos. My stomach's okay now. I'm hungry. And a game or two would get me back in the groove. Tomorrow's soon enough to take the case."

The Marcos was The Broken Wings' best hotel, and one of the best in The Arm. And that despite the limits imposed by the space and conservation regulations of a dome city.

Dome cities are planet-bound space vessels. Which translates as uncomfortable.

The lobby of the Marcos had been decorator-engineered to provide an illusion of openness. The wall facing the entrance was masked by a curving hologramic panorama from another world.

Mouse froze.

"What's the matter?"

The smaller man stared straight ahead. He did not reply.

"The Thunder Mountains seen from Edgeward City on Blackworld," Niven murmured, recognizing the scene.

It was a stark view, of black mountains limned by the raging star winds of a pre-nova sun. Blackworld was one of the least hospitable and most dramatically beautiful of the outworlds.

"Just surprised me, Doc." Mouse glanced around the lobby. "It was the Cathedral Forest on Tregorgarth when we checked in."

People stared. The two gave the impression of being invaders instead of guests. Their appearance labeled them hardcases barely able to get by on their wits. Men of that breed belonged in the warehouse district, not at the watering hole of the genteel.

The watery-eyed bellhop, who watched them stroll through the hologram to the elevators, did not belong either. He limped when he walked, but he was too solid, too *macho,* to be staff. His uniform was a size too small. His stance was a centimeter too assertive.

"Something's gone broomstick," Mouse said. The elevator doors closed with startling severity, as though issuing a declaration of war.

Meticulous preliminary research characterized a Beckhart operation. They had seen holos of, and reports on, all regular hotel staff.

"I saw him. What do we do?"

"Cut out a floor short."

Why not just get the hell out? Niven wondered.

"We'll take the stairs. We'll catch them from behind."

"You're taking a lot for granted."

"Anything to save a kick in the teeth."

Their floor was the fifth. The penthouse level. It contained four suites. Only theirs was occupied.

"The empty car will tip them," Niven remarked after Mouse had punched Four.

"Yeah. You're right."

"So?"

"Tell you what. Let's slide down and see if we can snatch the gimp. Shoot him with Nobullshit and see what he's got to say."

That was pure Mouse thinking, Niven reflected. Running was an alien concept.

They were both in Old Earther role. Holonet stereotype Old Earther role. But they had not received a full Psych-brief. Their speech patterns tended to meander between that appropriate to the role and that of Academy graduates. Their mission-prep had included only a limited Psych-brief. They remembered who they were. They had to think to maintain consistent images.

"We're getting sloppy," Niven observed. "Let's tighten up."

The elevator stopped on Three. They exchanged glances.

"Better stand back, Doc."

Mouse's eyes and face blanked. A subtle air of crouch, of tenseness enveloped him. He seemed to have gone to another world.

He had entered "assassin's mind." Which meant that he had become a biochemical killing robot.

Mouse was a physical combat specialist.

A dowdy, blubbery woman with two poodles and a make-believe fortune in cultured firestones waddled aboard. "Five, please." And, before Niven caught the wrong note, "You're new. Offworlders?"

Niven responded with an affirmative grunt. He had to think of some way to distract the woman while Mouse relaxed.

"How marvelous. Let me guess. One of the Inner Worlds?"

Niven grunted again. He stared at the door, hoping rudeness would be distraction enough. He took Mouse's arm gently as the door opened on Four.

"Stay where you are!"

A tiny needlegun peeped from a fat hand. The woman sloughed the dowager character. Suddenly she was as hard-edged as they.

"Move together." The doors closed. "Thank you."

Niven looked beyond costume and props and saw the enemy.

She was the Sangaree Resident for The Broken Wings, Sexon S'Plez.

Christ, you're slow, he told himself. *The fat alone should've warned you.*

Plez was suspected of being a proctor of the Sexon, which was one of the First Families of the Sangaree. That would make her the equal of a Planetary Senator...

The assignment of a heavy-duty Resident to a backwater world was what had stimulated Luna Command into sending in its shock troops.

How had she gotten onto them so fast? Niven wondered.

Two nervous heavies in ill-fitting hotel livery awaited the car on floor Five. They were a tall, pale, ginger-haired pair who had to be brothers.

"Which one's Niven?" the older asked.

"Out." The woman gestured with her weapon.

Wavering guns peered from all the brothers' four hands.

Careful, Niven thought. He raised his hands slowly. These men were amateurs. They might start panic-shooting.

"Chunky's Niven. The gook must be Piao."

The Starduster's associates were as shadowy as he, but one of the few names known was John Li Piao, reputed number-two man and chief bone-breaker. The face of the man who wore that name, though, was as much an enigma as the Starduster's.

"I don't want you should get upset," Niven said, trying to project terrified and outraged innocence, and having no trouble with the fear, "but I think you've got the wrong..."

"Stuff it, animal!" the woman snarled.

The Old Earth cant is catching, Niven thought.

The brothers' eyes narrowed. Their lips tightened. The insult included them. Animal was the Sangaree's ultimate racial slur.

Niven put on a bewildered face. "What's going on, anyway? I'm just a social researcher. Studying the effects of dome constriction..."

The brothers laughed tightly. One said, "Crap."

Mouse had gotten caught in the limbo between normalcy and assassin's mind. The state was one of semi-consciousness. It would take him time to push himself one way or the other. Niven knew which way Mouse would go. His stomach knotted.

"... to study the effects of dome constriction on immigrant workers." Mouse needed a distraction. "For Ubichi Corporation. This man is my secretary. We're not carrying any cash." That was the course, he thought. Protesting innocence of a connection with the trade would cause laughter. Protesting being robbed might make them hesitate the instant Mouse needed.

He did not feel that Mouse was doing the right thing. But Mouse did not know how to back down. He was a hitter. It would get him killed someday.

It might get them both killed, but he could not change Mouse's ways.

The older gunman wavered. "The yacht was a Ubichi charter."

"Cover…" the woman began. Too late.

Mouse exploded.

Flying, with a scream that froze them an additional second.

A fist disarmed the woman. Her weapon dribbled into the elevator. One foot, then the other, pistoned into the older brother's face. He triggered. Needles stitched the wall over Niven's head.

The younger brother managed only a half turn. Mouse bounced into him. He chopped weapons away with his left hand. His right went for the man's throat.

A gurgling scream ripped through a shattered windpipe.

Knowing what would happen did not help Niven. Mouse was *fast.*

The woman was running before Niven recovered her weapon. He crouched, trying to aim.

He was too sick to hold his target.

She had kneed him savagely. The agony numbed his mind.

He hit the button for One, left the brothers to Mouse. Maybe he could get her in the lobby…

Reason returned before the doors opened.

There was nothing he could do. Not in front of fifty witnesses. Aching, helpless, he watched the fat woman collect her limping accomplice and depart.

He began shaking. It had been close. Too damned close.

Mouse was human again when Niven reached Five. He was shaking too. "Get her?"

"In the lobby? With fifty witnesses?"

"From the elevator. They couldn't see you through the holo."

"Oh." That had escaped him. "What about those guys?"

"Got to do something with them."

"Hell, turn them loose. Won't make any difference…" He took another look. His sickness returned, centered higher. "Did you have to?…"

Defiantly. "Yeah."

Mouse was driven by a murderous hatred of everything Sangaree. It splashed over on anyone who cooperated with them.

He refused to explain.

"Better get them out of the hall. Staff might come through." He grabbed a leg, started dragging.

Mouse dabbed at bloodstains.

"The outfit won't like this," Niven said as he hauled the second corpse into the suite. "Number's going to be on us now."

"So? We've been on the bull's eye before. Anyway, we bought some time. They'll want to salvage the fat broad before they move. And they'll bring in somebody new. They're careful that way. We'll hustle them meanwhile."

"How? The number's on. Who'll talk? Anybody who knows anything is going to know that we're dead."

"You ain't dead till they close the box."

"Mouse, I don't feel right about this one."

"Doc, you worry too much. Let it stew. We keep our heads in and our backs to the wall, maybe a little something will blow our way. Just be on your toes. Like they said in the olden days, when you get handed a lemon, make lemonade."

"I don't think the hardcase course took," Niven said. "You're right, I mean. I shouldn't be so worried."

"Know what your problem is? You ain't happy unless you've got something to worry about. You're spookier than an old maid with seven cats."

THREE: 3048 AD
Operation Dragon, Blake City Starport

The terminal's sounds crowded benRabi. The smells and swirling colors dazzled him. The nervousness started.

It always did at the mouth of the lion's den. Or, this time, the dragon's lair. The briefing tapes had claimed that starfish, seen in space, resembled dragons two hundred kilometers long.

He shuffled forward with the line, finally reached the table. One of the Seiner men asked a few questions. He replied numbly.

"Sign and thumbprint this please, Mr. benRabi. Give it to the lady with the rest of your paperwork."

Shaking, he completed his contract. The Seiner girl at table's end smiled as she shoved his papers into the maw of her reducing machine. She said, "Just through that door and take a seat, please. The shuttle will be ready shortly."

He went, bemused. That pale Seiner girl, with her pale hair and harsh cheekbones, reminded him of Alyce, his Academy love. That was not good. More than a decade had passed, and still the pain could penetrate his armor.

Was that why he had trouble with women? Every affair since had, inevitably, fallen into emotional chaos. Each had become a duel with swords of intentional hurt.

But there had been no prior affairs to stand comparison. Maybe he was just consistent in picking unstable women.

He took a chair in the waiting room. Out came the tattered notebook, a traveling companion of many years. This time, he swore, he would finish *Jerusalem*.

> The unbreakable fetters which bound down the Great Wolf Fenrir had been cunningly forged by Loki from these: The footfall of a cat, the roots of a rock, the beard of a woman, the breath of a fish, the spittle of a bird.
>
> —*The Prose Edda*

Yes, the more he thought about it, the more he was sure that was the best possible opening quote. It had an indisputable universality.

Every life had its Loki capable of binding it with chains as tenuous but strong.

Those wormwood memories of Academy returned. They were indestructible memorabilia of an affair with a fellow midshipman who had been the daughter of the Vice Commandant and the granddaughter of the Chief of Staff Navy.

He had been an idiot. A pig-iron, chocolate-plated fool. How had he made it through? In the context of Alyce, he still thought his survival a miracle.

And the cost? What if he had not, as ordered, dropped the affair? What if he had persisted? She had demanded that he do so, defying what to him had been terrifying concentrations of authority.

To her those people had been family. Mother and grandfather. To him they had appeared as behemoths of power.

And the night beast with guilt-fangs longer than any of his other haunts: What of the child?

Come on, he grumbled at himself. *What is this? Let's ditch the memories and romantic nonsense.* He was a grown man. He should get back into *Jerusalem*; that would be a blow against the dread empire of his soul.

One of his favorites, from Pope's *Dunciad*:

Lo! thy dread empire, Chaos, is restored;

Light dies before thy uncreating word...

"Ladies and gentlemen."

He looked up. What now? Ah. A last-chance-to-get-out briefing.

It was conducted by an officer with a voice so infuriatingly scratchy that it had to be technically augmented. "We don't want you on our ship. You're not our kind of people," the officer said for openers.

"Why're you here? What are your motives?"

Good questions, benRabi thought.

"Two reasons. You're either bemused by the Seiner myth, which is a holonet fabrication, or you're here spying. I'll let you in on the secret now. This isn't going to be any romantic adventure. And you're not going to get at any information. All we're going to give you is a lot of hard work inside a culture unlike any you've ever known. We're not going to ease you into our world. We're not going to coddle you. We don't have the time."

The man was deliberately trying to upset them. Moyshe wondered why.

"We've assembled you for one reason. It's the only way we can meet next year's harvest quotas."

BenRabi had a sudden feeling. A premonition, he thought. The man had more than harvests on his mind. Some worry, or fear, was racketing around his brain. Something terrible and big had him half spooked.

Admiral Beckhart liked using benRabi because he had these intuitions.

Moyshe also sensed a ghost of disappointment in the speaker, along with a taint of distaste for landsmen. He spoke as if tasting the sour flavor of betrayal.

It was inarguable that these Seiners were desperate. They would never have sought outside technicians otherwise.

BenRabi quelled a surge of compassion.

The speaker's home was a harvestship somewhere out in the Big Dark. To survive it needed a massive input of competent technicians. The man was sour because of all of Confederation's billions, only two hundred people had come forward. And most of those could be considered suspect.

The Seiner fumbled in the pockets of his antiquated tweed jacket. BenRabi wondered if the man was an Archaicist. His preconceptions of the Seiners did not include the possibility that they were faddists too.

The man produced a curious little instrument. He thrust it between his teeth. He gripped it with his right thumb and forefinger, puffing while he held a small flame over its bowl. Only after he had begun expelling noxious clouds did benRabi realize what was happening.

"A pipe!" he muttered. "What the hell?" Tobacco stench assailed his nostrils. "I can't believe this much bad taste." He shuddered.

His reaction was not unique. His companions buzzed. A woman rose and started to leave, then gagged and returned to her seat. Even Mouse looked appalled.

How many of these crude horrors lay in ambush ahead? This was carrying Archaicism to the point of boorishness.

Much as the pipe disgusted him, benRabi applauded the psychology behind its appearance. The man was easing them in after all. The impact of later cultural shocks would be blunted a little.

"As I said," the Seiner continued, once his pause had his audience squirming, "there're spies here. Spy is a nasty word, I know. And spying is a nasty business. But a realist recognizes the existence of espionage, and we're all realists here. Aren't we? Espionage is all around us today. We're drenched in it. Up to our heinies in it. Because almost anybody with any power at all will do almost anything to get control of a starfish herd."

He assayed a little smile. It mocked them all. He was doing a show, putting on the pompous ass to prod somebody into reacting. BenRabi sensed a quiet, self-assured competence behind the showmanship. In fact, there was something about the man that screamed *Security Officer.*

"You spies won't learn a thing. Till your contracts terminate you'll see nothing but the guts of a ship. Even then you'll see only what we want you to see, when we want you to see it. Everybody. Hear this. Security rules will be observed at all times. That's the

Eleventh Commandment. Engrave it on your souls—if you have any. Even a slight irregularity might spook us into hasty reaction. Since we're not sure what information the spy-masters would consider valuable, we're going to do our damnedest not to give away anything at all."

BenRabi grimaced. Was the fool trying to impress them with Seiner paranoia and xenophobia? He could rave for a week and not intimidate the professionals.

"I reiterate: outside agents simply won't be given a chance to contact anybody who might possess critical information. There'll be penalties for trying to reach such people. Am I making myself clear?"

Someone made a snide remark.

The speaker responded, "You've got to realize that we consider ourselves a nation unto ourselves. We're not Confederation. We don't want to be Confederation. We don't give a damn about Confederation. All we ever asked from it was to be left alone. Which is what we ask of any gang of strongmen. Archaicism is our way of life, not just a crackpot hobby. Just for example, we still execute people once in a while."

That blockbuster fell into an ocean of silence.

BenRabi wondered how many times Confederation had tried coaxing these strange, fiercely independent people into the government fold. Dozens, at least. Luna Command was persistent. It was a long-toothed hound that did not turn loose of a bone.

And for a century and a half the Starfishers had managed to evade Luna Command's "protection," mostly by remaining so damned hard to find, but also by making it clear they were willing to fight.

Luna Command had never given up. It never would. Even these people had to recognize that, benRabi thought. They had to recognize the government's stake.

Nervousness pervaded the waiting room, fogging in like some unexpectedly conjured demon. The briefing officer met pairs of eyes one by one. The romantic flinched before his stare. They were finding their legend had teeth and claws.

No one executed people anymore. Even the barbarians beyond Confederation's pale recycled their human garbage, if only through cyborg computation systems.

The civilians were learning what people in benRabi's trade learned early. Adventures were more fun when it was somebody else getting the excelsior ripped out of his crate.

"In view of what I've said, and knowing that your futures may not be exactly what you anticipated when you applied," the man said, "anybody who wants to do so can opt out now. We'll cover expenses as advertised."

BenRabi smiled at his lap. "Thought that's where you were headed," he whispered. "Trying to spook the weaklings, eh?"

There was a stir in response, but no one volunteered to go home. The weaklings seemed scared that they would look foolish. The Starfisher shrugged, collected his notes, and said, "All right. I'll see you all upstairs." He left the room.

Time to sit, to wait for the shuttle; benRabi returned to his notebook and *Jerusalem*.

He was having trouble with the story. His mind seemed to be too ordered and mundane to produce the chaotic, nonobjective symbolism of a McGuhan or Potty Welkin. His maliciously intentional obscurantisms refused to remain obscure. That could have been because he knew what he wanted to say.

Maybe he should do the story as straight narrative, Moyshe thought. He could strive for what the Archaicist reviewers called "a refreshingly anachronistic flavor." It might then survive the Archaicist marketplace, where the unsophisticated arts of the past still had appeal.

Ykadabar Station is six months long and two years wide, fifteen minutes high and a quarter of nine forever; there are songs in its skies and trumpets in its walls. The Roads have neared their ends:…

Was he wrong? Was he alone in his feeling that all people were exiles in time? No matter. What could he do about it? Not a damned thing. That was the passion that should drive the story. Raging impotence.

People began moving excitedly. The volume of conversation picked up. BenRabi dragged himself back to reality. He muttered, "Shuttle must be ready."

Yes. His companions had begun filing onto the field already.

These Seiners were frugal. They had not bothered to lease an attached landing bay.

The air outside was cool and on the move. A raindrop touched his cheek, trickled like a tear. A ragged guerilla band of clouds hurried over, firing off a few scattered water-bullets that made little mud balls in the dust lying thick on the tarmac. An omen? Rainy weather at Blake City was almost a nevertime thing. Water was too scarce in this part of Carson's.

He laughed nervously. Omens! What was the matter with him? "Into the shuttle, caveman," he mumbled.

The ship had been an antique when his grandfather was wetting diapers. It was no commercial lighter, and never had been. Broomstick, from Century One, it was a go-powered coffin with no comforts from strictly-for-gun-power days. He saw nothing but stark functionalism and metal painted black or grey. It appeared to be Navy surplus, probably from the Ulantonid War.

The part of him that was still line officer noted that she was well maintained. Not a spot of dirt or corrosion showed anywhere. The ship had that used but kept-up look sometimes seen in rare antiques. These Seiners were lovingly careful of their equipment.

The passenger compartment was the antithesis of luxury. BenRabi had to suspend disbelief to credit it as suitable for human use. Yet the converted cargo bay did have ranks of new acceleration couches, and soothing music came from hidden speakers. It was old stuff, quiet, perhaps something by Brahms. It put a comforting gloss over the unsteady whine of the idling drives.

They would lift blind, he saw. Weedlike clumps of color-coded wiring hung where view-screens had been removed. They were taking no chances.

This seemed to be taking security a bit far. What the hell could the screens show if the Seiners kept them switched off? For that matter, what could they betray if turned on? He knew where he was. He knew where he was going, at least for the short run.

Was it some subtle psychological trick? A maneuver to accustom them to flying blind?

He dithered over a choice of couches.

The knot behind his ear, containing the non-dispersible parts of the instel-tracer, seized him with iron, spiked fingers. He had been switched on by the Bureau.

Why now? he wondered, staggering with the pain. They were supposed to wait till the lighter made orbit.

The thin, pale girl who had done the form reductions rushed toward him. "Are you sick?"

Her expression was one of genuine concern. He was more shaken by that than by this Bureau treachery. He had lived under the gun for years now. He was unaccustomed to strangers *caring*.

Her concern was not the bland, commercially dispensed pablum of a professional hostess, either. She *wanted* to help.

I want fired across his mind.

"Yes. A migraine attack. And my medicine is packed."

She steadied him. "Sit down here. I'll get you something."

He dropped onto the couch. A devil kicked the back of his skull with a steel-toed boot. It was a vicious little critter. It kept hammering away. He could not restrain a groan.

The headache became a bass drumbeat overshadowing his other pains. He looked up into the girl's pale blue eyes. They were perfectly suited to her pale complexion and colorless hair. He tried a smile of gratitude.

"Be back in a minute," she told him. "Hang on." Off she hurried, her hips moving in a languorous way that belied her haste. BenRabi's head left him no time to appreciate the nicety.

His frayed nerves jumped. They had migraine tablets on hand? That was strange. And her curiosity. Why was she interested in his health? She had become intrigued and apprehensive the instant he had mentioned migraine.

He had stretched the truth this time, but he had had headache trouble all his life. He had gobbled kilos of painkillers in his time.

Still, he had not been bothered recently. The susceptibility was noted in his medical file as a cover for the pain his tracer would cause...

Why the hell switch him on now?

His headaches were a mental thing, Psych had declared. They

were caused by unresolved conflicts between his Old Earth origins and the demands of the culture into which he had climbed.

He did not believe it. He had never met a Psych he trusted heaving distance. Anyway, he had had headaches even before he had begun to consider enlisting.

For at least the hundredth time he asked himself why the Bureau had implanted an imperfect device. He answered himself, as always, with the observation that the tracer was the only way they had to follow a Seiner ship to a starfish herd.

Completely nonmetal, the tracer was the only device that could be smuggled aboard without being detected.

There was no satisfaction in knowing the answers. Not when they were so damned unpleasant. He wished to hell that he could take a vacation. A real vacation, away from anything that would remind him of who and what he was. He needed time to go home and get involved in something with known, realizable, and comfortable challenges. He longed for the private universe of his stamp collection.

The Seiner girl returned with another of those big, warm smiles. She carried a water bottle in one hand, a paper pillbox in the other. "This should put that right," she said. That damned smile tried to eat him up. "I brought you a dozen. That should last the whole trip."

He frowned. How long would they be aboard this piece of flying junk?

"I asked if I could stay with you till we make orbit. Jarl turned me down. Too much else for me to do." She smiled, felt his forehead.

He had had a feeling she would report him to somebody. It was the way she had reacted to his mention of migraine.

What was so remarkable about a headache? Even a migraine? Something was wobbling on its axis and he could not get a grip. The pain just would not let him think.

Hell. He was probably just feeling the first ground tremors of culture shock. *Fly with it, Moyshe,* he told himself. *You've raced a sunjammer in the starwinds of the Crab...* What could the lady do that was less predictable, or more terrifying?

She was leaving. He did not want her to go. "Wait." She turned.

His heart did a teenager's flop. "Thank you. My name's benRabi. Moyshe benRabi." Now wasn't that a gimp way of feeling for an opening? But she responded with a quick little smile.

"I know, Moyshe. I remember from your papers. Mine's Coleridge. Amaranthina Amaryllis Isolte Galadriel de Coleridge y Gutierez." She yielded a half-laugh because of his rising eyebrows. "Mother was a reader. Amy's good for everyday."

There was a long, unsure moment. It was that period of uncertainty preluding potential relationship where he did not know if he dared open up a little more. She said, "I'm in Liquids Systems too."

He nodded. She had left the door open a crack. It was plain that it was up to him to use or ignore it.

Some words finally came, but too late. She was walking away. Maybe later, then.

I want returned to his mind, stimulated by the girl's invitation. Could a woman be his need? No. Not all of it, though having one around might be oil on the seas of his mind.

He had been hunting his Grail for a long time. Though he believed himself a cripple when dealing with them, the occasional woman had fallen his way. None of them had been panaceas. Alyce's ghost usually got in the way.

The Bureau supported his quest, knowing he was searching. Psych did not miss much. They might even know what he needed. Whatever, his masters were certain they would show a return on their investment.

Few of the Bureau's agents were sane in the accepted sense. It recruited obsessives intentionally. BenRabi did not think that sane men would make good operatives.

It took a madman to want into Intelligence in the first place. He smiled, mocking himself.

The lighter shuddered, rocked, shoved against his back. He was on his way to the orbiting Starfisher.

He watched Mouse, who was three rows ahead of him. The small man trembled as if suffering from a palsy. The getting off the ground part of space travel seemed to be the only terror his universe held. His reactions to everything else seemed as intense as those of a stone.

"So the Rat's chicken."

The Sangaree woman was on the other side of the aisle, smiling. He had not seen her sit down. Did he have to take this and the pain too?

FOUR: 3047 AD
The Olden Days, The Broken Wings

Mouse was right. The outfit didn't whisper for days. Niven's tension dissolved. He started living his cover.

He began reviewing psychiatric statistics at Angel City's medical center. Bureau planners had calculated the cover mission both to gather information of potential interest and to keep the opposition undecided.

On the surface there was no logical reason for a prime agent to spend all his time developing a mental-illness profile for an outpost city. And even less sense in it for the Starduster.

He found the data intriguing. He began enjoying it.

Then he met the woman.

She materialized at the edge of his vision for an instant. She was long, willowy, dark-haired. High, large, firm breasts locked a stunning holographic picture into his mind forever.

She vanished before he could get a better look.

His papers hit the floor. He grabbed, wondering if wishful thinking had bitten him. Those knockers...

It was lust at first sight.

Then she was peeking back around a grey metal cabinet in open-mouthed curiosity. Niven looked up into dark eyes. He dropped his notes again. Bewilderment danced across her features.

"Is something wrong?"

"Just clumsy. You startled me." He had never been comfortable with women. Especially those who attracted him so strongly, so suddenly.

It had been years since a woman had aroused him instantaneously. He considered himself with amazement.

The tough program did not keep his stomach from knotting, or his hands from shivering. It was silly. Adolescent. And he could not help himself.

He knew that he would bitterly recriminate himself for his weakness later. He always did.

He fumbled with the papers again.

She smiled. "Better let me do that." She knelt, shuffled his notes together.

Mona Lisa, he thought as he peered down her deeply cut blouse. *Her mouth is exactly the same. And her face has the same shape. But freckled.*

She wore no makeup. And didn't use anything but shampoo on her hair. She wore it brushed straight down. It hung wild and free, and had a hint of natural curl.

She's turned me into gelatin, he thought. He wanted to say something. Anything. He could think of nothing that did not sound juvenile, or insipid. But he wanted to know her. Wanted her.

"You work here?" he gobbled. His throat was tight and dry. He expected her to laugh.

He knew she was no employee. He had spent two days in Records already. She was the first person he had encountered, excepting the ratty old nurse who had explained the system, and who stole through now and then to make sure he did not leave obscene graffiti or drop a grenade down the toilet.

While he was keeping the cover, Mouse was alley-prowling, searching for the key that would open the operation. Prepared sound tapes made it seem he was hard at work in their suite.

"No. I came in to do some research. How about you?"

"Research. A project for Ubichi Corporation. Oh. Gundaker Niven. Doctor. Social Psychology, not Medicine."

"Really?" She smiled. It made her that much more desirable.

"I guess you've heard it before. You don't look it."

"Yeah." He did not have to force much sour into his reply. He was a born homeworlder. That much of the cover was easy to keep. "You're from Old Earth, everyone thinks..."

The social handicap of an Old Earth birth, properly exploited, could be converted to a powerful asset. For no logical reason Outworlders felt guilty about what had become of the motherworld. Yet Earth's natives had made it the hell it was.

Escape was available to the willing. The willing were few. People with adventure in their genes had gotten out in the first centuries of space travel, around World Commonweal's Fail Point, during First Expansion, and other early migrations. Modern departures came primarily through the Colonial Draft, as Earth's planetary government sold huge blocks of conscripted labor in return for forgiveness of indebtedness. Those few natives who wanted out usually chose military service.

Niven did not suspect that she might be Sangaree. He thought he had scored the Old Earth point.

"You must be an exceptional man... Excuse me. That's rude."

"That's prejudice."

She handed him his notes, huffed, "I said I was sorry."

"Forgiven. I don't expect an outsider to understand Old Earth. I don't understand it myself. Won't you introduce yourself?"

"Oh. Yes. Marya Strehltsweiter. I'm a chemo-psychiatrist. I'm doing my internship here. I'm originally from The Big Rock Candy Mountain." For an instant she fell back inside herself. "I have one more year to go."

"I've been there," Niven said. "It's magnificent." *Oops*, he thought. *That was a screw-up.* Dr. Gundaker Niven had never visited The Big Rock Candy Mountain.

"I miss it. I thought The Broken Wings would be exotic and romantic. Because of the name. You know what I mean? And I thought I'd get a chance to know myself. I never had time at home."

Niven frowned his response. He wanted to keep her talking, to hold her, but did not know what to say.

"The old story. I got pregnant young, got married, dropped

out of school. Had to find work when he took off… Did that and went back to school both…" She smiled conspiratorially, winked, "It didn't do any good to get away. The pain came with me."

"Friend of mine told me you can't run away. Because the things you want to get away from are always inside you."

"An Old Earther said that?"

"We're not Neanderthals."

"Sorry."

"Don't be. You're right. It's down the chute. If it weren't for Luna Command and Corporation Center it would be back in the Dark Ages. I've had it. Want to duck out for lunch?" He surprised himself. He was seldom that bold.

"Why not? Sure. It's a chance to talk to somebody who hasn't spent their whole life in this sewage plant. You know what I mean?"

"I can guess."

"You on expense account? Don't get me wrong. I'm not trying to be mercenary. But it seems like forever since I ate in a decent place."

"We'll find one." *Anything, lady. Just don't fade away before I get organized and start talking my talk.*

"Where the hell have you been?" Mouse demanded. Niven had wandered in after midnight. "I was getting scared they'd burned you."

"Sorry, Mom. Won't happen again."

"Shee-it. Doc found him a girlfriend."

"Hey! You don't have a copyright on…"

"All right. I know. Be cool. But give me a yell next time. Just so I don't get hemorrhoids from worrying. I got it."

"What? The clap?"

"Why we're here. It's stardust."

"We knew that. Why else this silly-ass double cover?"

"Not little stardust. Not small-time stardust. Stardust big enough to rate a Family proctor in an outback Residency."

"You mean the fat broad?"

"Yeah. She was here because Angel City depots distribution traffic for this whole end of The Arm. I'm talking a billion stellars' worth a month."

"You're talking out your butt. There isn't enough ship traffic to handle that kind of smuggling."

"Yes there is. If you don't really smuggle it. If you send it out from a legit source labeled as something legit. If you own the Customs people and the ships and crews and shippers…"

"Start over. You skipped chapter one."

"What's Stink City known for? Besides the smell?"

"Organic pharmaceuticals."

"Point for the bright boy. All the good organics they dredge out of the muck outside. The main reason Angel City is here. The Sangaree have gotten control of the whole industry. And most of the local officials.

"They parachute the raw stardust into the swamp. The dredgers bring it in. The field traffic controllers are paid to ignore strange blips on their detection systems. The stuff gets refined here, in the best labs, then they ship it out along with the finest label organics. Their people at the other end intercept it and get it into the regular stardust channels."

"How did you dig that out?"

"Ran into a man who knew. I convinced him he should tell me. Now, figuring how the Old Man works, he probably guessed most of it before he sent us out. So what does he want? The source. Us to find out where the stuff comes from before it gets here."

Niven frowned over the drink he had mixed while talking. "It is big, then. So huge it would take a cartel of Families… And you tried to tell me the Sangaree outfit here was…"

"The biggest, Doc. We just might be on the trail of the First Families themselves. And I know what I said. I was wrong."

"I'm thinking about retiring. We're really in it, and that's the only way out."

The Sangaree were a race few in number. They had no government in the human sense. Their major form of organization was the Family, which could be described as a corporation or boundaryless nation led by persons who were related. So-called "possessionless" Sangaree formed the working class.

The Family was strongly elitist and *laissez-faire* capitalist. Sangaree cut one another's throats almost as gleefully as they chopped up the "animal" races.

A Family Head was an absolute dictator. His followers' fortunes depended upon his competence. Succession was patrilineal. The existence of proctors only mildly ameliorated the medieval power structure.

The First Families were the five or six most powerful Families. Intelligence had never accurately determined their number. As a consortium they determined racial policy and insured their own preeminence among their species.

Very little was known of the Sangaree that the Sangaree did not want known.

"Oh, hey," Mouse enthused. "Don't even joke about getting out. Not now. Not when we've got an opportunity like this. This might be our biggest hit ever. It's worth any risk."

"That's subject to interpretation."

"It is worth anything, Doc."

"To you, maybe." Niven nursed his drink and tried to regain the mood he had had on arriving.

Mouse would not let be. "So tell me about your friend. Who is she? Where did you meet her? She good-looking? She give you any? What's she do?"

"I ain't telling you nothing. You birddog your own."

"Hey! Don't get that way. How long you known me?"

"Since Academy."

"I ever take your girl?"

"I never caught you." He mixed another drink.

"What's that supposed to mean?"

"Jupp did."

Mouse flashed him a black look. "Who?" He shook his head, indicated his ear. The room might be bugged. "Carlotta, you mean? She came after me, remember? And he didn't give a damn."

Jupp von Drachau *had* given a damn.

Their mutual acquaintance and Academy classmate had been crushed. He had hidden it from his wife and Mouse, though. Niven had been the receptacle into which he had poured all his pain.

Niven had never told Mouse that he was the reason that von

Drachau had abandoned wife and son and had thrown himself into his work so wholeheartedly that he had been promoted ahead of men far senior. Navy was the one institution that von Drachau trusted implicitly.

He was not alone in that trust.

The Services were the Foreign Legion of the age. Their people shared a hardy camaraderie based on their conviction that they had to stand together against the rest of the universe. Service was a place to belong. For people like von Drachau it became a cult.

Niven never would tell Mouse.

The evil had been done. Let the pain fade away.

It was not what Carlotta had done. Faithful, till-death-do-us-part marriage was an Archaicist fantasy. It was the *way* the hurt had been done. Carlotta had made a public execution of it, flaying Jupp with a dull emotional flensing knife, with clear intent to injure and humiliate.

She had paid the price in Coventry. She was still one of the social outcasts of Luna Command. Even her son hated her.

Niven still did not understand what had moved the woman. She had seemed, suddenly, to become psychotic, to collapse completely under the weight of her aristocratic resentment of her *nouveau-riche* husband.

Von Drachau, like Niven, was Old Earther. Even before the collapse of his marriage he had been climbing meteorically, surpassing his wife's old-line, fourth-generation Navy relatives. That seemed to have been what had cracked her.

"Well, don't get in too deep," Mouse warned, interrupting Niven's brooding. "We might not hang around long."

Later, as he drifted on the edge of sleep, trying to forget the trials of life in Luna Command, Niven wondered why Mouse had discussed their mission openly, yet had stifled any mention of von Drachau.

Protecting their second-level cover? Associates of the Star-duster certainly should not be personal friends of a Navy Line Captain.

Or maybe Mouse knew something that Admiral Beckhart had

not mentioned to his partner, Niven thought. The Old Man liked working that way.

The bastard.

"Probably both," he muttered.

"What?"

"Talking to myself. Go to sleep."

Beckhart always used him as the stalking horse. Or moving target. He blundered around, stirring things up for Mouse.

Or vice versa, as Mouse claimed.

He wondered if anybody had been listening. They had found only one bug in their sweeps. It had been inactive. It had been one of those things hotel managers used to keep track of towel thieves. But it was good tradecraft to assume that they had missed something live.

Niven was not in love with his profession.

It never allowed him a moment to relax. He did not perceive himself as being fast on his mental feet, so tended to overpress himself pre-plotting his situational reactions. He could not, like Mouse, just fly easy, rolling with the blows of fate like some samurai of destiny.

For him every venture out of Luna Command was an incursion into enemy territory. He wanted to go out thoroughly forewarned and forearmed.

Life had not been so complicated in his consular residency days. Back then friend and foe alike had known who and what he was, and there had been a complex set of rituals for playing the game. Seldom had anyone done anything more strenuous than watch to see who visited him and who else was watching. On St. Augustine he had worn his uniform.

There were different rules for scalp hunters. Beckhart's friends and enemies both played by the war rules. The blood rules.

And for reasons Niven did not understand, Beckhart's command was involved in a war to the death with the Sangaree.

Niven had had all the indoctrination. He had endured the uncountable hours of training and hypo-preparation. He even had the benefit of a brutal Old Earth childhood. But somehow his Academy years had infected him with a humanism that occasionally made his work painful.

A tendency to prolonged introspection did not help, he told himself wryly.

The campaign against the Sangaree could be justified. Stardust destroyed countless minds and lives. Sangaree raidships pirated billions and slaughtered hundreds. Through front men the Sangaree Families obtained control of legitimate business organizations and twisted them to illegitimate purposes.

The humanoid aliens had become a deadly virus in the corpus of human civilization.

Yet the very viciousness of Navy's counterattacks caused Niven grave doubts. Where lies justice, he wanted to know, when we are more barbarous than our enemies?

Mouse was fond of telling him that he thought too much and felt too little. The issue was entirely emotional.

Morning brought an indifferent mood. A depression. He simply abdicated all responsibility to Mouse.

"What's the program today?" He knew his partner meant to break routine. Mouse had had Room Service send up real coffee. Niven nursed his cup. "How are you going to get this past the auditors?"

"My accounts go straight to the Old Man. He stamps them ACCEPTED."

"Must be nice to be the Number-One Boy."

"It has its moments. But most of them are bad. I want you to hit the Med Center again. Business as usual. But try to audit their offworld drug traffic if you can. There's got to be records of some kind even if they only give us a side view. I think most of it is going out of the Center labs, so it's got to leave some kind of paper trace. If we can't find the source, maybe we can pinpoint the ends of the pipes."

"What about you?"

"I'm going to spend some of the Old Man's money. For hidey holes. For tickets out. You know. The insurance. That new Resident will show up pretty soon. We've got to be ready when it hits the ventilation."

"Are you getting close?" Feelings warred within Niven. He wanted out of Angel City and the mission, but not right now. There was Marya to get to know.

"No. Like I said, just buying insurance. I've got the feeling this'll get tight fast when they have somebody to tell them what to do."

"What do you mean, get tight? It already is. I had sticktights all day yesterday. Some of them stayed so close we could have worn the same shoes."

"That's what they get for using local talent. But I think that's part of their camouflage. We'd figure a place this important would have a battalion of high-powered types baby-sitting it. If somebody hadn't gotten onto S'Plez, they might have rolled along forever."

"I've got a feeling too, Mouse. And it ain't a good one. What happens if we get caught in a crunch between them and the Starduster?"

Mouse whipped a finger to his lips. "Let's not get back to tertiary cover yet," he breathed. Then he grinned. "Going to suicide? Look, if you have trouble, make the fallbacks. If I can't make them myself, I'll drop you a note somewhere. Otherwise, I'll catch you here tonight. It should be our last here, anyway."

Niven hit the lobby convinced that Mouse knew a lot more than he was telling. But that would be typical. Mouse was Beckhart's fair-haired boy. His perfectly expendable fair-haired boy.

He glanced back at the holorama. It was portraying one of the furious electrical storms in Ginunga Gap on Camelot. A herd of wind-whales quartered toward him through the rain and lightning.

For Beckhart the Bureau's work was a game. A vastly recomplicated form of the chess to which Mouse was addicted. The universe was his board. He would sacrifice his most precious pawn for a minuscule advantage.

He had been taking on the entire Sangaree race for a generation. And, with the implacability of a glacier, he was winning.

The prices of little victories left Niven appalled.

It took some sweet talk on his part to get to the Med Center's commercial records. He never was quite sure what made the old nurse give in. Somewhere along the line he said the right things. Pretty soon her death mask fell apart and reassembled itself in imitation of a smiling face. Then she fell all over herself explaining the data-retrieval system.

The information was there. A bonanza, and only thinly disguised. More than Mouse could have prayed for. This was the data center from which the whole operation was controlled. And it was not guarded by so much as a data lock.

The Sangaree were notoriously sloppy administrators. They had entered the interstellar community as predators, and had never really adapted to the demands of modern commerce. Action-oriented, they tended to ignore boring details, especially on worlds they believed safely in their pocket.

Like making sure no one without an absolute need had access to their records.

There had been a time when the need for protection would not have occurred to them at all, just as certain hues might not occur as existing to a color-blind man who had spent his entire life among others with the same affliction. But they were learning. Beckhart was teaching them via the Pavlovian method. The weakness was his favorite angle of attack.

The Sangaree did keep one secret. They wrote it down nowhere, and defended it to the death. The need to protect it was the one thing that could bring all the Families together. Even Families in vendetta would set aside their enmity long enough to keep Homeworld's location from becoming known.

On Borroway Sangaree children had murdered their younger brothers and sisters and had then committed suicide rather than face human interrogation, and that just because they had been afraid they *might* know something the human animals would find useful.

The hospital records were perfect. Niven unearthed few names, but did gather business intelligence pinpointing critical distribution points on more than two dozen worlds. Crimped there, the pipelines would require years of healing.

He found it incredible that a people could be so ingenious in marketing and so inept in administration. But the Sangaree were pure power people. They provided the muscle, money, guns, and merchandise. They let human underlings take most of the risks. And lumps.

From the Sangaree viewpoint their human associates did not

much matter. The tips of the kraken's tentacles were nothing but ignorant, expendable animals. They could be replaced by others just as ignorant, greedy, and expendable.

Only one or two people on a market world could point toward Angel City. Only from the back of the beast itself could the entirety of the monster be seen. And the beast was solidly in Sangaree pay.

Marya caught him before he finished. "What in the world?" she demanded when she found him immersed in the data, far from his usual orbit.

FIVE: 3048 AD
Operation Dragon, Lifting Off

"Sorry I startled you." A she-wolf's grin made it plain that the Sangaree woman felt no remorse whatsoever. "I'm Maria Elana Gonzalez. Atmosphere Systems. Distributions Methods. Sometimes I do a little Hydroponics Ecology. I don't have a Master's for either, though. Too busy with other things." She smiled her gunmetal smile.

Yes, benRabi thought, *the lady has other interests. Stardust and murder.*

"Moyshe benRabi," he replied, in case she had forgotten.

"An unusual name." She smiled that smile. "Jewish?"

"So I'm told. I've never been in a synagogue in my life."

"You wouldn't be a writer?" She knew damned well that he was. Or that he pretended to be. He had whispered to her about it... "The name sounds so literary, somehow."

"I try, yes." Was she going to expose the Pale Imperator?

No. She did not push it. Nor did she thrust with anything from her arsenal of needles.

"What made you decide to sign up?" she asked.

"Unemployment."

"A space plumber? You're kidding. You must be on the blacklist."

"Yeah. Sort of. Somebody's. What about you?"

42

"The money."

The vibrations of hatred had begun mellowing out. She was controlling herself superbly.

BenRabi let it flow. He hurt too much to fence, or to probe about her mission. The armed truce persisted till the lighter reached the Starfisher.

Moyshe did not forget that she was Sangaree, that she would drink his blood happily. He simply tabled the facts for the time being.

Hundreds of her people had died because of him. Her children were dying. She *would* do something. The Sangaree tradition of honor, of Family responsibility, would compel her...

But she would not act right away. She had come here on a mission. She would complete that first. He could relax for a while.

As introspective and morality-stricken as he sometimes became, he could not feel guilty about The Broken Wings. Nor about its aftermath. Humanity and Sangaree were at war, and the Sangaree had fired the opening shot. That it was a subterranean war, fought at an almost personal level, did not matter. Nor did the fact that only humanity perceived a war, that the Sangaree were just in business. Battles were battles. Casualties were casualties, no matter how or why they went down.

Most of his associates and contemporaries hated the Sangaree, but to him they were just people. People he had to hurt sometimes, because of what they did and represented.

He snorted. The most bigoted man alive could say the same thing and mean it.

The whole stardust trade turned his stomach.

"The trouble with me is, I don't love or hate anything," he murmured.

"What?"

"Sorry. Thinking with my mouth in gear."

His mood left nothing counting. Nothing could move him. The pain tablets had kicked him into nirvana. Or into a depthless black pit where the light of emotion simply could not shine. He was not sure which.

He did not care. He did not give a damn about anything. Instead, he immersed himself in the mystery he called Mouse.

BenRabi believed he knew Mouse better than did anyone but the Admiral. A lot of one another had leaked across during their teamed operations. These little flare-ups in the secret war were slowly melting them, molding them...

And still Mouse remained a mobile enigma.

Mouse scared hell out of benRabi.

Mouse was the only man he knew who had killed someone with his bare hands.

Killing had not become a social dodo. But the personal touch had been removed. Murder had become mechanized, its soul and involvement eliminated. It had been that way for so long that most civilians could not endure the emotions they suffered if they entered a killing rage.

Their brains shorted. They went zombie. And nothing happened.

Anybody could push a button and hurl a missile to obliterate a ship of a thousand souls. A lot of timid little anybodies had.

The same anybody could sleep without dreaming the following night. The involvement was with the button, not the bang.

Ample opportunities arose in nice remote space battles with Sangaree, McGraw pirates, or in the marque-and-reprisal antics of minor governments, for that kind of killing. But to do a man face to face, with hands or knife or gun... It was too personal.

Confederation men did not like to get too close to anyone. Not even to end a life. A man knew he was in too deep if the urge arose.

The People of Now wanted no faces on their haunts.

BenRabi was free-associating, and unable to escape the flight of his thoughts. Mouse. Interpersonal relationships. The two joined forces to kick him into a pit of fear.

He had known Mouse as early as their Academy days. They had shared their moments then, both in training and the play typified by sunjammer racing in the wild starwinds of an old supernova. They had crewed their sunjammer victoriously, and had shared celebrations during leave. But they had refused, persistently, to become anything more than acquaintances.

Friends were strange creatures. They became responsibilities. They became walking symbols of emotional debits and personal obligations.

He was getting too close to Mouse. Growing too fond of the strange little man. And he suspected that Mouse was having the same trouble.

Friendship would be bad for their professional detachment. It could get them into trouble.

The Bureau had promised that they would not be teamed again after the operation on The Broken Wings. The Bureau had lied. As it always did. Or this *really* was a critical, hurry-up, top-man job.

He wondered. The Admiral apparently would do or say, or promise anything to get the work done.

Always there was a rush but he had no good reason to complain. Hurry was inherent in the modern social structure. Change came about so swiftly that policy, operational, and emotional obsolescence developed overnight. Decision and action had to be sudden to be effective.

The system shuddered constantly under the thundering impact of precipitous error.

BenRabi was now involved in one of the Bureau's few old, stable programs. Catching a starfish herd had been a prime mission before his birth. He suspected it would continue to be one long after his death.

He might die of boredom here. He now saw little hope that he and Mouse would be recalled early. The presence of Sangaree altered all the rules.

He had abandoned all hope of enjoying the mission.

Somehow, sometimes, because of the Sangaree woman or otherwise, he or Mouse would get hurt.

A *clang* rang through the shuttle. The vessel shuddered. BenRabi ceased flaying himself with the tiny, dull knives of the mind.

The lighter nosed into its mother ship like a piglet to a sow's belly. Moyshe followed the crowd moving to board the starship. He worked his way close to the pale Seiner girl. Could he pick up where he had left off?

He wondered why she intrigued him so. Just because she had been kind?

Guides led the way to a common room where several high-powered command types awaited them. *Another lecture*, Moyshe thought. *Some more shocks set off by a lot of boredom.*

He was half right.

Even before they were comfortable, one of the heavy-duty lads said, "I'm Eduard Chouteau, your Ship's Commander. Welcome aboard Number Three Service Ship from *Danion*, a harvestship of Payne's Fleet." That was enough ceremony, evidently. He continued, "We've contracted you as emergency replacements for technicians *Danion* lost in a shark attack two months ago. Frankly, Fishers haven't ever liked or trusted outsiders. That's because outsiders have given us reason. But for *Danion*'s sake we'll do right by you till we get our own people from the schools. All we ask is that you do right by us."

BenRabi felt that little feather tickle again. Half-truths were fluttering around like untamed butterflies. The man had something on his mind. There was a smoke screen rolling tall and wide, and behind it something he and Mouse just might find interesting. He made a mental note.

The Seiner schools were unique. Most ground-siders knew a little about them. They made romantic, remote settings for holonet dramas.

Those shows, naturally, had borne little relation to reality.

The Seiner creches were hidden in dead planetoids somewhere in deep space. The old and the young of the Fisher fleets dwelt there, teaching and learning. Only healthy Seiners of working age spaced with the fleets and hazarded themselves against disasters of the sort that had overtaken *Danion*.

Unlike Confederation parents, Starfishers yielded their children to professional surrogates out of love. They did not see their young as dead weight that might hamper them as they shot the rapids of life.

BenRabi had never seen enough of his father to have developed an emotional attitude toward him. And what could he think about his mother? She could not help being what she was. His mother was the child of her society, shaped by a high-pressure environment. The years and prejudice had devoured their tenuous umbilical link... They were of alien tribes now. The barrier between them could no longer be breached, even with the best will on both sides.

Visiting her had been a waste of leave time, but then there was the kid.

How was Greta doing? Christ! He might not know for one hell of a long time.

Why had his mother's behavior so horrified him? He should have known better than to have gone. He had come out of that world. All Old Earth was a screaming rat warren packed with people seeking new thrills and perversions as escapes from the grim realities of narrow little lives.

"Lights!" the Ship's Commander snapped. BenRabi returned from introspection. A hologram took form in the center of the darkening common room. It developed like some fantasy magician's uncertain conjuration, flickering for several seconds, then jerking into sudden, awe-inspiring solidity.

"The stars you see here we retaped off a standard Second Level astrogation training module. Our holo people dubbed the ships from models used in an engineering status display at Ship's Engineering Control aboard *Danion*. This is *Danion*, your home for the next year."

The name *Danion* rolled off his tongue, freighted with everything the ship meant to him: home, country, refuge, responsibility.

A ship formed against the imaginary stars. It was a weird thing, making Moyshe think of octopi entwined. No. He decided it looked like a city's utilities systems after the buildings and earth and pavement had been removed, with the leavings flung mad among the stars. There were vast tangles of tubing. Here and there lay a ball, a cone, a cube, or an occasional sheet of silverness stretched taut as if to catch the starwinds. Vast nets floated between kilometers-long pipelike arms. The whole mad construct was raggedly bearded with thousands of antennae of every conceivable type. The totality was spectacularly huge, and dreadful in its strangeness.

In theory a deep-space vessel need not be confined in a geometric hull. Most small, specialized vessels were not. A ship did not have to have any specific shape, though the complex relationships between drive, inertial-negation, mass increase effect reduction, temporal adjustment, and artificial gravity induction systems did demand a direction-of-travel dimension slightly more than twice that of dimensions perpendicular to line-of-flight in vessels intended to operate near or above the velocity of light. But this was the first truly large asymmetric ship benRabi had ever seen.

It was a flying iron jungle. The streamlined ship had been preferred by mankind since space travel had been but a dream. Even now designers felt more comfortable enclosing everything inside a skin capable of generating an all-around defensive screen.

Even the wildest imaginings of novelty-hunting holo studios had never produced a vessel as knotted and strewn as this mass of tangled kitten's yarn.

BenRabi's astonishment was not unique. Silence died a swift death in that room.

"How the hell does that bastard keep from breaking up?" someone demanded.

"What I want to know is, how do you build something like that without a crew from every holonet in the universe turning up?"

Someone more technically smitten asked, "Ship's Commander—what sort of system do you use to synchronize drives? You'd have to have hundreds on a ship that big. Even with superconductor or pulse laser control systems your synch systems would be limited to the velocity of light. The lag between the more remote units…"

BenRabi lost the thread. Another surprise had jumped on him wearing hobnailed boots on all four feet.

He was aboard a ship he and Mouse had studied from the surface of Carson's. She was a typical interstellar vessel of an obsolete class now common only among the Rim Run Freehaulers.

A similar vessel had appeared in the hologram. It was approaching the harvestship.

The surprise was in their relative sizes.

The starship became a needle falling into an expanding, cosmic ocean of scrap. The service ship retained its holo dimensions.

Danion swelled till she attained epic proportions.

Moyshe could not begin to guess her true dimensions. His most conservative estimate staggered him. She had to be at least thirty kilometers in cross-section, twenty thick, and sixty long. That was impossible. There were countries on Old Earth smaller than that.

And stretching far beyond the dense central snarl of the ship were those spars spreading silvery sails and nets.

Did she sunjam on stellar winds?

She couldn't. The Starfish stayed away from stars. Any stars, be they orbited by settled worlds or not. They stayed way out in the Big Dark where they could not be found.

The whole thing had to be a brag show. Pure propaganda. It just had to be.

He could not accept that ship as real.

His normal, understandable operation-opening jitters cranked themselves up a couple of notches. Till that ship had declared itself he had thought he could handle anything new and strange. Change was the order of the universe. Novelty was no cause for distress.

But this mission held too much promise of the new and unknown. He had been plunged *tabula rasa* into a completely alien universe.

Nothing created by Man had any right being so damned big.

Light returned. It drowned the dying hologram. BenRabi looked around. His jaw was not the only one hanging like an overripe pear about to drop.

Despite prior warning, everyone had believed themselves *aboard* a harvestship. Cultural bias left them incapable of believing the Fishers could have anything better.

Moyshe began to realize just how poorly he had been prepared for this mission. He had done his homework. He had devoured everything the Bureau had known about Starfishers. He had considered speculation as well as confirmed fact. He knew all there was to know.

Too little had been known.

"That's all you'll need to know about *Danion*'s outside," the Ship's Commander told them. "Of her guts you'll see plenty, and you'll have to learn them well. We expect to get our money's worth."

They had the right to ask it, Moyshe figured. They were paying double the usual spacer's rates, and those were anything but poor.

The man talked on awhile, repeating the security officer's injunctions. Then he turned the landsmen over to ratings, who showed them to their quarters. BenRabi's nervousness subsided. He had been through this part before, each time he had boarded a Navy warship.

He got a cabin to himself. The Seiner assigned to him helped settle him in. From the man's wary replies, Moyshe presumed he could expect to be aboard for several days. Payne's Fleet was harvesting far from Carson's.

Once the man had left and benRabi had converted his barren cubicle into a Spartan cell, he lay down to nap. After looking for bugs and spy-eyes, of course. But sleep would not come. Not with all the great lumpy surprises his mind still had to digest.

Someone knocked. Mouse, he guessed. The man never used a buzzer. He made a crochet a means of identification.

Yes. It was Mouse. "Hi," he said. "I'm Masato Iwasaki. Oh. You're in Liquids too? Good." He stuck out a hand. They shook.

"BenRabi. Moyshe. Nice to meet you." Silly game, he thought. But it had to be played if they wanted people to believe that they had just met.

"You wouldn't happen to play chess?" Mouse asked. "I'm looking for somebody who does."

He was addicted to the game. It would get him into trouble someday, benRabi thought. An agent could not afford consistent crochets. But who was he to criticize?

"I've been up and down the passage, but I haven't found anybody."

No doubt he had. Mouse was thorough.

"I play, but badly. And it's been awhile." It had been about four hours. They had almost been late to the spaceport because of a game. Mouse had been nervous about liftoff. BenRabi had been holding his own.

Mouse prowled, searching for bugs. BenRabi closed the door.

"I don't think there are any. Not yet. I didn't find anything."

Mouse shrugged. "What do you think?"

"Broomstick all the way. Strictly from hunger. We're riding the mythical nova bomb."

"The woman? Yeah. Pure trouble. Spotted a couple McGraws, too. You think she's teamed?" He dropped onto the extra bunk.

"I don't think so. Not by choice. She's a loner."

"It doesn't look good," Mouse mused. "We don't have enough info. I feel like a blind man in a funhouse. We'd better fly gentle till we learn the traffic code." He stared at the overhead. "And how to con the natives."

BenRabi settled onto his own bunk. They remained silent for minutes, trying to find handles on the future. They would need every advantage they could seize.

"Three weeks," Mouse said. "I can handle it. Then a whole year off. I won't know what to do."

"Don't make your reservations yet. Marya... The Sangaree woman. She's one bad omen. Mouse... I don't think it's going to work out."

"I can handle it. You don't think I want to spend a whole damned year here, do you?"

"Remember what that character said down at Blake City? It could be the rest of our lives. Short lives."

"Bah. He was blowing smoke."

"Ready to bet your life on it?"

BenRabi's head gave him a kick. He was not sure he could take much more pain. And this compelling *need*...

"What's the matter?"

"Headache. Must be the change in air pressure."

How the hell was he supposed to work with his body in pain and his mind half around the bend? There was something to be said for those old-time sword swingers who did not have to worry about anything but how sharp their blades were.

"We'd better hedge our bets, Moyshe. Better start planning for the long haul, just in case."

"Thought you could handle it."

Mouse shrugged. "Got to be ready for everything. I've been poking around. These Seiners are as bad as us for special interests.

They've got coin clubs and stamp clubs and Archaicist period groups... The whole thing. They're crazy to get into the past. What I was thinking was, why don't we start a chess club for landsmen? We'd have a cover for getting together."

"And you'd have an excuse to play."

"That too. A lot of Seiners play too, see. Maybe we could fish a few in so we could pump them socially." He winked, smiled.

The Seiners he was interested in hooking were probably female.

BenRabi could not fathom Mouse. Mouse seemed happy most of the time. That was disconcerting. The man carried a load of obsessions heavier than his own. And somebody whose profession was hatchet work should, in benRabi's preconceptions, have had a happiness quotient approaching zero.

BenRabi never had been able to understand people. Everybody else seemed to live by a different set of rules.

Mouse shrugged. "Fingers crossed? Hope Beckhart will pull it off? Wouldn't bet against him."

BenRabi *never* knew where he stood in the Admiral's grand, tortuous schemes.

"Hey, I've been here long enough," Mouse said. "No point attracting attention straight off. I saw you get pills from that girl. What was wrong? Head?"

"Yeah. Might even be my migraine. My head feels like somebody's been using it for a soccer ball."

Mouse went to the door. "A game tonight, then?"

"Sure, as long as you don't mind playing an amateur." BenRabi saw him off, feeling foolish. There had been no one around to hear his parting speech.

The public address system announced dinner for passengers. Mouse turned back. "Feel up to it?"

BenRabi nodded. Though it had ached miserably seconds ago, the tracer was not bothering him at all now.

Somebody was trying to impress them. The meal was superb. It was the kind Navy put on when important civilians came aboard. Everything was hydroponics and recycle, yet supremely palatable. Each mouthful reminded benRabi of the horrors of a Navy mess six months out, after the fresh and frozen stores were gone. From some angles the mission had begun to show promise.

He looked for the Seiner girl, Amy, but did not see her.

Lazy days followed. There was little to do in transit. He stayed in his cabin most of the time, loafing, toying with *Jerusalem*, and trying not to remember too much. Mouse, and a few others he had met, occasionally came to visit, play chess, or just bullshit about common interests.

The landsmen began to settle in, to get acquainted. The unattached singles started pairing off. Mouse, never inclined to celibacy, found himself a girl the second day. Already she wanted to move in with him.

Individual quarters had been assigned everyone but the married couples. There was room. The ship had been prepared to haul a thousand people.

Mouse immediately established himself as a character and leader among the landsmen. His notion of a chess club, while no fad, caught on.

One of the joiners was the Seiner who had striven to rattle them at Blake City.

His name was Jarl Kindervoort. He did not hide the fact that he ranked high in *Danion*'s police department.

BenRabi marveled again at the size of the harvestship. A vessel so huge that it had a regular police agency, complete with detectives and plainclothes operatives   Just incredible.

They called themselves Internal Security. BenRabi saw nothing in what he learned of their structure to remind him of a security unit in the intelligence sense. The function was doubtless there, cobbled on in response to the arrival of outsiders, but the agency look was that of a metropolitan police force.

Mouse's club inspired a general movement. Half a dozen others coalesced. Each was Archaicist-oriented.

In an age when nothing seemed as permanent as the morning dew, people who needed permanence had to turn to the past.

BenRabi looked on the whole Archaicist movement with studied contempt. He saw it as the refuge of the weak, of moral cowards unwilling to face the Now without the strategic hamlets of yesterday to run to when the pressure heightened.

Archaicism could be damned funny. BenRabi remembered a

holocast of pot-bellied old men stamping through modern New York outfitted as Assyrian soldiery off for a sham battle with the legions of the Pharaoh of New Jersey.

Or it could be grim. Sometimes they started believing... He still shuddered whenever he recalled the raid on the temple of the Aztec Revivalists in Mexico City.

One morning he asked Mouse to read the working draft of his story. He had managed to push it all the way to an unsatisfactory ending.

Mouse frowned a lot. He finally said, "I guess it's all right. I don't know anything about non-objective art."

"I guess that means it isn't working. I'd better get on it and do it right. Even if you can't figure out what the hell it's about, it should affect you."

"Oh, it does, Moyshe."

His tone conveyed more message than did his words. It said that he thought benRabi was wasting his time.

Moyshe wanted to cry. The story meant so damned much to him.

SIX: 3047 AD
The Olden Days, Luna Command

He waited patiently in the line outside Decontamination. When his turn came he went to Cubicle R. No one else had done so. A sign saying OUT OF SERVICE clung to the door beneath the R.

That sign had been there more than twenty years. It was old and dirty and lopsided. Everyone in Luna Command knew that door R did not open on a standard decon chamber.

The men and women, and occasional non-humans, who ignored the sign were agents returning from the field.

He closed the door and placed his things on a counter surface, then removed his clothing. Nude, he stepped through the next door inward.

Energy from the scanner in the door frame made his skin tingle and his body hair stand out. He held his breath, closed his eyes.

Needles of liquid hit him, stung him, killing bacteria and rinsing grime away. Sonics cracked the long molecular helixes of viruses.

A mist replaced the spray. He breathed deeply.

Something clicked. He stepped through the next door.

He entered a room identical to the first. Its only furniture was a counter surface. On that counter lay neatly folded clothing and a careful array of personal effects. He dressed, filled his pockets, chuckling. He had been demoted. His chevrons proclaimed him a Second Class Missileman. His ship's patch said he was off the battle cruiser *Ashurbanipal*.

He had never heard of the vessel.

He pulled the blank ID card from the wallet he had been given, placed his right thumb over the portrait square. Ten seconds later his photograph and identification statistics began to appear.

"Cornelius Wadlow Perchevski?" he muttered in disbelief. "It gets worse and worse." He scanned the dates and numbers, memorizing, then attached the card to his chest. He donned the Donald Duck cap spacers wore groundside, said, "Cornelius Perchevski to see the King."

The floor sank beneath him.

As he descended he heard the showers go on in the decon chamber.

A minute later he stepped from a stall in a public restroom several levels lower. He entered a main traffic tunnel and walked to a bus stop.

Six hours later he told a plain woman behind a plain desk behind a plain room, behind a plain door, "Cornelius W. Perchevski, Missileman Two. I'm supposed to see the doctor."

She checked an appointment log. "You're fifteen minutes late, Perchevski. But go ahead. Through the white door."

He passed through wondering if the woman knew she was fronting. Probably not. The security games got heaviest where they seemed least functional.

The doctor's office made him feel like Alice, diving down a rabbit hole into another world.

It's just as crazy as Wonderland, he thought. *Black is white here. Up is down. In is out. Huck is Jim, and never the Twain shall meet...* He chuckled.

"Mr. Perchevski."

He sobered. "Sir?"

"I believe you came in for debriefing."

"Yes, sir. Where do you want me to start, sir?"

"The oral form. Then you'll rest. Tomorrow we'll do the written. I'll schedule the cross-comparative for later in the week.

We're still trying to get the bugs out of a new cross-examination program."

Perchevski studied the faceless man while he told his tale. The interrogator's most noteworthy feature was his wrinkled, blue-veined, weathered hands. His inquisitor was old...

The Faceless Man usually was not. Normally he was a young, expert psychologist-lawyer. The old men in the Bureau were ex-operatives, senior staff, decision-makers, not technicians.

He knew most of the old men. He listened to the questions carefully, but there was no clue in the voice asking them. It was being technically modified. He reexamined the hands. They offered no clues either.

He began to worry. Something had gone broomstick. They did not bring on the dreadnoughts otherwise.

His nerves were not up to an intensive interrogation. It had been a heavy mission, and the trip home had given him too much time to talk to himself.

Debriefing continued all month. They questioned him and counterchecked his answers so often and so thoroughly that when they finally let him go he no longer really felt that the mission had been part of *his* life. It was almost as if some organ had been removed from him one molecule at a time, leaving him with nothing but a funny empty feeling.

Five weeks after he had arrived at Luna Command they handed him a pink plastic card identical in all other respects to the white one he had received at Decontamination. They also gave him an envelope containing leave papers, money, bankbooks, and such written persona as a man needed to exist in an electronic universe. Included was an address.

An unsmiling amazon opened a door and set him free.

He stepped into the public tunnels of Luna Command. Back from beyond the looking glass. He caught a bus just like any spacer on leave.

The room was exactly as he had left it—except that *they* had moved it a thousand kilometers from its former location. He tumbled into his bed. He did not get out again for nearly two days.

Cornelius Perchevski was a lonely man. He had few friends.

The nature of his profession did not permit making many.

For another five days he remained isolated in his room, adapting to the books, collections, and little memorabilia that could be accounted the time-spoor of the real him. Like some protean beast his personality slowly reshaped itself to its natural mold. He began taking interest in the few things that made a unified field of his present and past.

He took down his typewriter and notebooks and pecked away for a few hours. A tiny brat of agony wrested itself from the torn womb of his soul. He punched his agent's number, added his client code, and fed the sheets to the fax transmitter.

In a year or two, if he was lucky, a few credits might materialize in one of his accounts.

He lay back and stared at the ceiling. After a time he concluded that he had been alone enough. He had begun to heal. He could face his own kind again. He rose and went to a mirror, examined his face.

The deplastification process was complete. It always took less time than did his internal mendings. The wounds within never seemed to heal all the way.

He selected civilian clothing from his closet, dressed.

He returned to public life by taking a trip to the little shop. The bus was crowded. He began to feel the pressure of all those personalities, pushing and pulling his own... Had he come out too early? Each recovery seemed to take a little longer, to be a little less effective.

"Walter Clark!" the lady shopkeeper declared. "Where the hell have you been? You haven't been in here for six months. And you look like you've been through hell."

"How's it going, Max?" A self-conscious grin ripped his face open. Christ, it felt good to have somebody be glad to see him. "Just got out of the hospital."

"Hospital? Again? Why didn't you call me? What happened? Some Stone Age First Expansioner stick a spear in you again?"

"No. It was a bug this time. Acted almost like leukemia. And they don't even know where I picked it up. You have anything new for me?"

"Sit your ass down, Walter. You bet I have. I tried to call you when it came in, but your box kept saying you weren't available. You ought to get a relay put on that thing. Here, let me get you some coffee."

"Max, I ought to marry you."

"No way. I'm having too much fun being single. Anyway, why ruin a perfectly good friendship?" She set coffee before him.

"Oh. This's the real thing. I love you."

"It's Kenyan."

"Having Old Earth next door is good for something, then."

"Coffee and comic opera. Here's the collection. The best stuff is gone already. You know how it is. I didn't know when you'd show up. I couldn't hold it forever."

Perchevski sipped coffee. He closed his eyes and allowed the molecules of his homeworld to slide back across his taste buds. "I understand. I don't expect you to hang on to anything if you've got another customer." He opened the ancient stamp album.

"You weren't out to the March of Ulant, were you, Walter?"

"Ulant? No. The other direction. Why?"

"Because of the rumors, I was curious. You know how Luna Command is. They say Ulant has been rearming. The Senators are kicking up a fuss. High Command keeps telling them it's nonsense. But I've had a couple of high-powered corporate executive types in and they say the Services are smoke screening, that there's something going on out there. A lot of heavy ships moving through here lately, too. All of them moving from out The Arm in toward the March."

"It's all news to me, Max. I haven't had the holo on since I got back. I'm so far behind I'll probably never catch up. These Hamburg... The notes all over the page. What are they?"

"Jimmy Eagle did that. Right after I picked up the collection. Lot of them are forgeries. The cancellations. Most of the stamps are good. He marked the reprints. You haven't heard any news at all?"

"Max, by the time I got back from Illwind I was so sick I couldn't see. I didn't care. I don't know why we've got an embassy on that hole, anyway. Or why they sent me there. The only natives I ever saw were two burglars we caught trying to blow up the Ambassador's safe. They need a military assistance mission like

Old Earth needs another Joshua Ja. Their methods of killing each other are adequate already."

"Then you haven't even heard that Ja is done for?"

"Hey? What happened? This I got to hear about."

Joshua Ja was one of Old Earth's more noxious public figures. The holonet newscasters had dubbed him the Clown Prince of Senegal. The nets followed his threats and posturing faithfully, using him as humorous leavening for their otherwise grim newscasts.

The self-proclaimed Emperor of Equatorial Africa was no joke to his subjects and neighbors. His scatterbrained projects and edicts invariably cost lives.

"He invaded the Mauritanian Hegemony while you were gone."

Perchevski laughed. "Sounds like one gang of inmates trying to break into another's asylum."

Old Earth was a nonvoting member of Confederation. Both Confederation itself and the World Government refrained from interfering in local affairs. World Government held off because it had no power. Confederation did so because the costs of straightening out the home-world were considered prohibitive.

Earth was one of the few Confederation worlds supporting multiple national states. And the only one boasting an incredible one hundred twenty-nine.

World Government's writ ran only in those countries deigning to go along with its decrees.

Centuries earlier there had been but two states on Earth, World Commonweal and United Asia. United Asia had remained impotent throughout its brief, turbulent history. World Commonweal might have created a planetary state, but had collapsed at Fail Point, so called because at that point in time agro-industrial protein production capacity had fallen below the population's absolute minimum survival demand.

"You missed the best part of it, Walter. During the first week the Mauritanians shot down half of their own air force. And the Empire lost a whole armored brigade in a swamp because Ja ordered them to march in a straight line all the way to Timbuktu. The holonets had a field day. That's the lilac brown shade there.

We've got a Foundation certificate for it."

Perchevski lifted the stamp and examined its reverse. "I already have a copy. I'm just looking."

"Anyway, the Mauritanians have been less klutzy than the Imperials. They're closing in on Dakar."

"What's the Council doing?"

"Laughing a lot. They're going to let him go down. The word's out that other countries shouldn't accept refugees from the Empire. Ja and his gang have done too much damage to Old Earth's image."

"Old Josh? You're kidding. How do you lower something that's already at the bottom?"

"You see anything you want?"

"You, my love."

"Smart ass."

"Wednesday night?"

"What've you got in mind?"

"A cribbage game."

"I'll call you. If it does any good. If you're not off to some weird place with a name like Toilet Bowl."

"Actually, I was thinking about going to the archaeological digs at Ley."

"Funny you should mention them. More coffee?"

"Sure. Why?"

"They broke into a new chamber last month. It was in pretty good shape."

"Is it open?"

"They put a transparent tube in. You can walk through and look, but you can't get close to anything or get in the way."

"Call me, then. If you want to go see."

"Excuse me, Walter." Another customer had come in. "Yes sir? May I help you?"

"How are you in Twenty-first Century France?"

Perchevski lost himself in the bits of paper that told tales of a remote, turbulent era. He finally selected seven pieces for his collection, paid for them from the Walter Clark account.

"Max, thanks for the coffee. And hold that Berlin piece, will you? I'll let you know as soon as I make up my mind. Like maybe Wednesday?"

"All right, Walter. I'll call you tomorrow."

"Leave a message if I'm not there."

"I will."

He clambered aboard a bus and returned the two hundred kilometers to his apartment.

You're a fool, he told himself. *To go all that way for an hour of gossip.*

But damn, did he feel better.

He had traveled a lot farther in the past. He doubted that Max had a ghost of a notion just what she meant to him. She was one of the few stable realities in his life. She was a landmark by which he guided himself back from the wildernesses of Bureauland.

He mounted his new stamps in his albums using a surgeon's care. He took down a notebook and marked their catalog numbers off his list of wants, noting the date and price he had paid for each. He entered the total in his cumulative ledger, then marked down the fact that two more album pages had been filled.

The detailed record keeping was necessitated by something within him, some compulsion to put down tiny proofs that he was interacting with the universe, if only through the hieroglyphics of numbers. He had other notebooks in which he kept other records. He did a lot of bookkeeping on the events of his life.

None of it ever left his apartment.

He wondered what the Bureau snoops made of the lists and notes. He was sure they checked them whenever he was away.

He finished his record keeping. He looked around the sterile room. It suddenly became very tight, very lonely.

He tried the holo, turning to the Luna Command news channel. He caught it in a low cycle. There was nothing on but an endless parade of public service messages, though once a commentator mentioned rumors of a forthcoming major news event involving Navy. Something big was expected, but its nature could not be determined. Security remained unusually tight.

"Sure," Perchevski growled at the cube. "The Chief of Staff will probably announce this year's winners in the Fleet Backgammon Playoffs."

Luna Command was heart and brain of Confederation. It was

headquarters for the Services, which were Confederation's bone and sinew. It was the hub of a human enterprise kept unified only by its military. And the only exciting thing that had happened there in Perchevski's lifetime had been the discovery of the prehistoric alien base on the moon's dark side.

The military did not control Confederation. But the only obstacle to absolute military rule was a gentlemen's agreement among the generals and admirals to accept the forms of democracy. High Command could do anything it damned well pleased, any time it pleased, were it to ignore custom. Out in the remote reaches, far from senatorial eyes, it often did. There were few sanctions the civilian sector could exercise.

Aggravated, Perchevski killed the holocast. He checked the lunar calendar for the best viewing site, recovered his tunic, and hit public transportation again. He took the high-velocity electric train the six hundred kilometers to the tourist observation dome overlooking Tycho.

The crater was not the attraction there. People did not come from Confederation's one hundred thirty-four member planets, and more than a hundred dominions, protectorates, associated states, and outright colonies, to look at a hole in the ground. The allies and tributaries were not interested in a crater either.

Neither was Perchevski.

Tycho observation dome offered a magnificent view of Old Earth. His homeworld. A world he had not visited in eight years.

Tycho, or its sister domes, was as close as most tourists cared to get to their biological roots.

Perchevski lay back in a lounger and half-listened to the canned commentary.

"...where the race of Man began... possibly also the planet of origin of the Sangaree... first successful extraterrestrial landing, July 20, 1969, in the old dating. Neil Armstrong... ascension of World Commonweal following World War III... Fail Point, July, 2194, led to the Collapse. Reinhardt Ships carried Commonweal refugees to interstellar colonies from 2187 through the end of the Luna Wars in 2226. The Treaties of Jerusalem of 2228 led to the chaotic exploration and random settlement we now call

First Expansion.

"A profligate expenditure of resources and racial will initiated a reactionary isolationism which spanned the twenty-fourth and twenty-fifth centuries. Space travel, even to Luna, was discontinued. Contact with the star worlds did not resume till 2613, when Vice-Admiral Takada Yoshimura brought New Earth's fleet back to Luna. A short time later Yoshimura encountered ships of the Palisarian Directorate.

"The old records in Luna Command revealed the locations of scores of settled worlds. The secondary colonies of the Directorate were under pressure from Toke at the time. The Directorate and New Earth concluded a xenophobic alliance, and began searching for other human allies.

"The concept, if not the fact, of Confederation had been created.

"We have our former enemies, the Toke, to thank for midwifing Confederation through its birth pains. The unrelenting determination of the Star Lords and Caste of Warriors united humanity. The conflict endured sufficiently long for Confederation to become a reality, with its military headquartered here in the tunnels of Luna.

"Confederation and Luna Command have been growing steadily since."

Perchevski stopped listening. He had heard it all before.

He knew he would hear it again. The viewing domes were the Meccas of regular hadjs.

He looked at the Earth and wondered how his parents were doing. He had not heard from either for a long time.

He slept while returning to his apartment. It had been a long day.

Two messages awaited him. The first was from Max. She wanted to see the xenoarchaeological digs Darkside. The other was from his employers. The printout said: SENIOR STAFF PARTY WEDNESDAY 8 PM ATTENDANCE MANDATORY CONTACT 864-6400-312 FOR FURTHER INFO.

He sighed, pecked out the number. Max would not like this. He tried her number after he had gotten the story.

"Max? Walter. Yeah. Thanks for calling. Hey, I've got a problem.

Just got word from my boss. I have to go to a staff party tomorrow night. Can't get out of it. I know. I'm sorry. Hey! Want to come along? All the big wheels will be there. The Chief of Staff Navy is supposed to come out with some big announcement. No. I don't think it has anything to do with the March of Ulant. That's all smoke screen, if you ask me. It's at the Command Club. Can you meet me there? Okay. 'Bye."

He lay back on his bed and wondered what the news would be, and why he had been ordered to make an appearance. He was a senior operative, but certainly not senior staff.

He also wondered how long it would be before they called him down and stuck him behind a desk. It didn't look as if his vacation was going to go through, and they did not like people just loafing around while they waited for an assignment.

Again he thought about his parents.

SEVEN: 3048 AD
Operation Dragon, Engagement

He could not write. He had too much free time. He always worked better when the minutes were quick and crowded.

Something was wrong with his head. Skeletons were coming out of their closets in there. Especially the Alyce affair. The unbreakable walls of Tyre were crumbling.

It had been years since he had thought about Alyce. Why now? That hasty Psych programing before the mission? Or were the edges of his sanity just fraying?

He had two bad days. There were moments when he did not know where he was or why, or, sometimes, just who he was.

He sometimes felt his life was managed by guardian devils. The Fates pursued him like indefatigable hounds, with malice their only joy.

The ship dropped hyper without warning. "Are we finally there?" he asked the air. He stepped into the corridor. Most of the landsmen were there.

Jarl Kindervoort's voice filled the ship. "Passengers, remain in your quarters. Strap in for acceleration. We're about to engage a Confederation squadron that has been following us."

"Engage?" Moyshe said. "What the hell? Mouse? What's going on? Jupp's not supposed to move for two weeks yet."

Mouse shook his head warningly. People were listening. The Sangaree woman appeared to be in a black rage.

"Wheels within wheels," benRabi whispered. "Beckhart's doing it to us."

"Let's hope we didn't suddenly get expendable," Mouse said. "What's going on?"

"Oh, damn! I figured *you* knew. Beckhart? Maybe Jupp thought he saw a chance? Maybe that frontier thing broke?"

"What? That's bullshit. The Ulantonids know better. It's the Old Man. Got to be."

"Better strap in. Say any prayers you know." BenRabi had seen several battles while in the line. They had ruined his taste for space warfare. Defeats were too total and final.

The vessel shuddered while he was strapping in. He recognized a heavy missile salvo departing. The ship clearly mounted weaponry not customary for her class.

Would the nasty surprises never end?

For a few seconds his mind fell apart completely, into absolute chaos. A tiny part of him seemed to be outside, watching the disorder.

All-clear bells and his door buzzer sounding bracketed the reassembly process.

A crewman stepped into his cabin. "Mr. benRabi? Will you come with us, please?"

He was as polite as the spider inviting the fly.

There was going to be trouble.

A half-dozen people wearing guns backed him. BenRabi joined them in the passageway.

Another group had collected a stoic Mouse.

How had they blown it?

Kindervoort was directing the pickup himself. He looked like a man with a compulsion to explain. And to ask. Moyshe hoped he would not get primitive.

Mouse seemed to fear that. But hatchetmen lived by the Old Testament: eye for an eye, live by the sword...

"Got you, boys." Kindervoort grinned toothily. He had an overbite.

BenRabi had an irrational aversion to the man. It had nothing to do with the situation. More like loathing at first sight.

Kindervoort had a colorless, fleshless face. His skin lay stretched drumhead tight over prominent cheekbones and a lantern jaw. Shadowed hollows lay between. He achieved a deathshead look when the light was wrong.

BenRabi automatically disliked anyone with that gaunt, graveyard look.

"Ah, here you are," said the Ship's Commander as they shuffled into his darkly decorated office.

The furniture was of mahogany-toned imitation woods crafted in antique styles. The walls and ceiling had been artificially timbered to suggest the captain's cabin of a sailing ship. There were reproductions of antique ship's lanterns, a compass, a sextant, a chart of Henry the Navigator, framed prints featuring caravels, clippers, and the frigate *Constellation*. "Any trouble, Jarl?"

"No sir. The Bureau doesn't employ fanatics. May I present Commanders Masato Igarashi Storm and Thomas Aquinas McClennon, of Confederation Navy? They're senior field agents of the Bureau of Naval Intelligence. Commanders, Ship's Commander Eduard Chouteau."

BenRabi pursed his lips. He had been afraid Mouse's real name might be Storm. Mouse had been conspicuously absent from Academy during their final year of school. That had been the year of the Storm-Hawksblood war in the Shadowline.

Moyshe had visited Blackworld after that war's end. There had been a Masato Igarashi Storm there at the time, but their paths had not crossed. That Masato had taken command of his father's mercenaries after Sangaree treachery had killed his father, brothers, and most of the family officers.

Kindervoort certainly had *him* pat, though the name McClennon seemed like a stranger's, like that of someone he had known a long time ago, in an age of innocence.

He felt less like Thomas Aquinas McClennon than he did Moyshe benRabi, Gundaker Niven, Eric Earl Hollenkamp, Walter Clark, or... How many men had he been?

"Take seats, gentlemen," Chouteau said. "And relax."

BenRabi dropped into a chair, glanced at his partner, Mouse, who also seemed stunned. The simple knowing of a secret name bore so many implications... The spookiest was that someone might have penetrated the Bureau deep enough to have gained access to its primary data system. That meant a mole of a generation's standing.

"Worrying about your Navy friends?" Kindervoort asked. "Don't. They're all right. They cut and ran. And I mean fast. Guess they figured there wasn't any point to a slugfest when they couldn't gain anything even if they won." He chuckled. So did Chouteau.

Had to be a deep mole. Nothing else would explain their perpetual success at evading Confederation.

Kindervoort planted himself in front of benRabi. He leaned close, frowning. Moyshe avoided his deathshead face by staring at Chouteau.

The Ship's Commander leaned back in his fat, comfortable chair and half closed his eyes.

Kindervoort said, "But we're not worried about von Drachau or Admiral Beckhart, are we?" He chuckled, again, moved to Mouse. "Why we wanted to see you was these tracers you've got built in. Walking instels they inflict on us. Ingenious."

They *did* have a mole.

Moyshe had thought he was the only human instel. Beckhart had pissed and moaned like the expense of it was coming out of his own pocket. Redundancy had not seemed plausible after that.

He hadn't really wondered why Mouse was along. Beckhart had issued an assignment. Nobody questioned the Old Man. Not in any way that might look like contradicting his will.

Mouse looked like death warmed over. Swell. It would do him good to get short-sheeted sometimes too.

How come Mouse had not been hurting?

Knowing Beckhart, the Pyschs had programmed the headaches. Maybe to divert attention from Mouse. Had Mouse known?

They had some talking to do.

Beckhart clockwork, jerking along, often was oiled by the confusion of its parts. Only the master knew all the secrets of his machinery.

Would there be more?

Silly question.

Beckhart's nature semed to demand twists on twists and gaudy smoke screens that concealed truths as slippery as greased snakes. His plots, however, while labyrinthine, had their own tightness and logic. They were mapped by the finest computers in Luna Command. He ran simulation models against even the most ridiculous contingencies.

Had Beckhart calculated a mole into this scheme?

BenRabi suddenly intuited that he and Mouse were not partners after all. This time they were voyagers sailing parallel but distinct courses. They had been programmed to hide from one another as much as from their targets. And they had been intended for exposure from the beginning.

Beckhart knew about the mole.

He wanted them taken captive. He wanted them to spend a year in Seiner service.

Moyshe got mad. That was a year stolen from his life!

"The thing's all biological, eh?" Kindervoort asked.

"What?"

"This instel. Remarkable gimmick. Our detectors didn't quiver when you came aboard. 'Course, that didn't matter in the long run."

He was smug, damn him. So was Chouteau, chubby-happy there in his plastic-antique, made for the Archaicist trade captain's chair.

"How the hell did you get my name?" benRabi demanded. They were in the mood for talking. They might give him something the computers could use to pinpoint the mole.

Kindervoort ignored his question.

"We began monitoring the hyper bands when we broke orbit at Carson's. We wanted to see if we could catch anything from von Drachau's squadron. Imagine our surprise when we found out somebody was sending from the ship."

"You were plain lucky, Jarl," Chouteau said.

"It wasn't luck that we knew they were coming, just that they started broadcasting in a ship small enough for us to pinpoint them."

How had they gotten the word?

Moyshe remembered a raggedy-assed Freehauler boat that had not lifted on schedule. Had the Freehaulers been the mole's couriers? *Black Mirage.* Remember that ship. Somebody would have to have a talk with her people someday.

Was there a relationship between Seiners and Freehaulers? Both certainly refused to stop giving grief to Confederation's policy makers.

Chouteau called out, "Doctor DuMaurier, come in here. Let's get on with this."

Kindervoort darted behind Moyshe and seized his shoulders. BenRabi did not resist. There was nothing he could do.

A doctor pushed into the room. He poked, pinched, and sprayed Moyshe's neck with an aerosol anesthetic. He removed an unsettlingly ancient lasc-scalpel from his medical bag. Then, quoting every doctor who had ever lived since the days when Incas trepanned one another with sharp stones, he said, "This will only take a minute. You won't feel a thing."

"That's what they told me when they put it in," benRabi grumbled. He could not go down without registering some kind of protest.

"We'll just pull the ambergris nodes," Kindervoort said. "Ed, what do you think? Is it proper to sell them back to Navy come next auction?"

Chouteau nodded amiably. "I think so. I like it."

Moyshe wished they would stop. It made him want to scream, "You're being unprofessional!"

They were not professionals. The harvestships apparently had no real intelligence-oriented security people.

There was justice in Kindervoort's suggestion. BenRabi and Mouse, and all the other agents aboard, irrespective of their allegiances, were after the same thing. Access to one of the herds of great nightbeasts that produced the critical element in the node being removed from benRabi's neck.

The Seiners called it ambergris. The name had evolved from that of a "morbid secretion" of Old Earth whales once used by perfumers. The word could mean anything anyone wanted now. The leviathans of the deep no longer had a claim. They had been extinct for centuries.

Star's amber, space gold, and sky diamond were other popular names. By any name ambergris was the standard of wealth of the age.

In the vernacular its name was short and pithy. It was the solid waste of a starfish. Crap.

This crap fertilized a civilization. Confederation could not have existed without it. Without it there would have been no fast star-to-star communication. Speed and reliability of communications ultimately define the growth limit of any empire.

BenRabi did not comprehend the physics of instel. He knew what the man in the street knew. A tachyon spark could be generated in the arc between an ambergris cathode and a Bilao crystal anode. The spark could be made to carry an FTL message. Neither ambergris nor Bilao crystal could be synthesized.

The crystal occurred naturally deep in the mantles of several roughly earth-sized worlds orbiting super-cool stars. Sierra was the only such world within Confederation. Mining the crystal, at depths exceeding thirty kilometers, was overwhelmingly expensive.

Bilao crystal was cheaper than ambergris. The Seiners had a monopoly. They were free market capitalists of the first water. Every node went to the highest bidder.

The demand for ambergris perpetually exceeded supply. Despite gargantuan capital demands, optimists often assembled the hard and software of an installation merely in hopes that an ambergris node would become available.

The combined Seiner harvestfleets, in their best year ever, had gleaned fewer than forty thousand nodes. Most of those had gone to replace nodes already burning out.

The Seiners sold their product at auction, on worlds declared temporarily neutral and threatened by all the firepower the fleets could muster. The bidders always went along with Seiner rules. The Starfishers might refuse to do business with someone who pushed.

Ambergris alone explained the flood-tide of operatives heading toward Carson's after *Danion* had begun advertising for groundside technicians. The agents had swept in like vultures, hoping to feed on the corpse of a betrayed Payne's Fleet.

That's what we are, benRabi thought. *Me and Mouse, we're vultures... No. Not really. We're more like raptors. Falcons flung from Beckhart's wrist. Our prey is information. We're to bring down any morsel that might betray a starfish herd.*

Moyshe tried to believe that Confederation *should* control the harvesting and distribution of ambergris. He tried hard.

Sometimes he had to tell himself some tall ones to get by. Otherwise he asked himself too many questions. He started worrying irrelevancies like Right and Wrong.

His soul, slithering past morality shyly, merely mumbled *I want.* There was a pain in it that he could not understand. It nagged him worse than did his ulcer.

BenRabi dreaded madness. He was afraid of a lot of things lately. He could not figure it out.

"There. One down." The doctor dropped Moyshe's node into a gleaming stainless steel tray. Plunk! Exclamation point to the end of a phase of the mission. He began suturing Moyshe's wound.

"How bad will that hurt when the anesthetic wears off?"

"Not much. Your neck should be a bit stiff, and tender to the touch. See me if it gives you any trouble." The doctor turned to Mouse. Mouse squirmed a little before he submitted. His conscience, benRabi supposed. He had to make a showing.

Doctors were another of Mouse's crochets. He had no use for them, as he often told anyone who would listen.

BenRabi suspected that was why Beckhart never had Mouse altered during his mission preps.

"We don't like spies," the Ship's Commander blurted. The way he said it made it sound both spontaneous and irrelevant, a non sequitur despite what was happening.

We, Moyshe thought. *These people always say* we.

The worm within him bit. He shifted uncomfortably. Somehow, Chouteau had taunted his need. Weird.

He tried to recapture it, to discover what it was that he wanted, but, like a wet fish, it wriggled through his fingers.

Nearly a minute later, Chouteau pursued his remark. "But *Danion* needs your expertise to survive. And we love her enough to give you another chance." He became less distant.

"Listen up. We're going to keep you alive. But you're going to work till you drop: till you forget why it was that you were sent here. And when we're done with you, we're going to ship you home just as ignorant as you were when you signed on.

"Men, don't give us any more trouble. Be satisfied being ignorant. We need you bad, but won't let you push. *Danion's* big. A couple men more or less wouldn't make much difference. Doctor, aren't you finished yet?"

"Just have to sew him up, sir. One minute."

"Commander McClennon, Commander Storm, go back to your cabins. Try not to aggravate me for a while."

BenRabi rose, touched the small bandage behind his ear. The numbness had begun to fade. He could feel a mild burning. It made him think of bigger cuts on his body and soul.

The doctor finished with Mouse. "There you go, Commander. Try not to strain it too much. I suggest you let your lady friends do the work for a few days." He spoke with a gentle sarcasm that may have masked envy.

"Word's getting around about you, Mouse," benRabi said.

Mouse did not respond. He was in no mood for banter.

They beat an unescorted retreat, seeking their cabins like wounded animals seeking the security of their dens. In the passage outside benRabi's cabin, Mouse asked, "What do we do now, Moyshe?"

BenRabi shrugged. "I don't know. I was hoping you'd think of something. Go for the ride, I guess. They've stalemated us."

"Just for now." Mouse stood a little taller. "We've got a year. They can't keep their guard up forever, can they?"

"They probably can." But a little false encouragement felt good. "Still, you never know. Something might turn up."

"Look at that."

The Sangaree lady was watching them from her doorway. She smiled, waved.

"Gloating," benRabi said.

"Think she knows what happened? Think she helped do us in?"

BenRabi shrugged, looked at the woman. Their gazes seemed to ring like meeting swords. Her smile broadened. "Yes. I'm sure she did."

EIGHT: 3047 AD
The Olden Days, The Broken Wings

Hoping Marya would make no sense of the data before him, Niven told her, "I'm checking to see where people go when they leave The Broken Wings. If a statistically significant number emigrate to certain worlds, we can begin to infer both their fantasies under dome conditions and what it is that attracts them to a particular type world. If it's environmental, then we've discovered a way to ease the negatives of dome life." He hoped he sounded tutorial. He cranked it up a notch to be sure. "Ubichi specializes in negative environment, high-yield exploitation operations. Employee turnover has become a major problem because of the expense of training and transportation for some of our field operations. It's in the corporate interest to reduce those costs by keeping our employees happy and comfortable."

Pretty glib, he thought. He congratulated himself. "What're you doing here?"

"Looking for you. We had a date."

"Not till… Holy Christ! Look at the time. Hey beautiful lady, I'm sorry. I got on the track of something. I worked right through lunch. Give me a minute, will you? I'll finish up, call my secretary, and we can get moving." He grinned. "I have to check in. Education didn't wear the Old Earth off of him. You wouldn't believe the hell he gave me last night!"

He no longer felt the smile. She was turning him to gelatin again.

Mouse did not answer his buzz. Niven would have been surprised had he done so. The call was simply a ploy to get the data out of Marya's sight, and to seize time to create a plausible structure of lies atop those he had just told.

He needed no story. Marya asked no questions except, "What do you want to do?"

He almost replied with the hard truth.

"I've had it with work, but we about covered everything last night. Angel City isn't swing-town." Gallantly, he added, "I'm content just being with you. You pick."

She laughed. "And they say there's no romance left on Old Earth. How about we just go for a walk? I feel like a good long one."

"Uh…" His hands started shaking.

He had gotten out young, but the lessons of an Old Earth's childhood died hard. People who did not learn them young also died hard. Not to walk the streets without a gang of friends was one of the strictest lessons of the motherworld.

This was not Old Earth. Death did not make the streets its home here. But the sticktights did lurk there, and they might up the ante in the game at any minute.

"How come you're grinning?"

"That's no grin, lady. That's what they call a rictus. Of fear. I'm Old Earther. You know how hard it would be for me to walk down a street without at least fifty guys to back me up?"

"I forgot. But there's nothing to worry about here, Gun."

"You know it. I know it here in my head. But down here in my guts there's a caveman who says we're both liars."

"If it's really that hard…"

"No, don't get upset. I didn't say I wouldn't try. I've got to get used to it. Hell, I force myself to get out as much as I can. I just wanted to warn you so you won't think it's your fault if I get a little jumpy and quiet."

"You'll settle down. You'll see. This is just about the dullest, least dangerous city in The Arm."

A few hours later, shortly after The Broken Wings' early night had fallen, Niven snarled, "What did you say back at the hospital? Something about the safest streets in the galaxy?"

The darkness of the alley pressed in. His frightened eyes probed the shadows for movement. The lase-bolt had missed his cheek by a centimeter. He still felt the heat of it. "Even my toenails are shaking, lady."

Marya fingered her hair. A bolt had crisped it while they were running. Niven's nostrils twitched as they caught the sharp burnt hair odor.

Marya's face was pallid in the glow of a distant streetlight. She was shaking too. And apparently too angry to respond.

"You got a jealous boyfriend?"

She shook her head, gasped, "This isn't Old Earth. People don't do things like this out here."

Niven dropped to all fours and crawled to the alley mouth.

Heavy work was not his province, but he had had the basic programs given all field agents. He could make a show if he had to.

He had to do something now. The alley was a cul-de-sac. And the rifleman might be teamed. A deathtrap could be closing.

A bolt scarred brick above his head. He rolled away, growling, "Starscope. Damn!" But he had spotted the triggerman. The bolt had come from atop a warehouse across the street.

"Can't be much of a shot," Niven mumbled. "That isn't fifty meters."

If he could survive the sprint across the street...

There was a startled exclamation from the gunman's position, then a choked wail of fear and pain. A body plunged off the warehouse roof and thumped into the street.

Niven was across in an instant, shoving himself into the warehouse wall while he studied the corpse.

The weak light revealed the limper from the Marcos lobby. His windpipe had been crushed.

Every man's signature is unique. And an assassin leaves a grim sort of signature on his victims. Niven knew this one. He peered upward.

Why would Mouse be shadowing him?

Not that he objected. Not right now.

Marya arrived. She averted her eyes. "You must have a guardian angel."

"One of us does." He stared at her. Something clicked. It was nothing he could define, just a tweak of uneasiness because she had not asked him why anyone would want to kill him. A civilian would have asked that right away.

He looked for the assassin's weapon, did not see it. "I'm going to try to get onto that roof."

"Why? Shouldn't we get out of here?"

Another click. Civilians started screaming for the police. Outworlds civilians, anyway.

"Yeah, I guess. If he had anybody with him we would have heard from them by now." But where to go? he wondered. Not the hotel. Not with the number officially on. Not with the war rules proclaimed. And not to a safehouse. He did not yet know what Mouse had arranged. And he could not make the fallbacks to find out with Marya tagging along.

The death threat had alerted the professional in him. Had raised barriers that would wall off the whole universe till he had sorted the friends from enemies and noncombatants.

"We could go to my place," Marya suggested.

Memories of countless spy and detective dramas battled for Niven's attention. Was it all a setup? Three misses at fifty meters seemed unlikely for even a clumsy assassin. But he did not want to believe that Marya was involved. She was such a magnetic, animal woman...

Believe it or not, only a cretin would have ignored the possibility completely. Survival had become the stake on the board.

He dared not let her know he was suspicious. "All right." He looked around fearfully, having no trouble projecting shakiness and confusion. "But I've got to do a couple of things first."

Their eyes met. And he *knew*. He did not want it to be, but it was true. She *was* the enemy. Right now she was trying to find an excuse to stay close to him that would not arouse his suspicions.

She was not a good actress. Under stress she could not control the body language signals that betrayed her thoughts.

He felt betrayed and hurt, though he had known her just one day.

He had always needed to be wanted. Not for whom or what he was, but just as a human being.

Human. Was she even human? There was no sure way of telling without complicated tests. Geneticists were certain that humanity and the Sangaree shared a prehistoric ancestry.

She might even be the new Sangaree Resident. The last one had been a woman.

"Where do you stay?" he asked.

She chose not to push. She explained how he could get to her apartment.

"You don't have to do this," he told her, then cursed silently. By saying that, he had tacitly admitted being the sniper's target. But sometimes it was necessary to take chances. He could at least feed her belief in his lack of suspicion. "It might be dangerous."

"That's all right. I've never been involved in anything like this." Feigned excitement illuminated her face. "What have I gotten myself into, Gun?"

It was smoke screen time. "Sweetheart, I don't know. I really don't. This is the second time I've been jumped, but nobody bothered to tell me why last time either. They tried it right in the Marcos before. The day we got here. And we don't even know anybody here. But people have been following me all the time, and… If you're an Old Earther, you sense things like that."

"Maybe it's not you. Maybe it's your friend."

"John? I never thought of that. I guess it's possible. I don't really know anything about him. The Corporation sent him. Anyway, whatever's going on, I mean to find out."

He had yielded just enough distorted truth, he hoped, to leave her with doubts. A lot depended on whether or not the opposition had been able to evade Mouse's bug-scans.

"Will you be all right, Marya? Should I walk you home?"

"I'll manage."

"Probably be safer without me, anyway. See you in a while."

He glanced at the dead man, then the streets. Not a soul was stirring.

It was odd how people sensed a gathering storm, then stayed inside where they would witness nothing and run no risks. Though this was a warehouse district, there should have been some traffic. Hell. Where were the security patrols? Where were the police cruisers?

He had seen the same thing happen on Old Earth, where the gangs went to their guns at the slightest provocation. Citizens and enforcers always kept a low profile till the stink of gunsmoke left the air.

Mouse was not at the first fallback, nor had he left a message. Niven did find a hastily scribbled message at the second. It told him that Marya was the new Sangaree Resident. And, as if in afterthought, Mouse went on to say that he was on the run from a dozen men who had gotten onto him after the incident at the warehouse.

Niven scratched a reply, explaining where he would be. The drop was large, so he left the notes he had taken at the Med Center.

Those had to be salvaged no matter what. Maybe by Chief Navy Recruiter for The Broken Wings. He was the Bureau Angel City station chief.

Niven began drifting, killing time in order to give Marya a chance to make a move that would illuminate the outfit's current thinking. After an hour he picked up a sticktight.

His shadow was a sleepy-faced thug pretending to be a derelict. A not-too-bright offworlder, Niven decided. Angel City was too young and thoroughly ordered to sustain even a one-man Bowery.

The man did not move in. They were hoping he would lead them to Mouse.

He observed his shadow's tradecraft more out of curiosity than concern. The man was a professional but unaccustomed to this kind of work. He was probably a shooter or runner grabbed simply because he was available. He could be shaken at leisure. Niven shifted him to the back burner of awareness.

He drifted toward Marya's apartment. His nerves settled. He

decided what he was going to do.

He did not relax completely. They might catch Mouse. Then his life would be worthless. But while Mouse remained at large, he was sure, they would not harm him.

He shook the sticktight, found a public comm, woke the Angel City station chief, explained where the Med Center information was hidden. He used a word code the other side would need hours to unravel—assuming they were tapping at all.

He reached Marya's apartment as dawn began coloring the dome. The molecularly stacked plastic glimmered redly. As the sunlight changed its angle of incidence, the plastic would alternate between transparency and a progression up an iridescent spectrum.

He was tired but still alert, and exhilarated because he had handled himself well.

Marya responded to his knock instantly. "Where have you been?" she demanded. "I've been worried sick." She peered over his shoulder, along the second floor hallway.

Checking for Mouse? For her backup?

"Somebody started following me around. I didn't know what to do, so I just walked around till he gave up. Or I lost him."

"Gun, I don't understand all this. Why?..."

"Honey, I don't know. And I've been thinking hard. All I can figure is maybe one of Ubichi's competitors thinks I'm after something besides that research data..." He paused, pretending to have been startled by a thought. "Hey! They never did tell me *why* they want the data. I just assumed... Maybe it's for a project that's stepping on somebody's toes."

Had he been what he claimed, the possibility would have been real. Ubichi maintained its own armed forces. The frontier corporations played rough.

Uncertainty filled Marya's eyes for a moment.

Bureau miscalculated, he thought. He could have convinced her had he *looked* like a social psychologist. His cover could be checked all the way back to his birth. The Bureau was thorough that way. Especially Beckhart's section.

But Niven looked like an Old Earth heavy. And that was the death of any other credential a man could present.

"Mom? What's going on?" A dark-haired girl of seven or eight stumbled into the room. She ground sleepy eyes with the backs of her fists. She was small for her age, a breastless miniature of her mother.

"Brandy, this is my friend Dr. Niven. I told you about him."

"Oh."

Less than enthusiastic, Niven thought. In fact, her expression said he was a threat to her world.

She was a beautiful child. Straight out of a toy ad.

Niven could not frame a compliment that did not sound inane. "Hi, Brandy. You can call me Gun. It's short for Gundaker."

"Gundaker? What kind of name is that?"

"Old Earth."

"Oh." She wrinkled her lip. "Mom called you Doctor. Michael's sick."

He turned to Marya. The woman still stood at the door. "My son. Brandy's younger brother. He's got some kind of bug. Looks like flu."

"I'm not that kind of doctor, Brandy. But if there's anything I can do…"

"Do you know any good stories? Michael don't like the ones I make up. And Mom's never here." She glanced at her mother accusingly.

She was good, Niven thought. Better than Marya. "What kind of stories? Pirates? Olden days? War stories? Richard Hawksblood and Gneaus Julius Storm? Did you know they fought a war right here on The Broken Wings?"

He mentioned it casually, conversationally, fishing for a reaction. The war in the Shadowline, the last great mercenary war, had taken place on Blackworld not long after the encounter on The Broken Wings.

Sangaree interests had taken a beating because of the Shadowline. But one or two Families had begun recouping here before the shock-waves from Blackworld had died.

Getting caught with their hands in there had cost them control of numerous legitimate corporations and the lives of several Family chieftains. The disaster had been so huge and widespread that it had become Sangaree legend.

The girl just shrugged, implying that Blackworld meant nothing to her. "Pirates, probably." She seemed to lose interest.

She left the room. Cooking sounds followed her departure.

Must not have heard about the Shadowline, Niven thought. What Family did Marya represent? A minor one crowding the First Families because of their loss of face on Blackworld? Surely not one that had been involved there.

"She's a doll," he told Marya. "You thought about getting her into modeling?"

"No. She wouldn't. Sit down. Relax. I'll fix you something to eat. Then I'll move Michael in here. You can sleep in the kids' bed."

Brandy brought coffee. It was real.

He discovered what Marya had meant about Brandy. He had not caught it earlier because she had not looked his way.

The girl's one eye trained wildly walleyed and appeared blind.

He showed no reaction to her pained, defiant stare. Her sensitivity screamed at him. He supposed the damage was recent.

Niven indulged in tradecraft during the few seconds when Brandy had returned to the kitchen and Marya had not yet returned. He examined his surroundings critically.

The time would come when he would have to report, accurately, where every speck of dust had lain.

The apartment was cramped. That was typical of dome city living quarters. It was sparsely populated by ragged second hand furniture. That was to be expected of poor folks. And Marya, clearly, was not an obsessive housekeeper. Cobwebs hung in the ceiling corners. Junk cluttered the chairs and floors.

Her sloppiness had nothing to do with poverty or lack of time, only with habit. Sangaree at home had animal servants who picked up after them.

Marya shared her roof with whole tribes of roaches. Dirt streaked the plastic walls. The curtains were frayed and soiled.

It was exactly the sort of place where a busy, impoverished woman would come to rest. She was crafty, this one. She had converted her ethnic liabilities into assets.

But would a poor woman serve real coffee? When coffee had to come all the way from Old or New Earth?

He did not call her on it. He might give something away by revealing that he recognized the real thing when he tasted it. Most Old Earthers would not, because every ounce went into export.

They were fencing now, subtly, with rapiers consisting of little tests.

One of the rules of his profession was never to yield anything concrete.

She was not giving him anything either. Certainly not enough to understand her.

Who could comprehend the Sangaree mind? The Admiral had been trying for decades. He barely got by.

Like Mouse, though, Beckhart did not want to understand. Not really. He wanted to destroy. Comprehension was just a weapon in his arsenal.

They sat in silence for several minutes. He watched Marya over his cup. She considered him. He wondered what strange thoughts might be running through her alien brain.

"I'd better check on Michael, Gun."

He followed her as far as the bedroom door.

The room was tiny. It contained two dilapidated beds. One for Marya, one for her children.

Marya settled on the edge of the one containing a pale five-year-old. The boy watched Niven warily.

"Michael, this is my friend Dr. Niven. He's going to stay with us for a while."

"Hi, Mike."

"Not Mike." The child's voice was weak but angry. "Michael. After my great-grandfather."

Marya winced.

Michael radiated pride.

Niven controlled his surprise. "Right. Michael it is."

He had been wrong. Almost fatally wrong. These Sangaree would know the Shadowline well.

There had been but one Sangaree with the human name Michael. Michael Dee. The man who had engineered the war. The man who had been both the pride and despair of his race.

The man who had paid the ultimate price for failing.

"Brandy says you like pirate stories. I knew a pirate once. Only he wasn't a pirate when I met him. That's what he is now. I grew up and went to school, and he grew up and became a pirate."

"I don't think he's ready for that right now, Gun." Marya seemed honestly worried. "I'm going to have to call a doctor, I think."

Niven was surprised at himself. He was concerned too. "You want me to call a cabcar?" What was he doing? The kid was Sangaree. His purpose in life was to help guide that species to a final solution. Little ones became big ones.

"Oh, no. There's one from the hospital who lives right upstairs. I don't know her very well, but…"

"Go get her, woman. I'll manage here."

She stared. Something within her softened momentarily. The hidden woman, the one behind the one behind the one she was trying to portray, showed through. She kissed his cheek. "Thanks, Gun." When he pulled her closer, "Later. I'll be back as soon as I can."

He had not been after a kiss. He had attached a tiny chameleon transmitter to the back of her collar.

She closed the apartment door behind her. Niven inserted a receiver into his ear while pretending to scratch.

Smiling wryly, he patted himself where she had touched him. Had she done the same to him?

There was no reason why she should have to go out for a doctor. She would have sufficient medical background herself—if there was any truth to her cover.

He smiled again. Marya was no tactician, either.

"Are you my mom's new lover?"

He was surprised. Little girls did not ask questions like that. "No. Not yet."

"She needs one. Do you think she's pretty?"

"I think she's gorgeous." He was uncomfortable. He did not know how to socialize with children. The only child he knew was Jupp's boy, Horst-Johann.

"Maybe she should get married again. Are you married?"

Marya had reached a public comm. She was briefing someone. Following her part of a conversation and trying to guess the other half while carrying on another with Brandy proved impossible. He did hear Marya ask for a deep trace on his cover. That meant he had won a round. She had doubts. Or wanted to have them, which came to the same thing.

"No. I never met the right lady." This was one bold child. Did she know she was not human? Probably. From the little he had heard, Sangaree had no childhood in the human sense. Their children were shielded from nothing. They were treated as, and expected to behave as, miniature adults.

"Don't know if I'd like you, though."

Honest, too, he thought. He went to check on Michael. The boy still watched him with wide, wary eyes.

He was bad sick. Marya would not risk a human doctor otherwise. There were few greater risks the underground Sangaree could take. Physicians could sometimes spot the subtle differences between species.

Marya returned with the doctor before Niven's conversation with Brandy became impossible.

The doctor, he decided, was "tame." She worked with a confidence and quickness that betrayed her.

Niven whispered to Marya, "Brandy's been matchmaking."

She laughed. "Husband-shopping for me again? She never gives up."

"I don't think I passed the exam."

"Doesn't matter. I won't get caught in that trap again."

"Why'd you bring them out here?" On Old Earth parents usually put their children into public care as soon as they were born. Niven had had an unusual childhood in that he had spent much of it with his mother. He still kept in touch with her, but had lost track of his father years ago.

The shedding of children was a common practice on the tamed outworlds, too. Fewer than a quarter of Confederation's children were raised by their biological parents.

Marya was shocked. Her Sangaree sense of Family had been outraged. But she could not tell him that. "I forgot. You do things differently where you come from. Yeah, it would be convenient sometimes. But they're *my* kids."

"Don't try to explain. Just call it one of the differences between the Inner Worlds and the frontier. I'm getting used to them."

The doctor returned from the bedroom. "I gave him a broad-spectrum antibiotic, Marya. And an antiviral. It's nothing serious. See that he gets plenty of bed rest and lots of fluids, and keep an eye on his temperature. It'll go up. Give him some aspirin if it gets too high. Do you need a thermometer?"

Marya nodded. She portrayed embarrassment beautifully.

You did that well, lady, Niven thought. *Too poor to afford a thermometer. But you serve genuine coffee.* He smiled. She was doing a chemo-psychiatric internship, but had to summon an outside doctor... Was she driven by some secret death wish?

"Nice to have met you, Doctor Niven," the doctor told him.

"You too." He watched her go to the door. There was no pride in the way she walked.

"You want to get some sleep now, Gun?" Marya asked.

"Going to have to." But would his nerves permit it here in the heart of enemy territory?

They would. After he had skinned down to his underwear, had flopped into Marya's bed, and had told Michael, "Good night, Captain," the lights went out.

He wakened once, hazily, when Marya slipped into bed beside him. He mumbled foggily, then knew nothing for hours.

He wakened slowly. Gradually, he realized that The Broken Wings' truncated day had sped by. It was night again. He did not remember where he was till he rolled against the woman.

That simple movement initiated three tempestuous days.

Marya was insatiable. The only word he found to fit her was "hungry." He had never encountered a woman who had such a need for a man.

Niven astounded himself. Their lovemaking became so savage, so narrowly scoped, that it was more like combat. As if, "Let he who first cries 'Hold! Enough!' be damned forever."

They seemed to do nothing but sleep and copulate, making attack after attack in some sort of sexual war. The outside world seemed to have lost all meaning.

Yet there was method. There was rationality. In struggling to please Marya, who was struggling to distract him, Niven kept himself motivated by remembering who she was. He kept trying to convince himself that he was doing this to sabotage the enemy chain of command.

He knew Marya was not motivated entirely by lust either.

Oh, but they did have one hell of a good time on the rumpled sheets of that battlefield.

In the interims Niven sometimes wondered what had become of Mouse. Mouse, he reflected, sure had the free hand he always wanted.

Brandy, recognizing the way of things, had taken her brother out the first night. They were staying upstairs with the doctor. Michael, looking a little better, sometimes wandered in, moped around without saying much, then wandered out again. Brandy stayed away all the time.

"What are we doing?" Niven once muttered to himself. They were enemies to the death. That was the prime rule, the blood rule, by which he and she were supposed to live and die. Yet they were denying it, or sublimating it in the form of love…

He began to dread mission's end. Debriefing… He would have to answer questions. He would have to explain.

Niven was snoring. He had one arm beneath Marya's neck.

The building shuddered like a dog shaking off water. A window cracked. Tableware clattered onto the kitchen floor. The whole neighborhood reverberated to the explosion.

Niven jerked upright. "D-14," he grunted.

"What?"

"What was that?"

"An explosion."

They dressed, almost racing. Reflections of dancing firelight colored the cracked window. Marya looked out. "Oh, Holy Sant!"

"What?"

"The warehouse…"

"Eh?"

"I'll be right back… What's that?"

A yell had come from somewhere downstairs. Cries and screams followed it.

Niven knew that first yell. That was Mouse in assassin's mind.

Earlier, he had seen the shape of the needlegun lumping her underwear in a dresser drawer. He beat her to it.

The door crashed inward. A ragged, battered, bloody Mouse hurtled through. He was so keyed for action that he looked three meters tall.

"Easy," Niven said, gesturing with the needlegun. "Everything's under control, Mouse."

Mouse was not hurt. The blood was not his own. "Got everything," he croaked through a dry throat. "Message away. Got to bend the bitch and get out."

That was their business, but... Niven could not permit the woman's murder. That she was Sangaree seemed irrelevant. "No. There's no need. Not this time."

Mouse was coming down. Thought was replacing action. He glanced at Niven's weapon, at the woman. "All right. You're the boss, Doc. But I've got to get something out of this. Where're the damned kids?"

"Upstairs. But I won't let you kill children, either."

"Wouldn't think of it, Doc. Wouldn't even drown a puppy. You know old John. So tie her up, will you? Can't have her coming after us." He backed out the door.

Siren howls tortured the streets. The grumble of a gathering crowd slipped tentacles into the room. "Sorry it had to end this way, Marya. But business is business."

"I almost believed..." She stared at him. For an instant she looked small and defenseless. He reminded himself that she was Sangaree, that she would become instant death if he were careless. "I suppose you're soothing your conscience. I wouldn't if the tables were turned. You've hurt us too much already."

Not a smart thing to say to somebody pointing a gun at you, Niven thought. He shrugged. "Maybe. It's not conscience, though. A different weakness. You'd probably have to be human to understand." He left it to her to figure out what he meant.

Mouse returned with the children and doctor. In the process he had acquired a weapon. "Tie these three, too, Doc."

The doctor was more frightened than Brandy or Michael. Humans on the fringes of the Business generally imagined operations by and against the organization to be more deadly than they were.

Brandy asked, "What're you doing, Gun?" Straight out, emotionlessly. As if she were used to being under the gun.

"Business, dear."

"Oh." She sped her mother a disgusted look.

"He's the Starduster," Marya told her.

"And you fell for his story?"

Niven tore sheets into strips, tied the doctor, then the girl, then Michael. "Told you I knew a pirate, Captain."

"Good," Mouse said. "Let me have the gun, Doc."

"Eh? Why?"

"Because I need it."

Puzzled, Niven handed the weapon over. Mouse tossed it into the hallway.

Niven shook his head, said, "We'd better get moving. They won't stay disorganized forever."

"One thing first." Mouse shoved his weapon under his arm. He took a hypo from the doctor's bag and filled it from an ampule he carried in his pocket. "This one's for your great-grandfather, kids. And all his brothers and sisters, nieces and nephews."

"What the hell are you doing?" Niven demanded.

"Just business, Doc. Turnabout's fair play, right? We should expand our own markets." He raised Michael's sleeve.

Marya understood instantly. "No! Piao! Not my children. Kill me if you want, but don't…"

Mouse answered her with a tight smile. "Just business, lady. Gag her, Doc. Hurry. We got to get the stuff out before Navy pops to we've cut out the instel here."

Niven suddenly understood what Mouse was doing. "Hey! You can't…" He wanted to stop it, to protest, to refuse, got confused by the reference to Navy. "Stardust?"

Mouse nodded, smiling wickedly. His hand strayed toward his weapon.

"Oh." How could the man be so cruel? That was murder in the worst possible way.

Marya needed gagging desperately. Her screams could attract attention…

Dazed, Niven silenced her. Her flesh seemed icy beneath his

fingertips. He felt the rage and hatred boiling inside her. She started shaking.

For an instant he thought she was having a seizure.

Mouse injected the children. That wicked little smile kept playing with his lips. He was blissfully happy in his cruelty.

Why did he hate so much?

"Come on, Doc. They're on their way down. Can't you hear them?"

The crowd noise and sirens were yielding to the rumble of assault landing craft descending on penetration runs. The Broken Wings' atmosphere howled its protest of the violation.

Jupp was on his way.

Someone stuck his head through the doorway. Mouse shot, missed, jumped into the hallway and shot again. "Doc, will you come on?"

"I'm sorry, Marya. Really. It's the way things had to be." He snagged the needlegun in passing, skipped a fresh corpse, and pursued Mouse into the emergency stairwell.

Later, as they waited in the crowd watching the invaders pour through the main city locks, Niven asked, "What was that crap about getting off before Navy finds out?"

"We're supposed to be the Starduster and Piao, remember?"

"But they'll know when..."

"Not yet. Look." The Marines entering the city wore uniform gear, but it was not Service issue. It was like nothing Niven had ever seen.

Mouse had chosen the waiting place with care. A man loaded with brass headed directly toward them. "Mr. Piao?" He avoided looking at Niven. His attitude seemed one of mixed awe, fear, and loathing. "You have the material for my officers?"

"That I do, Colonel." Mouse proffered a thick package. "Congratulations. Your men are as efficient as ours."

The Colonel reddened. His mouth snapped open, but he caught himself. Carefully, he said, "More so, Mr. Piao. As you'll someday learn."

"All things are possible to those who believe."

The Colonel riffled through a stack of copies. Other officers gathered behind him. He started passing them papers.

"Let's drift, Doc. They can handle it."

Niven did not miss the wariness in all those Marine eyes. "What was that all about?"

"Oh. They think we're Piao and the Starduster too. They think we worked a deal with Luna Command so we could knock over the Sangaree and take control of their nets."

"What's all the smoke screen for?"

"We've got to keep the Starduster story alive, at least till Jupp makes his hit. Otherwise they might evacuate their production facilities. By the way, I wanted to say you did a job digging all that info out. The Old Man is going to love you."

Niven did not follow it. "It's too Byzantine for me. Are the Sangaree supposed to find out that they're Marines? And then figure we didn't say anything about the production facilities because that would cut off our own supply?"

"Wait till you're in on one of the Old Man's complicated ones."

"Mr. Piao?" a Marine non-comm asked.

"Yes."

"If you'll follow me, sir. Your transportation." Marines surrounded them. A precaution against assassination, Niven supposed. Those bounties still existed.

Sounds of sporadic fighting came from the city. Believing the raiders to be Starduster men, the Sangaree minions would battle hard. The Starduster's viciousness toward collaborators was legend.

The Marines guided them into an armored personnel carrier. They had it to themselves. It rumbled away toward Angel Port.

"Mouse, I get the feeling the Admiral threw in a few twists just to make it interesting. What happens when the Starduster finds out that we've been using his name in vain?"

Mouse was in a bright, expansive mood. He had had a beautiful day. He had carved his initials on the Sangaree soul. He had vandalized their house of crime. "I'll tell you a secret, Doc. If you promise you won't ever let the Old Man know you know." He looked at Niven expectantly.

"All right. I give. What?"

"You really *are* the Starduster."

"What?"

"The Starduster. Piao. The Old Man invented the whole thing. The Starduster is whoever he points at and says, 'You!'"

"Well, shit. Mouse, I really needed that. Here you've had me scared to death that the son of a bitch was going to crawl out of the woodwork and cut my throat. I got a year's vacation coming after debriefing. And, dammit, as soon as it goes through, I'm going to…"

"Don't count on it, Doc. Not when you're working for the Old Man."

October 3047. Captain Jupp von Drachau, commanding Special Action Task Force IV, with a heavy siege squadron attached, surprises and commences reduction action against Sangaree manufacturing facilities hidden in the inner asteroid belt surrounding Delta Sheol, a white dwarf in the mini-cluster called the Hell Stars. Destruction is swift, savage, and complete. At the same time Confederation and local police agencies begin closing down the drug networks formerly rooted on The Broken Wings.

Admiral Beckhart has taken every point in a victorious round against his oldest and most favored enemy.

NINE: 3048 AD
Operation Dragon, *Danion*

BenRabi started to push into his cabin, still glaring at the
Sangaree woman.

"I should've bent her on The Broken Wings," Mouse snarled.
"You should've…" He had not forgiven Moyshe the weakness
that had left her alive.

"I can't stomach contingency assassinations, Mouse."

"Yeah? Look over there and think about it some more. How
much mischief could she do?"

"All right. So it makes a perverted kind of sense. If you figure
a ghost like The Broken Wings will come back to haunt you."

"It will. It always does. Maybe I'll settle this up…"

BenRabi shook his head. "Not here. Not now. Not after what
we just went through."

"I didn't mean right now. I'm not a fool, Moyshe. It would
look like an accident."

"Let it be, Mouse."

There was no compassion in Mouse. *I should be flint too,*
benRabi thought. *But I don't have his knack for hating.*

BenRabi found the things and people in his life too transient
for more than mild aversion.

"She'd better move fast when we hit dirt again, then." Mouse growled. "One getaway is all she gets... I hope we find Homeworld before I check out."

BenRabi felt a twinge of jealousy. Mouse knew the nature of his Grail. His feet were set inalterably on the path that led to it, though it was a cup of blood.

"For your sake, I hope so." Moyshe laughed softly, bitterly. Sometimes he had to, or scream. "See you later." He pushed into his cabin.

He hoped their year cooped up here would soften Mouse, but feared there was no hope. Marya would not let time work. Memories of her children would lead her on...

Mouse's hate was old and strong, and deeper than Confederation culture usually ingrained. If he were indeed a Storm, that would explain it. The Storms of the Iron Legion had had an old-fashioned, Biblical way of looking at things.

Sangaree manipulations, during the war in the Shadowline, had destroyed the family.

But Mouse did not have to be a Storm. His hatred could be stardust-related.

"The joy that burns, the dream that kills," Czyzewski had called the drug only seconds before his own addiction had carried him into the big, endless dream of death. The drug was the leading plague of the age, and had touched virtually every human being. It had taken more lives than had the bitter Ulantonid War.

Stardust was the pusher's dream. It was immediately addictive. One flight and the user was hooked forever. An addict could not taper off. Neither could he withdraw cold. Nor could he substitute another, less fearsome drug in its place.

For the poor Inner Worlder addiction ended hard: by suicide, by being slain while trying to steal enough to finance another fix, or by finding death in the constant dogfighting among have and have-not addicts. And many times the end came slowly, screamingly, in an institution where the warders could do nothing but watch, protect the world by keeping the addict restrained, and try to develop hearts of stone.

The sordid facts of stardust addiction tickled the Sangaree conscience not at all. They had a product to market, a stellar to turn.

They were not innately cruel. They simply did not see humans as anything but animals to be exploited. Do the cattleman, butcher, and customer consider themselves cruel to the beef animal? Sangaree thought their customers better than cattle. More like what Renaissance Europeans thought of black Africans. Semi-intelligent apes.

BenRabi lay on his bunk and wondered about his partner. Mouse claimed his assignments were all counter-Sangaree. To date they had been, and Mouse had prosecuted them with a savage zeal, with cruel little touches, like the injection of Marya's children. But what was he doing here, now, working against the Starfishers? That did not compute.

Following the announcement of von Drachau's raid, Mouse had been in the clouds, as if he were a skying addict himself.

The Sangaree were the demons of the Confederation era. They passed as human easily. Their Homeworld lay somewhere outside The Arm. Compared to humanity, they were few in number. It was rumored that they could breed only under their native sun.

The Sangaree produced little for themselves. They preferred instead to raid, to deal in drugs and slaves and guns.

Confederation resented them bitterly. Man was their prime victim. The nonhuman races considered them merely a nuisance.

Someone softly knocked on Moyshe's door. "Come in," he said. "Mouse. Thought it was you." It was the first he had seen Mouse since Kindervoort's inquisition.

"The word's around," Mouse told him. "They've all decided that we're evil, mean, bad, wicked, nasty, crude, rude, and unattractive spies." He laughed.

"The Sangaree woman passed the word, I suppose."

"Maybe. Why don't you slide out there and see what's going on? It's good for a laugh. Hell, you'd think we were as rare as dodos and smelled like skunks."

"Don't we? Morally?"

"Ahh… Moyshe. What the hell is it with you these days? Hey! You should see the competition laughing up their sleeves. But we get the last laugh. They're on their way. Kindervoort's troops snatched a couple beekies this morning. Same way he got us. Knew they were coming. Looks like he knew about everybody, except Strehltsweiter."

"Mouse, they've got to have a mole in Luna Command. Somebody deep."

"That's what I figure. It's the only answer that adds up. Moyshe, you should see the kids with their holy attitudes. Like they think they're a plane above us. Poor innocents." Mouse smiled at a memory. "You know that Williams girl? I shocked the hell out of her. Asked her her price. She missed the point. That's real innocence."

"Ah, youth. Mouse, what happened to *our* innocence and idealism? Remember how it was in Academy? We were going to save the universe."

"Somebody found our price." He frowned, dropped onto the spare bunk. "That's not really true. We're doing it, you know. It's just that the mechanics of it aren't what we thought they'd be. We didn't understand that everything has to be a trade-off, that whenever we changed things to what we thought they should be, we had to do it at somebody else's expense... Hell, you've got me doing it."

"What?"

"Thinking. Moyshe, what's happening with you? You always were a moody guy, but I've never seen you like you've been lately. Ever since we left Carson's..."

BenRabi's defenses stood to arms. He did not dare open up. Two reasons: you just did not do that these days, and he was not sure what was happening himself. So he masked the shadowed walls of *Festung Selbst* behind a half-truth.

"I'm just depressed. Maybe because I didn't get my vacation. Maybe because of Mother... I had a bag full of things I wanted to take home. Some stamps and coins I picked up in Corporation Zone. Some stuff I managed to get back from The Broken Wings. This beautiful hand-carved bone trivet from Tregorgarth, and some New Earth butterflies that would be worth a mint anywhere else..."

"Bullroar, my friend. Bullroar." Mouse peered at him from

beneath lowered brows. "I'm getting to know you, Moyshe benRabi. I can tell when something's got you by the guts. You better do something. It'll eat you alive if you keep it locked up inside."

Mouse was right about one thing. They were getting to know one another. Too well. Mouse was reading him now, and wanting to help. "Maybe. When's your next chess thing? I'll come lose a few games, tip a few brews with the troops."

Mouse frowned. He knew a light show when he saw one.

Getting too damned close!

Mouse glanced at *Jerusalem*, at which benRabi had been scribbling. "Well, I didn't mean to porlock, Moyshe." He rose. "I don't know if we'll have any more tournaments. Kindervoort says we'll make *Danion* sometime tonight. That's why I came over. Thought you'd want to know."

BenRabi brightened. "Hey, good." He pushed the *Jerusalem* papers back, rose, started pacing. "The waiting is getting to me. A little work…"

The rendezvous with the harvestship was anticlimactic. There were no brass bands, and no curious crowds at the receiving bay. The only Seiners around were those who had been sent to show the landsmen to their quarters and brief them about their job assignments. No one of any stature came to greet them. Moyshe was disappointed.

His guide did his work quickly and efficiently and told him, "You'd better turn in. This is the middle of our night. I'll be back early to help walk you through your first day."

"Okay. Thanks, Paul." Moyshe examined the man. Paul was much like the Seiners he had met before.

The man examined him, too, and struggled with prejudices as he did so. "Good night, Mr. benRabi."

"See you in the morning."

But he did not. Amy showed up instead, and took both benRabi and Mouse under her wing.

"Keeping an eye on us, eh?" Mouse asked.

She colored slightly. "Yeah. Sort of. Jarl said he wanted to keep you together so you'd be easier to watch."

"You don't have to be embarrassed. We understand."

"This isn't my kind of thing, Commander Storm. I'm a plumber, not a counterspy."

"Call me Mouse. Please. Or Mr. Iwasaki."

"Whatever you want. Mouse. Are you ready for breakfast?" She turned to Moyshe.

"I'm still Moyshe benRabi. All right? Yes. I could eat three breakfasts."

Work commenced immediately after tool issue and a brief class in how to find one's way around the harvestship. It never let up.

Moyshe forgot his screaming need in the pressure of the following week's labors. The memories that had been gnawing the underbelly of his soul vanished from consciousness. He flew easy, not thinking, not observing, not questioning. He stayed too busy or too tired. The Seiners were true to their promise to work the landsmen hard.

The mind-quirk he thought of as the image of the gun bothered him some, but only mildly, as he wandered through daydreams while replacing wrecked piping or damaged flow meters. He seized the vision, played with it, wrapped a few extended daydreams around it. It helped pass the time.

Kept busy, he began to enjoy life again.

"Something strange is going on here, Mouse," he whispered once when Amy was out of hearing.

"What's that?"

"This ship isn't hurt as bad as they want us to think. Look around."

"I couldn't tell. I never did any time in the line. All I know about ships is you get on, and after a while you get back off someplace else."

"What it amounts to is, there's a lot of damage, but nothing that would put something this size out of action. They could've handled it themselves. Just might have taken them a couple of years."

"So?"

"So, maybe we're here for some other reason. My intuition has been sniffing around that ever since Carson's."

"Why would they bring outsiders in if they didn't absolutely have to?"

"I don't know. The only reason you overstaff a ship is so you have personnel redundancy in case you take battle casualties. But on a ship this big two hundred people, or even a thousand, don't mean a thing. And who would the Seiners fight? Confederation? Not with a bunch of fifth columnists aboard."

"Give it time. It'll come to the top. No matter what they hope, they can't keep everything hidden forever."

"Can it. Amy's coming." Curious, he thought. Mouse did not seem interested in Starfisher motives at all.

BenRabi's first week did have its rough edges. Every encounter with the Sangaree woman became a crisis. And she could not be avoided. Her team, repairing air ducting, was working the same service passages as his.

She would not leave Mouse alone. And the certainty of purpose which made Mouse's responses predictable taunted benRabi with worries about his own incompleteness.

She did not bait him. She knew that he would do nothing but look at her soulfully, reflecting the pain-giving back at her.

She appeared from a cross-passage only seconds behind Amy.

"Damn!" Moyshe swore. "Her again."

"Restrain me, Moyshe."

"You got it, partner. Be my ass in the fire, too."

"Well, the Rat again." The Sangaree woman stood with her hands on her hips, defying him to act. Backing her were several idealistic youngsters. She had sold them a simpleminded anti-spy package. "What an unpleasant surprise. Butchered anyone lately, spy? There're lots of non-Confies aboard. You ought to be as happy as a hog knee-deep in slop."

A curious metaphor, benRabi thought. She must have chosen it especially for the Tregorgarthian kids.

The youths looked at one another, embarrassed. They shared her views, and were a rather rude bunch themselves, but their society had taught them that too much bluntness could get a person killed. Tregorgarth was a rough world.

"You could start with me. You know what I think about your

fascist military dictatorship. Or don't you have the guts?"

She knew damned well that he had, but assumed that he would not respond in front of witnesses—or that she could take him if he did. She was fooling herself there, benRabi thought. She believed Mouse strictly a strike-from-behind man. He was a lot more. Two decades of training and several thousand years of combat experience had gone into making him the perfect organic killing machine.

Moyshe did not know of a weapon, or a system of close combat, that Mouse did not know as well as any man who had ever lived. Short of pulling guns, there was little she and her whole crowd could have done were he to lose his temper.

BenRabi could sense the aching in Mouse, could feel Mouse's need to show her. But his partner controlled himself. That, too, had been part of his training.

BenRabi had to exercise some self-control himself. The woman's behavior had eroded his compassion.

She was playing a more dangerous game than she suspected. It would backfire on her if she did not ease up.

BenRabi was sure the woman was working to some carefully prepared plan. Her acting had not improved. Her easy confidence betrayed.

But she was vulnerable. Her Achilles Heel was her hatred. BenRabi was sure Mouse would exploit it...

"Miss Gonzalez," Amy said. "If you're quite finished? We have work to do. And I suggest you return to yours before there's cause for an inquiry into the absence of your supervisor."

The Sangaree woman backed down. She was not ready to jeopardize her mission.

"I feel like a fool," benRabi muttered.

Eyes downcast, Mouse said, "So do I. I can't take it forever, Moyshe."

Then Amy told them, "I'm glad you restrained yourselves. Things are ugly enough without our getting physical."

She intrigued benRabi. He watched her a lot when she was not looking. He was glad she did not go for chest-pounders. He was not the type, and in the back of his mind he had begun formulating designs upon her.

Over a flow chart thick with black X's indicating trouble spots, while Amy was off requisitioning a special wrench, Mouse muttered, "It's getting hard, Moyshe. I know what she's doing, but... She's trying to make us take ourselves out of the play."

"Hang on."

"One of these nights..."

Indefatigable Mouse. When benRabi finished work he had barely enough energy to eat, then tumble into bed. But Mouse got out and mingled, made new acquaintances (mostly female), and found new interests. He sponged up every bit of information that crossed his path.

His latest thing was the Middle American football popular with Seiners. They had arrived just in time for the pre-season excitement. His interest gave him an excuse to move around.

Moyshe was afraid. Having established his pattern of mobility, Mouse might arrange a fatal encounter with Marya somewhere far from the usual groundling stomping ground.

Moyshe wondered if he should catch her alone and try to make her understand.

He remembered The Broken Wings.

He was her primary target. She was trying to get at him through Mouse. The hurt he had done her was more personal, more ego-slashing than what Mouse had done. By her reasoning, what had happened to the children could be laid at his doorstep. He could have prevented it.

He would have to watch his back. Mouse was not the only one who could arrange an accident.

"Is she alone?" Mouse asked. "They like lots of backup."

"I haven't spotted anybody yet. They could be playing it close. What I want to know is, why is she here? Everybody else has tried something. But she just keeps on being obnoxious."

"She's waiting."

"For what?"

Mouse shrugged. "We'll find out the hard way, I guess."

"Here's a notion," Moyshe said. "It just came to me. A way to warn her."

"How?"

"Tomorrow's recreation day, right?" They had been promised

one day off a week. This would be the first.

"And?"

"Those kids. You know how Tregorgarthians are. They're challenging everybody to meet them in a martial arts elimination tournament. Think you could manage them? Without hurting anybody?"

Mouse thought. "I don't know if I can pull the punches anymore."

"It would be good for the boys, too."

Tregorgarthians away from home tended to become bullies. Their homeworld schooled them to believe that those who did not fight at the drop of a hat were cowards. Smacked around a little, they civilized fast.

"Might give them second thoughts about letting her suck them in," benRabi mused. "They've got to know she's up to something."

"They'd back off if they knew I was dangerous, eh?"

"I'm hoping. Sex seems to be her main hold on them. I see one sneaking out of her room almost every morning."

"Who's sneaking out of whose cabin?"

Amy had returned. "Just gossiping," Moyshe replied. "One of the girls has an assembly line going."

She bit. "Landsmen! They're right about you being immoral."

Moyshe forbore observing that the Seiners seemed to be just as loose as his own people. Amy's priggishness was personal, not cultural. She was the only Starfisher he knew who talked that morality nonsense.

Mouse did not forbear. "When did you lose yours, Miss Morality?"

"Huh? My what?"

"Your cherry. You're no more pure than Old Earth air."

She sputtered, reddened, mumbled something about all landsmen being alike.

"You're right. Satyrs and nymphs, the lot of us." Mouse licked his lips, winked, asked, "What're you doing tonight?"

BenRabi grinned. Mouse was teasing her, as he had been all week long, but she did not realize it. He used a subtler approach when he really wanted a woman.

Something within her clicked, as it did each time Mouse put her on the defensive. A different, colder personality surfaced long enough to carry her past the rough spot. "Sleeping. Alone. Did you decide where you want to cut that water main?" Then another quick change of subject. "Oh. Jarl said to tell you to sharpen your teeth. He's bringing some people to play you tomorrow. You too, Moyshe."

Mouse had become chess champion of Service Ship Three. The Seiners had been excited about it. They were fond of the game and eager for new challenges.

"Why me? I'm no good."

"Better than you think. Anyway, we like everybody to find their place in the pecking order." Her hardness faded as quickly as it had come.

"I wanted to go over to Twenty-three West. If I could get permission." He pulled the excuse off the wall, for the salving of his ego. He did not like losing all the time, even at games. "I heard there's a guy over there with some early English coins. Victorians."

She looked puzzled.

Mouse laughed. "Didn't you know? We're both mad collectors. Coins and stamps mostly, because they're easy to lug around."

Frowning over them, Amy reminded benRabi of Alyce. So many of their facial expressions were similar. "It looks like you're mad everything. Chess. Archaicism. Collections. Football and women."

"That's him, not me," benRabi said.

"What about people?" Amy asked.

"Aren't women people?" Mouse countered.

She shook her head. She was a Starfisher, and Starfishers could not understand. Even Archaicism was just a hobby for them. Landsmen plunged themselves into things because they did not want to get involved with people. People hurt. The growing closeness between Mouse and benRabi, and the apparent friendships that had taken shape among the other foreigners, had confused Amy. She did not recognize their lack of temporal depth.

A critical difference between Confederation and Starfisher

relationships was that of durational expectancy. The idea of a close relationship that could be severed quickly, painlessly, as easily as it had been formed, would not occur to a Starfisher. But they lived in a closed, static culture where a severely limited number of people passed through their lives. Friendships were expected to last a lifetime.

BenRabi was leery of the morrow. The isolation of the landsmen, far out in a remote residential cube, had minimized cultural friction during the week. But Kindervoort, for whom the outsiders had become a pet project, planned to make recreation day a gigantic college smoker, with floods of Seiners being exposed to landside ways.

Still trying to gentle everyone in, Moyshe supposed. Kindervoort was a rather thoughtful, admirable cop. He might get to like the man yet.

TEN: 3047 AD
The Olden Days, A Victory Celebration

"Max! You're beautiful."

"Don't sound so damned astonished, Walter."

"Oh. I didn't mean… I just never saw you dressed up before."

"Quit while you're ahead, friend. By the way. I notice you've changed a little too, Commander." She stared pointedly at the double sunbursts on his high collar. "I thought you said you were a dip."

"Naval Attaché. You know that."

"No, I didn't. Naval Attaché. Isn't that the same thing as head spy? Bureau of Naval Intelligence?"

Perchevski reddened. "Not always. Some of us…"

"Don't mind me, Walter." She smiled. "I'm just thinking out loud. That would explain some of the mysteries about you."

"Mysteries? About me? Come on, Max. I'm as mysterious as a pumpkin. Here we are."

A Marine accepted his ID badge, poked it into a slot. He eyed a readout screen somewhere out of sight. "Thank you, sir. Is this Miss Travers, sir?"

"Yes."

He consulted the screen again. "Thank you, sir. Have a nice

evening, sir. Ma'am." A door slid open.

"Ma'am?" Max asked. "Do I look that old?"

"Come on, Max."

"Isn't he going to check me?"

"He did. You're all right. You don't have a bomb in your purse."

"Thanks a lot. What do they do to you in Academy? Why can't officers be polite like that nice young Marine?"

"You were just complaining... Max, you're sure contrary tonight. What's the matter?" He handed his over-tunic to the Marine corporal in the cloak room, helped Max with her cape.

"I'm scared, Walter. I've never even been near the Command Club. I don't know how to talk to Senators and Admirals."

"Know something, Max?"

"What?"

"I've never been here before either. We'll lose our virginity together. I'll tell you this, though. Admirals and Senators put their pants on one leg at a time, same as us, and they'll paw your leg under the table the same way I do."

"Male or female?" She seized his arm as they entered the huge Grand Ballroom. Her grip tightened.

"Both, the way you look tonight." He slowed. The place had no walls. An all-round animated hologram concealed the room's boundaries. Portrayals of Navy's mightiest ships of war lay every direction but downward. Perchevski automatically scanned the starfields. He saw no constellations he recognized.

Max's grip became painful. "I feel like I'm falling, Walter."

Local gravity had been allowed to decline to lunar normal to reinforce the deep-space effect.

"Somebody's really putting on the dog," Perchevski grumbled.

"Commander. Madam," said another polite Marine, "may I show you to your seats?"

The place was thronged. "Of course. How many people going to be here tonight, First Lance?" He was getting jittery. He still did not know why he was one of the elect.

"Nearly two thousand, sir. Here, sir." The Marine pulled a chair for Max.

"But…" He had scanned the faces of his tablemates. His jaw refused to continue working.

A few of them he knew personally. The Chief of Staff Navy and the Director of Naval Intelligence he recognized from the holonetnews.

Max recognized them too. She leaned and whispered, "Who the hell are you really, Walter?" She was so awed she could not look at the high brass.

Perchevski stared at his place setting, just as awed. "I'm starting to wonder myself."

"Thomas?"

Only one man alive insisted on calling him by that name. Perchevski forced his gaze to rise and meet that of his boss. "Sir?" He flicked a sideways glance at Mouse, who was eyeing Max appreciatively while whispering to his own ladyfriend.

"How are you doing, Max?" Mouse asked.

"You too, Yamamoto?"

"Thomas, the CSN and DNI want to be introduced."

"Yes sir." He evaded Admiral Beckhart's eyes by fixing his gaze on the one seat still vacant. He moved around to shake hands with the brass while Beckhart murmured the introductions.

"This is the man," Beckhart said. "He made it all go."

"Congratulations, Commander," the CSN told Perchevski. "And thank you. I understand you'll receive the Swords and Diamonds. Not to mention the prize."

Perchevski could not conceal his bewilderment.

They've got to be talking about the operation, he thought. *Swords and Diamonds to the Lunar Cross, right?* More chest hardware. With another medal and fifty pfenning he could buy a cheap cup of soy-coffee. Or pay half a Conmark without.

"Thank you, sir. I'd rather have my vacation, sir."

His boldness startled him even more than did his bitterness.

The DNI peered at Beckhart. "Up to your tricks with the troops, Admiral?"

"Ma'am?"

Perchevski grinned. The mission was worth it after all, just to get here and see that look on Beckhart's face.

"This man obviously doesn't have the faintest damn notion of what he's doing here."

Perchevski threw oil on the flames by nodding behind his boss's back.

He entered his commander's presence only rarely, which was just as well. The Admiral brought out the contrariness in him.

"It'll be clear soon enough," Beckhart said. "I just thought it would be a nice surprise. Go back to your friend, Thomas. I see she knows Mouse."

As Perchevski departed, he heard the DNI snap, "And see that they get some time off. The whole human race can't keep your pace."

"Yes, Ma'am."

Perchevski winced. He would get time, all right. And he would pay for it. Beckhart would get it back with interest.

"What was that about?" Max asked. "You looked like they were talking about the firing squad."

"They're going to give me a medal. There's something about medals… They just don't seem adequate."

"For surviving a virus?" She wore a sarcastic grin.

The high brass fell silent. People began to rise. Mouse abandoned the finger game he had been playing with his companion. Perchevski turned. "Jupp!"

Von Drachau looked old and haggard. His face had grown pasty since last they had met. "Hi, Tom." He greeted no one else at the moment.

The holograms faded. Perchevski spied the news crews and cameras they had concealed. "I begin to understand," he muttered.

"What?" Max asked.

"Lady, you're about to see the full might of the Luna Command propaganda apparat in action."

Von Drachau dropped into the empty chair. "Mouse," he said by way of greeting. "Tom, you seen Horst-Johann?"

"Sorry, Jupp. I haven't had a chance," Perchevski replied. "Was it bad?"

"From hunger. And they drag me down here without a chance to…" He considered the seniority of the rest of his tablemates, closed his eyes, leaned back.

"Who's he?" Max whispered.

"Jupp von Drachau. We were classmates in Academy."

"Was he in on the same thing you were?"

"Yeah. Sort of."

Navy stewards began serving dinner. It was a smorgasbord sort of meal, with the diners offered a chance to select from trays bearing bits and pieces from different Confederation worlds.

"Whatever you do, don't miss the January wine," Perchevski told Max. "They always let you have a little at these things."

"Thought you'd never been here before."

"Mouse has."

"Mouse?"

"Yamamoto."

"Oh? You know him too?"

"We were classmates too."

The holo cameras started whining. They faded behind a new holo scene.

This one was no animation. It was a speeded recording of events that had taken place inside a warship's situation-display tank.

Green friendly blips were approaching a huge chunk of asteroidal material circling a white dwarf sun. More white dwarves blazed in every direction. Perchevski could almost feel the heat, the smash of the solar winds.

"The Hell Stars," he murmured. "That's where it was."

The asteroid began sparkling. Large red blips scuttled away behind the cover of a storm of red pinpoints.

Fast green blips raced after them.

The asteroid coruscated.

"Christ!" Perchevski said.

"What?"

"The place was an arsenal."

Max did not understand. She was a Navy brat, but had not done Service herself. "What's going on, Walter? Or whatever your name is."

"That's where Jupp was. It's a display record of a battle."

The Confederation warships began their assault. Jupp had had his share of firepower.

The guests munched complacently while watching the memory

of the death of a Sangaree station.

The fast boats trying to carry children to safety did not outrun Navy's blood-hungry hounds. Nor could the station's defenses stand up to the pounding delivered by a heavy siege squadron. But the Sangaree fought like a cat cornered by dogs, and left scars on von Drachau's command.

Here, there, Navy's professionals commented on the action like detached spectators at a ball game. Perchevski glared at his plate.

Von Drachau, he noted, was less excited than he.

The steward kept bringing the courses. He had to remind Max to drink her wine. The vintages of January were Confederation's finest and rarest.

The Sangaree persisted despite an overwhelming attack. It seemed impossible that they could have survived so long, let alone have continued fighting back.

Take no prisoners. That was the general order to all command grade officers who engaged Sangaree.

Christ, we're bloodthirsty, Perchevski thought He looked around. His neighbors were enjoying the spectacle even though they had no idea what it was all about.

Mouse looked like he was poised on the brink of orgasm.

How that man could hate! The Marine assault boats went in in time for dessert.

Hand-held camera recordings replaced the sterile display replay. Marines stalked Sangaree and their hirelings through smoky, ruined corridors. The fighting was hand-to-hand and bitter.

The camera technicians seemed inordinately fond of torn corpses and shattered defensive installations.

An assault team blew its way through an airlock.

Beyond, running for kilometers, brightly lighted, lay the hugest artificial environment farm Perchevski had ever seen. A voice boomed, "Sithlac fields."

The holos expired. Lights came up. A spot trained on the DNI. She rose. "Ladies and gentlemen. Comrades in arms. That is what tonight is all about. An operation in the Hell Stars that destroyed the biggest stardust production facility we've ever located. The raid was carried out twelve days ago. Police forces throughout The Arm are rounding up the people who processed and sold the drug produced on that asteroid."

She continued with a Navy-aggrandizing speech that Perchevski strove to ignore. Her theme was one of thank God for the Bureau's vigilance and determination.

The CSN said the same things in other ways, and praised von Drachau and the fleet people who had acted on the information the Bureau had supplied.

The hows and whys of the intelligence coup got no play. The details could not be divulged for security reasons. The agents responsible would receive decorations.

"You're a dip, eh?" Max whispered.

Perchevski shrugged. The near-worship in her face astounded him.

"I had a kid brother, Walter. He got hooked on stardust."

"Oh." He checked the time and was surprised to find that it had not been dragging after all.

The CSN insisted on presenting Captain von Drachau to Confederation's billions. Jupp accepted his decorations reluctantly.

"Instant celebrity," Perchevski mused. "Instant millionaire. And they won't remember his name in six months."

"Why're you so sour?" Max demanded. "You ought to be kicking your heels. Look what you did."

"I know what I did. I was there. Let's talk about something else. What about that Polar Flight airmail set you've been promising me for the last two years?"

"I bet you get a ton of prize money. How much? Do you know yet?"

"No. I didn't know about the raid till tonight."

"You'll be able to buy my whole shop."

"Probably." He had won prize money before. He was, by most standards, a wealthy man. He did not realize it. Money did not mean much to him. He could buy whatever he wanted when he wanted it, so economic problems never intruded on his life.

"Aren't you excited?"

"No."

"I am. When are we going to the Darkside digs?"

"I don't know. I think they're going to put me to work." He had come to a decision. He was going home. To his birthworld. One last time. Maybe there, where not one person in a billion gave a damn about Sangaree, or the March of Ulant, or McGraw pirates, or anything else going on offworld, he could get away from himself.

And maybe he could refresh his memory of just what it was that had sent him into a life he so loathed now. Maybe he could relearn what the choices were.

The show for the benefit of the holonets wound down. Then came the private postmortem, when he and Mouse shook hands with the mighty and received their medals and prize-money estimates.

Max patiently waited it out.

"You should have gone home," he told her when he finally broke away. "You can't spend your life waiting for me."

"I wanted to. I'm coming with you." She squeezed his hand.

"Sonofabitch," he said softly. His mood skyrocketed.

He had been firing on her for years. She had teased and led him on with smiles and gentle touches and had never given in. The occasional friendly date was as close as he had ever come.

Max made it a rewarding evening after all.

ELEVEN: 3048 AD
Operation Dragon, *Danion*

BenRabi groaned when he cracked an eye and saw the time. Noon already. He had wasted half his recreation day.

He flung himself out of bed and into the shower. Minutes later he was shuffling his *Jerusalem* papers, trying to find where he had left off.

The door buzzer whined. "Damn! I just got started. It's open."

The door slid aside. Jarl Kindervoort, Amy, and a half dozen unfamiliar Seiners grinned at him. They wore gaily colored period costumes. Moyshe laughed. "You look like refugees from a blood-and-blades epic." Except for one little fellow way in the back, grimy-gruesome in Billy the Kid regalia. "What the hell? Is King Arthur aboard?"

"It's recreation day, Moyshe," Amy said, using that smile that melted him. "We decided to drag the old grizzly out of his den."

How could he stay angry in the face of that smile? It was so damned disarming and warm. "I was going to work on the story." She had been impressed by his being a published author. "Anyway, I haven't got anything to wear." He realized they were offering him something. He grew wary.

114

"Eh?" Kindervoort asked, cupping his ear. "What's that? No matter, Moyshe. No time for it. Come on. We're late for the party now."

Amy chanted, "We're late, we're late, for a very important date…"

Kindervoort caught Moyshe's arm, pulled him through the doorway. He ignored benRabi's protests as he led him along a passageway crowded with young Seiners in wild costumes, zigging and zagging through to the common room serving as the landsmen's cafeteria, gymnasium, rec room, and lounge. It was a big place, but today Moyshe felt the walls pressing in. He had never seen it so crowded.

Most of the landsmen were there, lost among five times as many curious Seiners. The mixer had been going awhile. It had gotten organized. Not far from the door, at a long table where a dozen chess games were in progress, benRabi spied Mouse and the harem he had recruited.

"Where does he find the time?" he murmured.

Kindervoort and Amy herded him toward the table.

"Hey," Mouse said. "You dug him out. You have to use explosives?"

"He gave up without a fight," Kindervoort replied, laughter edging his voice. "Who should he play first?"

"Now wait a minute…"

"Get serious, Moyshe," Mouse snapped. "You're going to go Roman candle freaker if you stay locked up. Come on out and say hi to the world. Go on down there and beat the guy at the end of the table."

There was a tightness around the corners of Mouse's eyes. And an edge to his voice. Moyshe recognized a command. He moved down the table.

He did not like being pushed, but Mouse had a point. The mission was not dead. He would not get his job done sitting in his cabin.

He took the empty seat opposite the youth at the foot of the table, smiling wanly. His opponent had black. Moyshe opened with king's pawn. Four moves. "Checkmate." He could not believe it. Nobody fell for a fool's mate.

"Good, Moyshe," Amy said over his shoulder. "Tommy, wake up. Moyshe isn't a subtle player. He's more your kamikaze type."

BenRabi turned. "Really?" She was leaning on the back of his chair. Skullface Kindervoort and his troops had vanished.

"From the games I've seen you play."

Tommy's mouth finally closed. The swiftness of his defeat had shattered him.

"Let's say that's just for practice," Moyshe said. Tommy smiled weakly.

"Too generous of you," he murmured. "I deserved what I got."

BenRabi beat him again, easily, but took longer. Then he moved up the table, playing Seiner after Seiner, quickly, and one landsman whom he had beaten before. The Starfishers, while enthusiastic, were even less subtle than he. They played the game like checkers, going for a massacre. He won every match he played.

"Break time, Amy," he said. "I'm getting calluses on my butt."

"That was kind, what you did for Tommy," she said as she guided him toward the refreshments line.

"What's that?"

"Giving him a second chance. Playing badly on purpose."

"I did that?" He was glad they had dragged him in. The noise, the excitement of new people… It was infectious.

"You did. I know something about the game. Tommy's eager, but a little short. You know." She tapped her temple. "He's my second cousin. I feel sorry for him. Someday he'll realize that he won't ever beat anybody. It'll really hit him. The only thing he can really do better than anybody is handle the animals."

"Animals?" benRabi demanded incredulously.

"Sure. The zoo animals. In Twelve South, over by Sail Control. We've got the space for it. That's one thing we don't lack. We've got botanical gardens and feral forests and football stadiums and all kinds of space wasters. Our ships are built to be lived in."

"You remind me of somebody," he mumbled, remembering Alyce. Alyce had had that same elfin nose, those same high cheekbones, that same slim, small-breasted body.

"What?"

"Nothing." He tried to cover up by downing half a cup of steaming coffee. It scalded him. He sprayed the man in front of him. He mumbled apologies, felt small, and rubbed his lips and tongue.

Amy guided him away before he humiliated himself.

Swinging a hand to indicate the crowd, he said, "Reminds me of an Archaicist convention. For which read madhouse. Does this go on every week?"

"Except last week, when they were getting ready for you to come aboard. You should see it during sports season."

"How do they find people to play those games? From what Mouse told me…"

"People isn't the problem. Every residential cube has teams. They can pick and choose their players. It's a big thing, being a sports hero. Specially if you make one of the All-Star teams that play against the other harvestships. We've got every game you can imagine. You ever try nul-grav handball?"

"I've played. Maybe not by the same rules… Mouse and I play sometimes."

"Who wins?"

"He docs. Most of the time. I don't have the killer instinct. I just play for fun."

"He's always dead serious, isn't he? Completely determined. And yet he seems to enjoy life more than you."

He scowled. "What is this?"

"Sorry. Where was I? Oh. There's even an Olympics. And intership games whenever we're in The Yards, and Fleet games while we're harvesting."

"The yards?"

"Enough said. That's secret stuff."

He did not press. But the agent in him red-tagged her words.

Amy led him to a cluster of tables under a banner proclaiming: COLLECTOR'S CORNER. It was quieter there. The people were older and less flashily dressed. Moyshe spied coins and stamps and other odds and ends of milemarks from Old Earth's past. Coin and stamp collections had been popular, lightweight links with the motherworld during early space days, when mass and volume had been critically important.

"Not a nibble," he overheard one man complain to another. The listener nodded tautly, as though he were hearing it for the *n*th time. "Told you it would be a waste of time, Charley. They're all hedonists." The speaker glared at a raucous group of Archaicists. "We won't see one thing new before next auction."

His table caught benRabi's eye and interest. The man had laid out a display of British coins and stamps. "Excuse me, sir."

"Yeah?" the complainer growled. Then he recognized Moyshe as an outsider who might have something to offer. BenRabi could see excitement rising in him. More companionably, "Sit down. Sit down. Name's George. What's your field?"

"Victorians. Tell me, how does a Starfisher come by…"

A quick, conspiratorial smile flashed across the man's face. "I would've bet you'd ask that, friend. I got lucky one time. I bought this unclaimed trunk when I was on The Big Rock Candy Mountain. Opened it up and, Holy Christ!" George launched a narrative which included the minutest detail of his lucky day. Collectors were that way, and every one had his story.

Moyshe studied him. How had he gotten down onto a Confederation world? Why? Was this another tidbit that should be red-tagged? Did Starfishers make many surreptitious visits to the worlds of their hunters?

"I didn't know if I'd run into any collectors out here," Moyshe said, "but I brought my trading stock just in case. I'm more into stamps than coins. British and American and German. If you know anybody. I've got some good stuff."

"Know anybody? Look around you. See all those birddogs on point?"

I'm a champion fool, Moyshe thought suddenly. *I could retire on my collection if I could sell it at market. Hell. I'm rich.*

Prize money had a way of piling up. He only used his to support his hobbies.

"Come on, friend. Sit. How many times do I have to tell you? Paul, get the man some coffee." All warmth now, George practically forced him into a chair. Moyshe surrendered. Amy attached herself to its back.

She must be assigned to me, the way she's sticking, benRabi thought. *It's not my overwhelming charm keeping her here.*

"Like I said, I'm George. Grumpy George, they call me. But I kind of grow on you after a while."

"BenRabi. Moyshe benRabi. I was noticing this stamp here…"

He and George swapped stories for an hour.

"I'm glad you dragged me over here," Moyshe told Amy afterward.

"Good. I'm glad you're enjoying yourself." Her tone said she was not having fun.

"What're you doing tonight?" he blurted. He felt as nervous as a youngster trying to make his first date. "About the ball, I mean. One of the Archaicist groups is having that American Deep South Civil War thing…"

She smiled a sad smile. "I don't have any plans, if that's what you mean. But you don't have a costume."

"Is it mandatory?"

"No. You know Archaicists. They'll put up with anything to interest people in their pet periods. That one's already popular. The American ones are here. Our ethnic roots mostly go back to North America. Are you asking me?"

"Yeah. I guess."

"Good." She laughed. "I'll pick you up at eight."

"What? Shouldn't the man?…"

"Not when he's a landsman. The rules. You'd get arrested if you went running around looking for me."

"Oh. All right. What now?"

"There isn't much happening. Unless you want to join the Archaicists, or go to a ball game."

"Let's just circulate." He might pick up something interesting.

They milled in the press, watching several Archaicist performances, Mouse handling the Tregorgarthian youths, a fencing tournament, and the endless chess matches. Life aboard *Danion* was little different from that aboard a warship on extended patrol. The limits just were not as narrow.

Amy introduced Moyshe to scores of people whose names he forgot immediately. "This is getting to be like an overgrown cocktail party," he observed. "I hated them when I was line. You *had* to attend. They're the reason I decided to be a spy. Spies don't have to be nice to people they don't like."

Amy looked at him oddly.

"Just joking."

"Your friend is good at everything he does, isn't he?" She had become impressed with the way Mouse had handled the Tregor-garthians.

"When he gets interested in something he gives it everything. He's got a knack for switching on and off to complete commitment."

"And the girls. How does he find the time?"

"I don't know. If I did, I'd be cutting a swath myself."

His answer did not satisfy her. She kept trying to pry something out of him. She wasted her time. He had been in the spy business so long that the information shutdown was reflexive.

"You want to find out about Mouse, go to the horse's mouth," he finally told her.

"I don't think so, Moyshe."

He smiled. Mouse would talk about himself all night, not tell a word of truth, and seduce her three times in the process. "Probably not. We're different, him and me. I'm the type that would rather observe."

Amy linked her arm with his. "Observe for me, observer."

"About what?"

"You came to watch Seiners. Tell me about us. What do we look like to you?"

"Uhm. Happy. At peace with yourselves and the universe. Here's a thing. About laughter. It's different here. Not anything like at home. Like your souls are part of it. Like my people only laugh to push back the darkness. The guy who was doing the comedy routine?"

"Jake?"

"Whatever his name is. The one who told the story about Murph, the guy who knew everybody. He even made me laugh. And you know why? Because he was poking fun at things I wouldn't even have thought about. Or wouldn't have the nerve to criticize. I'm a moral coward."

"Whoa. What're you talking about? What brought that on?"

"I just started thinking about my boss. Very dignified

gentleman. When he wants to be. All the big-timers are in Luna Command. Only their dignity is almost always pomposity in disguise. Ever since I was a midshipman I've had this fantasy about being the king's secret agent. I'd go around disguised as Joe Citizen. I'd keep a list. Whenever a civil servant or sales person was obnoxious, I'd put their names down and the king's men would come and get them. I'd also be a sort of wandering clown who made pompous bigwigs expose themselves for what they were. The Bureau would be my first target."

"You have hard feelings against the people you work for?"

Moyshe did not answer. The intensity of Amy's question scared him off. She was too keen, too tense, too eager all of a sudden. "Let's change the subject."

She did not press. A while later she suggested, "Why don't you go back to your writing now?"

"Trying to get rid of me?"

"No! That's not what I meant. Did it sound like that? I'm sorry. I just thought you might feel better now."

He reflected for a moment. "I do. Maybe it'll go better. I hate to admit it, but I've had a good time, Amy. Thanks."

He allowed her to escort him to his cabin, where he immediately attacked his story. It went well.

He hardly seemed to have begun though, when Amy pushed his buzzer. "Moyshe. Wake up," she called from the passageway.

"It's open. Time already?"

In she bounced, charmingly dressed as a southern belle, in lots of pink and petticoats. "Been going good? You've got papers everywhere." She had a Confederate uniform over one arm, and swords and things under the other.

"Smoking."

"I borrowed some things... What's the matter?"

For an instant he had seen her as Alyce. His past hit him like a tsunami.

Her smile persisted, but did not ride her voice as she asked, "Moyshe, what's behind you?"

"Nothing. That costume for me? Give it here and I'll change."

"I've been watching you, Moyshe. Something's eating you.

Don't let it. Puke it up. Get it out where you can stomp on it, chop it up, and kill it."

That was the difference between Amy and Alyce. Alyce would never have asked. She would have waited till he wanted to talk.

"What about you?" he demanded. "Want to tell me what's behind you?" Best defense is a good offense, he thought, mocking himself.

She ignored it. "Tell me something." She spoke softly, with concern, just as she had done that day on the shuttle.

"I have walked with joy down the passion-shaded avenues
Abounding in the City of Love. My heart was young,
And She was beside me; together were we,
And in that was my totality."

"Czyzewski," she observed. "Yes. I read too. It's from *Sister Love*. They say he wrote it before he went into space and lost his mind—if a guy who brags about a love affair with his sister isn't crazy already. What do you mean by it, Moyshe? Is an old love affair bothering you? That's silly. You're not fifteen…"

"I'm perfectly aware of that. Intellectually. 'I was then, stark in the gardens of the moon,'" he quoted out of context. "Now I'm a tired old man, far from home, futureless, with no friend but a chess-mad Archaicist triggerman I never see except during working hours…" *Hold it*, he thought. *The mouth is playing traitor here.*

"Give me that costume. Let me get ready. Please?"

"All right." She put a lot into those two words. It reminded him of the professional mother who had taken care of him occasionally while his natural mother had chased ghosts of vanished Earths. She had been able to say the same words the same way, implying that nothing good could possibly come of whatever he planned. She had been able to say almost anything in a way that made it sound like he was condemning himself to the clutches of the Devil, or some equally nasty fate.

"Well. You make a striking officer," Amy said when he returned from the bathroom. "If you had a beard you'd look a little like Robert E. Lee."

"Yeah? Can you do something about this damned sword? How the hell did they get around without falling on their faces all the time?"

She giggled as she made adjustments. "What?"

"Just wondering how many Jewish generals there were in the Confederate Army."

"There're a lot... Oh, you mean that Confederation. I don't get it. Why should that be funny?"

"You have to know the period."

"Well, you've lost me. I only know it from military history at Academy. I can tell you why Longstreet did what he didn't do at Gettysburg, but not what religion he was. Anyway, I'm not Jewish. And you know it."

"What are you, then? Do you believe in anything, Moyshe?"

Poking again. Prying. For her own sake, he guessed. Fisher Security probably would not care about his religion.

He wanted to make a snappy comeback, but she had struck too close to the core of his dissatisfaction. At the moment he did not believe in anything, and himself least of all. And that, he thought, was curious, because he had not had these kinds of feelings since coming out of the line. Not till this mission had begun. "The Prophet Murphy," he said.

"Murphy? I don't get it. Who the hell is Murphy? I expected death and taxes."

"The Prophet Murphy. The guy who said, 'If anything can possibly go wrong, it will.' My life has been a testimonial."

She stepped back, shook her head slowly. "I don't know what to make of you, Moyshe. Yes I do. Maybe. Maybe I'll just make you happy in spite of yourself."

"Blood from a turnip, Lady."

He had had enough talk. Taking her arm, he headed for the ball, for the moment forgetting that he did not know where he was going. Then he saw that she had brought an electric scooter. The Seiners used them whenever they had to travel any distance. There were places in *Danion* that were literally days away by foot.

Red-faced, he settled onto the passenger seat, facing backward.

They did not exchange a word during the trip. Moyshe suffered irrational surges of anger, alternating with images of the gun.

That thing scared the hell out of him. He was no triggerman. It seemed to have less contact with reality than did his wanting.

He had become, on a low-key, reflexively suppressed level, convinced that he was going insane.

Time seemed to telescope. The unwanted thoughts would not go away. His hands grew cold and clammy. His mood sank...

Amy swung to the passage wall, parked, plugged the scooter into a charger circuit. It became one of a small herd of orange beasts nursing electrical teats. "Good crowd," he said inanely, taking a clumsy poke at the silence.

"Uhm." She paused to straighten his collar and sword. "Come on." Her face remained studiedly blank, landside style. It was a bit of home for which he was ungrateful.

The ball seemed a repeat of the morning's get-together. The same people were there. Only a hundred or so were in appropriate costume. Twice as many wore every get-up from Babylon to tomorrow, and as many again wore everyday jumpsuits.

Moyshe froze just inside the doorway.

"What is it?" Amy asked.

"I'm not sure. I don't have the right, but... I feel like something's been taken away from me." Had all those Vikings and Puritans and Marie Antoinettes stolen his moment of glory? Had he been bitten by the Archaicist bug?

"It's our history, too, remember?" Amy countered, misunderstanding. "You said everybody's roots go back to Old Earth."

A hand took Moyshe's left elbow. "Mint julep, sir?"

BenRabi turned to face Jarl Kindervoort, who wore buckskins and coonskin cap. *Dan'l Deathshead*, he thought. *Scair 'em injuns right out'n Kaintuck.*

"The damn thing fits you better than it does me," Kindervoort observed.

"It's your costume?"

"Yeah. Let's see what they've got at the bar, Moyshe."

Amy had disappeared. And Kindervoort's tone implied business. Feeling put-upon, benRabi allowed himself to be led to the bar.

That was another unpleasantness. The setup was Wild West, with a dozen rowdy black hat types attached, busy making asses of themselves with brags and mock gunfights. Acrid gunsmoke floated around in grey-blue streamers.

Of all the period crap that Archaicists bought, Moyshe felt Wild West was the worst. It was all made-up history, a consensus fantasy with virtually no foundation in actual history.

His mother's first Archaicist flier had been Wild West. It had come during his difficulties at Academy, when he had desperately needed an anchor somewhere. She had not given him what he had needed. She had not had the time.

To top it off, the Sangaree woman was there. She had assumed the guise of The Lady Who Goes Upstairs.

"Appropriate," benRabi muttered. Her awesome sexual appetites had grown since The Broken Wings.

She was watching him with Jarl. Was she getting a little worried? Wondering when he would turn her in? He smiled at her. Let her sweat.

There was a stir at the door. "Jesus," benRabi said. "Will you look at this."

Mouse the attention-grabber and most popular boy in class, with no less than six beauties attached, had just swept in outfitted as a diminutive Henry VIII.

"We're lucky this isn't a democracy," Kindervoort observed. "Your friend would be Captain by the end of the year, riding the female vote."

Moyshe ignored the pun. Sourly, he said, "Aren't you?" He was getting irritated with Mouse's antics. The man was flaunting his successes... Envy was one of benRabi's nastier vices. He tried to control it, but Mouse made that hard.

He faced the bar, found himself staring at some horrid-looking swill in a tall glass. "Mint julep," Kindervoort explained. "We try to drink according to period at these things." He sipped from a tin cup. The gunfighters were tossing off straight shots. At bar's end a hairy Viking type waved an axe and thundered something about honey mead.

"Bet it all comes out of the same bottle."

"Probably," Kindervoort admitted.

"It's your ballpark. What do you want, Jarl?"

Kindervoort's eyebrows rose. "Moyshe, you're damned hard to

get along with, you know that? Now you frown. I'm getting too personal. How do you people survive, never touching?"

"We don't touch because there're too many of us. Unless you're Mouse. He grew up with lots of elbow room and not wanting for anything. I don't expect you to understand. You couldn't unless you've lived on one of the Inner Worlds."

Kindervoort nodded. "How would you like to get away from all that? To live where there's room to be human? Where you don't have to be an emotional brick to survive?" He took a long sip from his cup, watching Moyshe over its rim.

He had to wait a long time for an answer.

Moyshe knew what was being offered. And what it would cost.

The demons of his mind rallied to fiery standards, warring with one another in an apocalyptic clash. Ideals, beliefs, desires, and temptations stormed one another's strongholds. He struggled to keep that armageddon from painting itself on his face.

He was good at that. He had had decades of practice.

It occurred to him that Kindervoort was Security, and Security men did not deal in the obvious. "Get thee behind me, Satan."

Kindervoort laughed. "All right, Moyshe. But we'll talk about it later. Go on. Find Amy. Have a good time. It's a party."

He vanished before Moyshe could respond. Amy appeared on cue.

"Rotten trick, Amy Many-Names, letting that vampire get ahold of me." Kindervoort's retreat raised his spirits. He felt benevolent toward the universe. He would let it roll on awhile.

"What did he do?"

"Nothing much. Just tried to get me to defect."

She just stared at him, apparently wondering why he was not shrieking with joy. Seldom did a landsman receive the opportunity to become a Seiner.

It was human nature to think your own acre was God-chosen, he realized. And Amy's was one he would not mind entering—though not on Kindervoort's terms. He was not in love with Confederation or the Bureau, but he would never sell them out.

"Let's dance," Amy suggested. "That's what we came for."

Time drifted away. Moyshe began to enjoy himself. He discovered that he was spending the evening with a woman who mattered more than the bag of duffel with sex organs she had been when they had arrived.

Somewhere along the way one of Amy's cousins invited them to a room party. No longer tense and wary, he said, "Why not? Sounds good." A moment later he and Amy were part of a gay crowd on scooters, shooing pedestrians with rebel yells. The partiers were mostly youngsters recently graduated from the creche schools, almost as new to the harvestship as Moyse. In a small group, confined to a cabin, he found them less reserved than the older Seiners he met while working.

They seemed to have Archaicist tendencies oriented toward the late twentieth century youth cults. At least the cabin belonged to someone fond of the approximate period. Moyshe could not identify it for certain.

Liquor flowed. Smoke filled the air. Time passed. Quiet in a corner, with Amy most of the time but sometimes without, observing, he gradually settled into a strange mood wherein he became detached from his environment. The bittersweet smoke was more to blame than the alcohol. It was dense enough to provide a high without his having to toke any of the odd little cigarettes offered him.

Marijuana, someone called them. He vaguely remembered it from childhood, as something the older kids in his gang had used. He had never done dope himself.

His companions coughed and gasped and made faces, but persisted. The drug was part of the period cult. He drifted farther from reality himself, floating free, till he swam in a mist of uninhibited, irrational impressions.

The touch of a woman on his hand—sail on, silver girl—and the flavor of whiskey on his tongue. Dancing light, harsh in a distant corner, all shadows and angles beside him. His fingers slipped into the warm place at the back of Amy's neck. She purred, moving from the arm of the chair into his lap. He thought sex… No. He was not drunk enough to forget Alyce. Fear arose. Shadows grew, beckoning. In their hearts lurked dark things, wicked spirit-reavers from the deeps of the past come to stalk him along the shores of the future. There was a magic at work in that room. He and Amy were suddenly alone amid the horde.

Alone among the golden people, all of them ten years their junior, each with a newly minted shiny innocence—on some becoming tarnished. He did not care.

They talked, she a little deeply, and he with scant attention. He was not ready to explore her yet. But it seemed, from hints she dropped, that their pasts might read like sides of the same coin. An unhappy affair lay behind her, and something physical, sexual, that she was not yet ready to yield, was troubling her now. He did not press. His own midnight-eyed haunts were lurking in the wings.

On. On. Near midnight, in a moment of clarity, he noticed her left-handedness for the first time because of the way she offered him a can of Archaicist-trade beer. Left-handed, pop the top, shift hands, offer with a bend of the wrist because he was right-handed. He marveled because he had not noticed it earlier. He was supposed to be an observant man. It was his profession. October thoughts died as his interest increased and he became aware of the intenseness of Amy's every move.

She laughed a lot, usually at things that were not funny. Her own fanged shadows were closing in, memories that she had to exorcise with forced mirth. She was trying to keep her devil out of sight, but he found its shaggy edges familiar. It was a cousin of his own.

While a dozen people silently considered the songs of someones named Simon and Garfunkel, or Buddy Holly, he discovered how nicely they fit. She spent an hour in his lap without making him uncomfortable. His left hand touched the back of her neck, his right lay on the curve of her left hip, and her head rested nicely on his left shoulder, beneath his chin. Her hair had a pale, pleasant, unfamiliar scent.

Weren't they a little old for this?

Shadows in the doorways, shadows on the walls. Don't ask questions. He listened to her heartbeat, three beats for his two.

He shivered as his monster shuffled closer. Amy moved, wriggling nearer. She chuckled softly when he grunted from the pain-tweak of her bony bottom shifting in his lap.

The partiers began drifting out, off to their private places, to be lonely, or frightened, or together till the reality of morning swept them back to work and today. Soon there were just three couples left. Moyshe shivered as he lifted Amy's chin. She resisted a moment, then surrendered. The kiss became intense. The shadows retreated a bit.

"Come on," she said, bouncing up, yanking his arm. They darted into the passageway, boarded the scooter, and flew to his cabin. She went in with him, locking the door behind her.

But the time was not yet right. They spent the night sleeping. Just cuddling and sleeping, hiding from the darkness. Neither was ready to risk anything more.

She was gone when he awakened. And his wants and haunts were strangely quiet.

Where would they go from here? he wondered.

TWELVE: 3047 AD
The Olden Days, The Motherworld

Perchevski shuffled from foot to foot. He was too nervous to sit. He had not realized that going home would unleash so much emotion.

He glanced around the lounge. The lighter would be carrying a full load. Tourists and business people. The former were mostly Ulantonid and Toke. They huddled in racial clumps, intimidated by Old Earth's xenophobic reputation, yet determined to explore the birth world of Man. The Toke nerved themselves with bold talk. Their every little quirk or gesture seemed to proclaim, "We are the Mel-Tan Star Warriors of the Marine Toke Legion. We are the Chosen of the Star Lords. The delinquents of a decadent world cannot frighten us."

But they were scared.

No enemy could intimidate the Toke. The Toke War had proven that. Only the stroke of diplomatic genius that had made a place for them in Service, and a place for Toke in Confederation, as equals, had saved the Warrior Caste from extinction.

It's a pity we can't work something like that for the Sangaree, Perchevski thought.

But there had been no hatred in the Toke War. It had been an almost clinically unemotional contest for supremacy in the star ranges of the Palisarian Directorate.

The Ulantonid were less bellicose than the Toke. Their war with Confederation had been unemotional too. Another blood-flavored wrestling match for supremacy.

These looked like a Catholic group headed for Rome, Jerusalem, and Bethlehem.

"Shuttle Bravo Tango Romeo Three One is now ready for boarding for passengers making a Lake Constance descent. Passengers for Corporation Zone will please assemble at Shuttle Bay Nine."

"I'd like to meet her," said a stranger near Perchevski.

"Who's that?"

"The woman who does the announcing. She can put her shoes under my bed anytime."

"Oh. The voice." It had been a soothing, mellow, yet suggestive voice. Similar voices did the announcing in every terminal Perchevski had ever visited.

The tourists and business people boarded first. Luna Command made a habit of doing little things that avoided irritating civilians. The individual Serviceman was supposed to remain unobtrusive.

Only one check on Luna Command's power existed. The operating appropriation voted by a popularly elected senate.

The Toke Marines stood aside for Perchevski, who had come in his Commander's uniform.

It was a long, lazy twelve-hour orbit to Lake Constance and Geneva. Perchevski read, slept, and pondered the story he had recently begun. He tried not to think about the world below.

The holonets could not begin to portray the squalid reality that was Old Earth beyond the embattled walls of Corporation Zone.

The shuttle dropped into the lake. A tug guided it into a berth. Perchevski followed the civilians into the air of his native world. He had come home. After eight years.

Geneva had not changed. Switzerland remained unspoiled. Its wealth and beauty seemed to give the lie to all the horror stories about Old Earth.

It was a mask. Offworld billions cosmeticized the Zone, and

Corporation police forces maintained its sanctity at gunpoint. The perimeters were in a continuous state of siege.

There were times when Luna Command had to send down Marines to back the Corporation defense forces. The excuse was protection of Confederation's Senate and offices, which were scattered between Geneva, Zurich, and the south shore of the Bodensee.

Once there had been a social theory claiming that the wealth coming into the Zone from the Corporations headquartered there would eventually spread across the planet. A positive balance of trade would be created. And the positive example of life in the Zone would act as a counter-infection to the social diseases of the rest of the planet. Change would radiate from Switzerland like ripples in a pond.

The theory had been stillborn, as so many social engineering schemes are.

No one here gives a damn, Perchevski reflected as he entered his hotel room. All that kept Earth going was trillions in interplanetary welfare. Maybe the whole thing should be allowed to collapse, then something could be done for the survivors.

The motherworld's people still played their games of nationalism and warfare. They loved their Joshua Jas. And they flatly refused to do anything for themselves while Confederation could be shamed into paying support.

The too often told tale of welfarism was repeating itself. As always, provision of means for improvement had become an overpowering disincentive to action.

Perchevski spent his first day at home doing one of the guided tours of the wonders of Corporation Zone. With his group were a few native youngsters who had been awarded the tour as contest prizes.

They surprised him. They were reasonably well-behaved, moderately clean, and not too badly dressed. A cut above the average run, and not unlike kids elsewhere. The Security guard was not called upon to practice his trade.

The tour group lunched in the restaurant at the Nureyev Technical Industries chalet atop the Matterhorn.

"Excuse me, Commander."

Perchevski looked up from his sausage and kraut, startled. A girl of sixteen, a tall, attractive blonde, stood opposite him. He was eating alone. His uniform had put off everyone but two Toke Marines, who were still trying to explain their need to a cook who was appalled at the idea of permitting raw meat out of his kitchen. He suspected the Marines wanted to stay near him for a feeling of added security. The Toke were a strongly hierarchical people, and among them warriors were the most respected of castes.

"Yes?"

"May I sit here?"

"Of course." He was stunned. She was one of the prize winners. Most Old Earthers so hated the Services that even the best intentioned could not remain polite.

Is she a prostitute? he wondered.

Whatever her pitch, she needed time. She was so nervous she could not eat.

She suddenly blurted, "You're Old Earth, aren't you? I mean originally."

"Yes. How did you know?"

"The way you look at things. Outworlders look at things different. Like they're afraid they'll catch something, or something."

Perchevski glanced at the other prize winners. Disgust marked their faces. "Your friends don't..."

"They're not my friends. I never saw any of them before yesterday. How did you get out?" Words tumbled out of her all strung together, so fast he could hardly follow them.

"Out?"

"Of this. This place. This world."

"I took the Academy exams. They accepted me."

"They didn't stop you?"

"Who?"

"Your friends. The people you knew. I tried three times. Somebody always found out and kept me from going. Last time three men stopped me outside the center and said they'd kill me if I went in."

"So there's still hope," Perchevski murmured. He knew what she wanted now.

"Sir?"

"I mean, as long as there's somebody like you left, Old Earth isn't dead. You've made my trip worthwhile."

"Get me out. Can you get me out? Anything is better than this. I'll do anything. Anything you want."

She meant it. Her desperate promise was so obvious it hurt.

He remembered his own desperation at an even younger age. When you chose the unpopular path you had to cleave to it with fanatical determination. He was moved. Deeply.

"I entered every contest there ever was just so I could get this far. I knew they wouldn't keep me from coming here, and I thought maybe I could find somebody…"

"But you were too scared to do anything when you got here."

"They were all outworlders."

"You leave Earth, you won't meet anyone else. I've only run into two or three Earthmen in twenty years." He eyed the group with which the girl had been traveling. The youths seemed to have caught the drift of her appeal. They did not like it.

"I know. I'd get used to it."

"Are you sure?…"

Three young men drifted to the table. "This slut don't belong here, Spike."

Perchevski smiled gently. "You just made fuck-up number one, stud. Don't get smoked."

That startled them. One snarled, "You'll shit in your hand and carry it to China, Spike."

"May I be of assistance, Commander?"

The Toke Marine dwarfed the three youths. Adam's apples bobbed.

"I don't think so, Fire Cord. I'd say the Banner is secure. The young men have said their piece. They were just leaving."

The Toke Major glared down. At two and a quarter meters and one hundred thirty kilos he was a runt for a Star Warrior. His aide, though, was the kind they put on recruiting pamphlets meant for circulation through the Caste Lodges. He stood quietly behind his officer, filled with that still, dread equanimity that made the Star Warriors unnerving to even the most hardened human Servicemen.

"'Go you silently, Children of the Night,'" Perchevski quoted from an old song used as a battle anthem by half the youth gangs on the planet. "You, especially, talking head."

The slang had not changed much. Unlike the Outworlds, Old Earth had become locked into static patterns.

The youths understood. There had been a time when he had been one of them.

They left, strutting with false bravura. Perchevski thought he caught a glint of envy in the spokesman's eye.

"Thank you, Fire Cord." The Security man, busy talking shit to a restaurant girl, had missed the encounter.

"We share the Banner, Commander. We will be near."

"Fire Cord?"

"Sir?"

"Don't call them on their own ground."

"This is my third visit, Commander."

"Then you know." He turned to the girl again, who seemed petrified. The two huge, leathery-skinned Marines moved to the nearest empty table.

The girl finally blurted, "Why did you come back?"

"I don't know. To remind myself? Looking for something I left behind? Roots? I'm not sure. I wanted to see my mother. It's been eight years."

"Oh." She sounded envious. "I couldn't find out who my parents were. I never met anybody who did know. Not my age, anyway."

He smiled. "Do you have a name? After that scene, you'd better stay close to me or the Marines. We'll have to call you something besides Hey Girl."

"Greta. Helsung. From Hamburg. Are they real Star Warriors?"

He laughed softly. "Don't let them hear you ask a question like that, Greta from Hamburg. They're as real as the stink in the sink. I'm Commander Perchevski. If you don't change your mind, I'll take you to see somebody when we get back to Geneva."

"I won't change it. Not after all the trouble I had…"

He peered at her intently. This was too breathtaking, too real, too dream-come-true for her. She did not quite believe him. He could almost hear her thinking he would use her, then dump her.

The use temptation existed. She was fresh and beautiful.

"I mean it, Greta. And don't be scared. You're young enough to be my daughter."

"I'm not a child. I'm old enough…"

"I'm aware of that. I'm not young enough. Eat your knockwurst. The meat came all the way from Palisarius."

"Oh, God! Really? I didn't know what I was ordering. I just asked for something that I didn't know what it was. Just for something different. They didn't show any prices. It must be awful expensive." She looked around guiltily.

"So don't waste it." Then, "Price doesn't matter to most people who eat here. If they couldn't afford it, they wouldn't come. Go on. Enjoy yourself."

Her tour expenses would be covered. Luna Command would pick up the tab. The Services sponsored the contests that gave Zone vacations as prizes. Some inspired social theorist had decided to fish for Old Earth's Gretas, for the one-in-a-million children who had adventure in their genes and dreams in their hearts.

The program was as successful as the normal recruiting procedures. It gave interested youths a chance to escape peer pressure. Computers watched and cross-checked the contest entries. Undoubtedly, someone would have contacted Greta if she had not come to him.

He eyed her and thanked heaven that someone out there still cared.

He felt pretty good.

Greta remained nearby throughout the tour, milking him for every detail about outside. Her former companions were not pleased, but the Fire Cord was always too close for their nerve.

Terrorism was a popular Terran sport. Toke, though, refused to be terrorized. They bashed heads. Their reputation did not make them immune, but it did force the natives to respect them.

Perchevski took the girl to the Bureau's front business office that evening. "A potential recruit," he told the night desk man, who recognized him from a holo portrait that had preceded him down. "Greta Helsung, from Hamburg. Treat her right."

"Of course, Commander. Miss? Will you take a seat? We can get the paperwork started."

"It's that easy?" she asked Perchevski.

The desk man replied, "You'll be sleeping on the moon tomorrow night, Miss. Oh. Commander. You're leaving?"

"I have an eleven-thirty to Montreal."

Greta looked at him in silent appeal.

"Will you sponsor, Commander?"

He knew he shouldn't. It meant accepting legal and quasi-parental responsibility. The Admiral would be furious... "Of course. Where do I print?" He offered his thumb.

"Here. Thank you." Something buzzed. The desk man glanced to one side, read something from a screen Perchevski could not see. "Oh-oh." He thumbed a print-lock. A drawer popped open. He handed Perchevski a ring.

"Why?" It was a call ring. It would let him know if the Bureau wanted him on the hurry up. It would give them a means of following his movements, too.

"Word from the head office. Ready, Miss Helsung?"

"Greta, I'll see you in Academy." He wrote a number on a scrap of paper. "Keep this. Call it when you get your barracks assignment." He started to leave again.

"Commander?"

He turned. Soft young arms flung around his neck. Tears seeped through his uniform. "Thank you."

"Greta," he whispered, "don't be scared. They'll be good to you."

They would. She would be treated like a princess till her studies began.

"Good-bye. Be good."

Four of the tour youths caught him outside. He had to break one's arm before they got the message. He was nearly late for his flight. He had to wait to shift to civilian clothing till after he had boarded the airbus.

North American Central Directorate showed his mother living

at the same St. Louis Zone address. He went without calling first, afraid she might find some excuse for not seeing him. Though their intentions were friendly enough, their few visits had been tempestuous. She could never forgive him for "turning on his own kind."

The passage down the last light canyon was like a journey home along an old route of despair.

The playgrounds of his childhood had not changed. Trash still heaped them. Kid gangs still roamed them. Crudely written, frequently misspelled obscenities obscured the unyielding plastic walls. Future archaeologists might someday go carefully through layer after layer of spray paint, reconstructing the aberrations of generations of uneducated minds.

He labored to convince himself that this was not the totality of Old Earth.

"Some of it's worse," he murmured. Then he castigated himself for his bigotry.

Sure, most Terran humanity lived like animals. But not all. There were enclaves where some pride, some care, some ambition remained. There were native industries. Earth produced most of its own food and necessities. And there were artists, writers, and men of vision… They just got lost in the barbarian horde. They formed an unnaturally small percentage of the population.

Not only had risk-taking been drained from the gene pool, so had a lot of talent and intelligence.

The average I.Q. on Old Earth ran twenty points below Confederation mean.

Perchevski overtipped his driver. It was enough to convince the man that he had conveyed some criminal kingpin. Crime was one profession where a man could still win some respect.

His codes still opened the building's doors. After all these years. He was amazed.

It was another symptom of what had become of his mother-world. Terror had become so ubiquitous that no one tried very hard to resist anymore.

His mother was drunk. She snapped, "You're not Harold. Who the hell are you? Where's Harold? Nobody comes here but Harold."

He looked past her into the space where he had spent most of his childhood. Three meters by four, it was divided into three tiny rooms. It had seemed bigger back then, even with his father living at home.

He said nothing.

"Look, brother... Holy Christ! It's you. What the hell are you doing here?" She sounded angry. "Don't stand there looking. Get in here before somebody burns us."

He slipped past her, plopped himself down on the same little couch that had been his boyhood bed.

The apartment had not changed. Only his mother had. For the worse.

It was more than age and unrelenting poverty. It was a sliding downhill from the inside.

She had begun to go to fat. Her personal habits had slipped. Her hair had not been combed in days...

"Let me clean up. I just got outta bed." She vanished behind the movable screen that made a bedroom wall. "What have you been doing?" she asked.

"Better I should ask you. I sent letters." And hard Outworlds currency. Neither had drawn any response.

"I never seem to get around to answering."

At least she did not make outrageous excuses, like not being able to pay a writer. He knew she took his missives to a reader. She cared that much. But not enough to reply.

"I did write twice. Once right after you were here last time, and two or three years ago, after your father was killed in the Tanner Revolt. I didn't care anymore, but I thought you might."

"He's dead?"

"As a stone. He got hung up in the Revanchist Crusade. They were getting pretty big. Then most of them got themselves killed attacking Security Fortress."

"I didn't get the letter. I didn't know." He had never heard of the Tanner Revolt or Revanchist Crusade. He asked about them.

"They were going to turn things around. Bring back the golden age, or something. Unite Earth and make it the center of the galaxy. A lot of people think you Loonies were behind it. They say the whole Archaicist thing was started by your meddling."

Archaicism had had its infancy on Old Earth concurrent with his own. If it had been more social engineering, the plan had backfired. The motherworld had not been awakened by the glory that was. It had merely found a new way to escape the reality of now.

The romantic pasts were popular. Men liked playing empires. Women liked glamour.

Men died when groups like Stahlhelm, SS Totenkopf, or Black September ganged up on Irgun or Stern… The smallest and most obscurely referenced groups were the most dangerous.

The ladies seemed to prefer Regency Balls, French Courts, and seraglio situations.

A search for uniqueness combined with the need for belonging had driven people to probe the remotest corners of Earth's history.

During his flight he had watched a live newscast of a raid on Mexico's Aztec Revivalist Cult. The police attackers had battled their way into the temple too late to save the sacrifices.

Perchevski's mother returned. She wore an outfit that looked ridiculous on a woman her age. The blouse was see-through. The skirt fell only to mid-thigh. He concealed his consternation. No doubt this was her best.

"I don't get into that kind of thing. Not my line. I do know a few guys who make a hobby of trying to save this dump from itself."

She did not like his attitude. "What are you calling yourself this time?"

"Perchevski. Cornelius Perchevski." He stared at her, and saw Greta forty years from now. Unless… If the kid enlisted, he would feel his own life-choice was justified. He would have rescued someone from becoming this…

"What are you into?" he asked. "I don't recognize the period."

"Beatles and Twiggy."

"Eh?"

"Twentieth century. Seventh decade. Anglo-American, with the beginning in England. One of the light periods."

"Youth and no philosophy? I gathered that much, though I'm

not familiar with it."

"It's all the rage now. It's so very outré. So clish-clash with itself. So schizophrenic. You speak English, don't you?"

"We have to learn. Most of the First Expansion worlds have some memory of it."

"Why don't you stop all that foolishness? All those ugly Outsiders... You could do well teaching English here. *Everybody* wants to learn."

Here we go, he thought. *She's picking up where she left off eight years ago. It'll only get worse. Why did I come here? To punish myself for getting out of this hell-hole?*

She recognized the look on his face. "It's news time. Let's see what's happening." She whistled a few bars of a tune he did not recognize.

The editing was unbelievable. This Archaicist group had done this. That one had done that. The Bay Bombers had beaten the Rat Pack 21-19. There wasn't a word about von Drachau, or anything else offworld, except mention of a Russian basketball team trouncing the touring team from Novgorod.

"Big deal," he muttered. "Novgorod's gravity is seventy-three percent of Earth normal. They'd have to play midgets for it to be fair."

His mother flared up. She hated foreigners almost as much as she hated Outworlders, but the Russians were, at least, good Old Earthers who had had the sense to stay on the motherworld...

He tuned her out, again wondering if he had a masochistic streak.

Would she try to understand if he explained how much in the middle he was? That Outworlders disliked Old Earthers just as much as she loathed them? That he had to reconcile those attitudes both within himself and with everyone he met?

He did not think she would help. He knew her cure. Give it up. Come back home. To squalor and hopelessness...

"Mother, I am what I am. I won't change. You're wasting your time when you try. Why don't we go out somewhere? This place is depressing."

"What's wrong with it? Yes. All right. It's a little old. And I have the extra credit over S.I. basic to move. But it's so *big*... I like having all this room to knock around in. I wouldn't have that in a new place."

Perchevski groaned to himself. Now came the Mama Marx self-criticism session during which she would confess all her failings as a Social Insuree. Then she would segue into her shortcoming as a mother, ultimately taking upon herself all responsibility for his having gone wrong.

He shook his head sadly. In eight years she should have found a new song. "Come on, Mother. We did this last time. Let's go somewhere. Let's see something. Let's do something."

She dithered. She fussed. It was getting dark out. Only rich Old Earthers, who could afford the armor, went out after the sun went down.

"Here," he said, opening his bag. "I've got my own house now. I brought some holos to show you."

The pictures finally penetrated her façade.

"Tommy! It's beautiful! Magnificent. You really are doing all right, aren't you?"

"Good enough."

"But you're not happy. A mother can tell."

Holy shit, he thought. *I'm grown up twice over. I don't need that.* "You could live there if you wanted."

She became suspicious immediately. "It's not in some foreign place, is it? Those mountains don't look like the Rockies or Sierras."

"It's on a world called Refuge."

"Omigod! Don't do that! Don't talk that way. My heart... Did I tell you that the medics say I have a weak heart?"

"Every time you've ever needed an excuse for..." He stopped himself. He refused to start the fight.

"Let's don't fight, Tommy. We should be friends. Oh. Speaking of friends. Patrick was killed just last week. He went out after dark. It was so sad. Nobody can figure out what made him do it."

"Patrick?"

"That red-haired boy you were friends with the year before you... You enlisted. I think his last name was Medich. He was living with his mother."

He didn't remember a Patrick, red-haired, Medich, or otherwise.

He did not belong here. Even the memories were gone. He had changed. The kid who had lived with this woman was dead. He was an impostor pretending to be her son.

She was bravely playing the game, trying to be his mother. He was sure there were other things she would rather be doing. Hadn't she been expecting a Harold?

Maybe that was why they tried to keep people from going. They became somebody else while they were gone.

"Mother..." His throat clamped down on the word.

"Yes?"

"I... I think I'd better go. I don't know what I came looking for. It's not here. It's not you. It's probably something that doesn't exist." The words came rumbling out, one trampling the heels of the next. "I'm not making you happy being here. So I'd better just go back."

He tried to read her face. Disappointment fought relief there, he thought.

"I'm an Old Earther when I'm out there, Mother. But I'm not when I come back here. I can see that when I'm here. I guess I should just stop remembering this place as home."

"It *is* your home."

"No. Not anymore. It's just the world where I was born. And this is just a place where I lived."

"And I'm just somebody you knew back when?"

"No. You're Mother. You'll always be that."

Silence existed between them for more than a minute.

Perchevski finally said, "Won't you even consider coming to my place?"

"I couldn't. I just couldn't. I belong where I am, being what I am. Useless as that is."

"Mother... You don't have to get old out there. We have a rejuvenation process..."

She showed genuine interest when she asked, "You've recovered the secrets of the immortality labs?"

"No. They're gone forever. All this process does is renew the body. It can't stop nerve degeneration. It's been around for centuries."

"How come nobody's heard about it?"

"Here? With Earth overpopulated and everybody doing their damnedest to make more babies? Some people probably know, though. Some maybe even benefit. It's not a big secret. But nobody here ever listens about Outside. Everybody here is part of this big conspiracy of blindness."

"That's not fair…"

"It's my world. I have the birthright, if I want, to point a finger and call names. Are you going to come with me?" He had begun to think about Greta. That was making him mad.

"No."

"I'll leave in the morning, then. There's no sense us carving each other up with knives of love."

"How poetic!" She sighed. "Darling, Tommy. Keep writing. I know I almost never answer, but the letters… They help. I like to hear about those places."

Perchevski smiled. "It must be in the genes. Thanks. Of course I'll write. You're my number-one lady."

THIRTEEN: 3048 AD
Operation Dragon, *Danion*

BenRabi muttered: " 'Aljo! Aljo! Hené ilyas! Ilyas im gialo bar!…' "
Over a joint with stripped threads.

"What the hell?" Mouse asked.

"A nonsense poem. By Potty Welkin. From *Shadows in a Dominion Blue*. Goes:

" 'Nuné! Nuné! Scutarrac… ' "

"Never heard of it. Think we ought to cut new threads?"

"Let's put in a new fitting. It was a political protest thing. Not one of his biggies. It was a satire on Confederation. The poem was his idea of what a political speech sounded like."

"What's that got to do with anything?"

"It's just the way I feel this morning. Like a poem without sense or rhyme that everybody's trying to figure out. Including me. There. That's got it. What do we do next?"

Beyond Mouse, Amy consulted her clipboard. She had been staring at him with questioning eyes. "A cracked nipple in a lox line about a kilometer from here."

"Uhn." BenRabi tossed his tool kit into the electric truck, sat down with his legs dangling off the bed. Mouse joined him. Amy took off with a lurch that bounced spare fittings all over the truckbed. She had been angry and uncommunicative all week.

Moyshe had been as wary himself, as unsure. He *thought* she was upset because he had not tried to seduce her.

Mouse had let it be for three days. Now, whispering, he asked, "What happened between you two?"

"Nothing."

"Come on, Moyshe. I know you better than that."

"Nothing. Really. That's the trouble." He shrugged, tried to change the subject. "I still can't believe we're inside a ship. I keep feeling we're back in the tunnels at Luna Command."

"What did you mean by that poem?"

"What I said. People keep trying to figure me out. So they can use me."

The ship *was* a lot like Luna Command, with long passageways connecting the several areas that had to be big to function.

"I don't understand," Mouse said.

"Who does? No, wait. Look. Here's Skullface, trying to get me to cross over…"

"So? He tried me too. He's trying everybody. Looks like part of their plan. I just told him I couldn't meet his price. I don't know anything that would be any good to him anyway. So what's the big deal? It's all part of the floor show. We've been through it before."

But there's something different this time, benRabi thought. *I've never been tempted before.* "Why was she hustling me?" He jerked his head toward Amy.

Mouse laughed wearily, lowered his head, shook it sadly. "Moyshe, Moyshe, Moyshe. Does it have to be a plot? Did the Sangaree woman burn you that bad? Maybe she likes you. They're not all vampires."

"But they'll all get you hurt," benRabi mumbled.

"What? Oh. You ever stop to think maybe she feels the same way?"

BenRabi paused. Mouse could be right. Mouse knew how to read women, and it paralleled his own impression. He wished he could assume a more casual, no-commitment attitude in his personal relationships. Mouse managed, and left the girls happy.

"Speaking of women. And her." The Sangaree woman gave them

a bright gunmetal smile and mocking wave as they glided past her work party, "What to do?" She had been less obnoxious since Mouse's recreation-day demonstration, but had not abandoned her plot.

"Just wait. We're making her nervous. You think old Skullface knows about her? We might make a few points by stopping her when she moves."

"It's a notion," Mouse said, becoming thoughtful. As they rolled to a stop, he suggested, "Why don't you come by for a game tonight?"

His partner was still very much devoted to the mission, Moyshe realized.

Amy plugged the truck into a charger circuit. "That woman. Who is she?"

"Which woman?" Mouse countered, tone idle.

BenRabi scanned the area. It looked like the site of a recent elephant riot. The passage had been open to space. Liquids had frozen and burst their pipes.

"We'll be here a week, Amy. How come we didn't bring any replacement pipe?"

"They're sending a Damage Control team up after lunch. They'll bring what we need. We just worry about the lox line now. It's got to be open by noon. You didn't answer my question, Mouse."

"What's that?"

"Who's that woman?"

BenRabi shrugged, said, "Maria Gonzalez, I think."

"I know her name. I want to know what's between you three."

BenRabi shrugged again. "I guess she hates spies. A lot of people have scratched us off their Christmas lists." Avoiding her eyes, he handed Mouse a wrench.

"Who does she work for?"

The question took him by surprise, but he was in good form. "Paul Kraus in atmosphere systems. He could tell you whatever you want to know."

Mouse chuckled.

A muscle in Amy's cheek started twitching. "You know what

I mean. Answer me."

"Take it easy, Amy," Mouse said. "Your badge is showing."

'What?"

"A little professional advice, that's all. Don't press. It puts people off. They clam up. Or play games with you, leading you around with lies. A good agent never pushes unless he has to. You don't have to. Nobody's going anywhere for a year. So why not just lie back and let the pieces fall, then put them together." He had selected the tone of an old pro advising a novice. "Take our situation. Give me a twenty-centimeter copper nipple, Moyshe. You know we're Navy men. We know you work for Kindervoort. Okay..."

"I what?"

"Don't be coy. Torch, Moyshe. And find the solder. You give yourself away a dozen times a day, Amy. The greenest apprentice wouldn't have fallen for that left-handed wrench thing."

BenRabi chuckled. Amy had torn through all three tool kits trying to find the mythical wrench. Then she had gone down to Damage Control and tried to requisition one. Somebody down there had gone along with the gag. They had passed her on to Tooling...

Amy had been given a crash course in plumbing, but she had not learned enough to fool the initiate.

Fury reddened her face. It faded into a soft smile. "I told him I couldn't pull it off."

"He probably didn't expect you to. He knows we're the best. Doesn't matter anyway. We're out of it now. Just a couple spikes here working. Okay, we know where we stand. Where's the flux, Moyshe? So why don't you do like we do? Don't push. Pay attention. Wait. It'll come in bits and pieces. No hard feelings that way. And that closes Old Doc Igarashi's Spy School and Lonely Hearts Club for today. Be ready for a surprise quiz tomorrow. Ow! That's hot."

"Watch the torch, dummy," Moyshe said. "This T pipe is an odd size. We'll have to choke it down to two centimeters somehow."

"Here," Amy said. She made a checkmark on one of the sheets on her clipboard, handed Moyshe a reduction joint with a number tag attached. "Special made. See. I'm learning." She laughed. "No more questions. Mouse. Moyshe. I feel better now. Not so sneaky."

"Good for you," Mouse said.

Danion suddenly groaned and shivered. BenRabi whirled, looking for a spacesuit locker. Mouse crouched defensively, making a sound suspiciously like a whimper. "What the hell?" he demanded. "We breaking up?"

Amy laughed. "It's nothing. They're shifting mindsails and catchnets."

"Mindsails?" BenRabi asked. "What's that?"

Her smile vanished. She had, evidently, said too much. "I can't explain. You'd have to ask somebody from Operations Sector."

"And that's off limits."

"Yes."

"Got you."

The shuddering continued for a half hour. They lunched while waiting for the Damage Control people. Amy began to lose her reserve toward benRabi. Soon they were chattering like teenagers who had just made up.

Mouse did a little poking and prodding from the sidelines, as skillfully as any psychologist, maneuvering Amy into inviting Moyshe out next recreation day.

BenRabi went to Mouse's cabin after supper. They played chess and, lip reading, discussed what Moyshe was putting down, using the venerable invisible ink trick, between the lines of his drafts of *Jerusalem*. They also attacked the problem of the Sangaree woman, and found it as stubborn as ever.

Recreation day came, with all its mad morning chess tournaments and its afternoon sports furor, its Archaicist exhibitionism, and its collectors' excitement. BenRabi concluded some business with Grumpy George, got deadlocked over some stamps, and managed a handsome cash settlement on some New Earth mutant butterflies he had brought along for trading.

That evening he and Amy attended another ball. This one was Louis XIV. He went in his everyday clothing. Amy, though, scrounged a costume and was striking. From the ball they went to her cabin so she could change. They had been invited to another party, by the same cousin.

"How did you people get involved in the Archaicist thing?" Moyshe asked while she was changing.

"We're the originals," she replied from her bathroom, her voice light with near-laughter. She had been mirthfully happy all day. Moyshe, too, had been feeling intensely alive and aware. "It starts in creche. In school. When we act out history. We haven't really been around long enough to have any past of our own, so we borrow yours."

"That's not true. We all have the same history."

"I guess you're right. Old Earth is everybody's history if you get right down to it. Anyway, it's a creche game. A teaching method. And it carries over for some people. It's fun to dress up and pretend. But we don't live it. Not the way some people do. Know what I mean?"

"You remember Chouteau? That Ship's Commander who brought us here? He had as bad a case as I've ever seen."

"An exception. Look at it this way. How many people go to these things? Not very many. And they're most of the Archaicists aboard. See? It's a game. But your people are so serious about it. It's spooky."

"I'll buy that." Curious, he thought. In these two weeks he had seen nothing culturally unique to the Seiners. They lived borrowed lives in a hash that did not add to a whole. His expectations, based on landside legends, rumors, and his Luna Command studies, had been severely disappointed.

But Amy had a point. He had encountered only a narrow selection of her people. An unusual minority. The majority, remaining aloof, might represent something different.

She came from the bathroom. "Zip me up, okay?" Then, responding to a question, "We're not complete borrowers. It's partly because you're just seeing a few people, like you say. And partly because this is the fleet. You wouldn't judge Confederation by what you saw on one of your Navy ships, would you? The Yards and creches are different. Except when we're working, we try to make life a game. To beat the boredom and fear. Can't be that much different for Navy men. Anyway, you're not seeing the real us, ever. You're just seeing us reacting to you."

What were these Yards? They kept slipping into Seiner

conversation. Did the Starfishers have a world of their own, hidden somewhere out of the way? It was not impossible. The records revealing the whereabouts of scores of early settlements had been destroyed in the Lunar Wars... He was about to ask when he recalled Mouse's advice about pressing.

There was much, much more to the Seiner civilization than anyone in Confederation suspected. The bits he and Mouse had collected already would be worth fortunes to the right people. If he kept learning at this rate...

They were going to give him another medal when he got back. He could see it coming. He would rather have that damned year off.

The party was a carbon of the previous one. Same people. Same music. Same conversation and arguments. Only he and Amy were different. They watched their drinking and tried to understand what was happening to them.

The partiers were younger than he or Amy, and uncomfortable with the gap, though Amy's cousin did her best to make them part of things. Moyshe never felt unwelcome, only out of place. He supposed he had been as much an anomaly before, but had been too preoccupied to notice.

Had Amy manipulated the invitation? If so, why? Another Kindervoort ploy? Both Jarl and Mouse seemed eager to push them together.

Why did he question everything? Even the questioning? Why did he feel that he was losing his grasp on his place in the universe?

They cuddled. They drank. The shadows closed in. They probed one another's pasts. He learned that she had once had an abortion after having been tricked into pregnancy by a man who had wanted to marry her, but whom she had loathed. He resisted the temptation to ask why she had been in bed with him in the first place.

He also learned that she was afraid of sexual intercourse because of some failing in herself. What? She shied away from explaining. He did not press.

Time marched. The sun of the party zenithed and hurried on. He and Amy stayed till everyone else had gone.

They feared leaving more than overstaying their welcome. That room locked them into a cell with well-known walls. Their interaction was defined by rules of courtesy toward their hostess. The limits would expand a pale of hurt.

Yet courtesy demanded that they leave before Amy's cousin found their presence painful.

The subtle differences between weeks coalesced and came to a head when they reached benRabi's cabin. Amy was frightened, unsure. So was he. This time, they knew, something would happen. The Big It, as they had called it when he was first becoming sexually aware.

Like kids, they were eager and afraid. The pleasant sharing they wanted carried with it a big risk of pain.

Thus did the sins of the past leave their marks. Both were so frightened of repeating old mistakes that they had almost abandoned trying anything new.

Moyshe watched the processes of his mind with mild amazement. The detached part of himself could not comprehend what was happening. He had survived affairs. Even with the Sangaree woman. Why this retrogression to the adolescent pain and confusion of the Alyce era?

There was a long, pale, tense moment when the night balanced on the edge of a double-edged blade. Amy stared at him as he slowly dismounted from the scooter. Then, with a grimace, she jammed the charging plug into a socket.

Moyshe yielded to a surge of relief. She had saved him the need to make a decision. She would bear the blame if anything went wrong.

They remained nervous and frightened. The tension had its effect in temporary impotence and difficult penetration. They whispered a lot, reassuring one another. BenRabi could not help remembering the first time, with Alyce. Both of them had been virgins.

Now, as then, they managed the main point only after trying too hard. Experience made it easier from there.

The truly cruel blow did not fall till the ultimate moment.

At the peak instant Moyshe felt a flood of hot wetness against his groin, something he had thought the exclusive domain of pornography.

Amy started crying. She had lost bladder control.

Ego-mad with that stunning proof of his manhood, benRabi laughed and collapsed upon her, holding her tightly.

She thought he was laughing at her.

Her nails ripped his skin. Angry words filled the air. She tried to knee him. He rolled away, baffled and babbling.

Hair streaming, wet with their sweat, trailing a damp, wrinkled sheet, Amy fled into the corridor. By the time benRabi got into his jumpsuit and started after her, she was a hundred meters down the corridor, scooter forgotten, trying to wrap herself in the sheet as she fled.

"Amy! Come back. I'm sorry."

Too late. She would not listen. He started after her, but gave it up when people began coming out to see what was going on.

He went back and pondered what he had done.

He had given her a gut-kick in a festering wound. This must have happened before and have caused her a lot of grief. This was why she had been so frightened. But she had come to him anyway, hoping for understanding.

And he had laughed.

"Fool," he said, flinging a pillow against a wall. Then, "She should have warned me..." He realized that she had, in her timorous way.

He had to do something before her anger ossified into hatred.

He tried. He really tried. He returned her clothing with a long, apologetic note. He called, but she would not answer. He visited Kindervoort and asked his help, but that seemed to do no good.

Their paths no longer crossed. She did not return to work. He could not corner her and make her listen.

The sword had fallen.

His new supervisor, another of Kindervoort's people, was a small, hard character named Lyle Bruce. Bruce was uncommunicative and prejudiced. He was intolerant and grossly unfair. Repairs had to be done his way even though he was less skilled than Amy.

Mouse and benRabi took it all and smiled back. So Bruce tried harder. "His turn in the barrel will come," Mouse promised. "This is just some test Kindervoort is putting on."

BenRabi agreed. "He won't last. I'll sweet him to death."

BenRabi was right. Next week Bruce was replaced by a man from Damage Control. Martin King was not exactly friendly, but neither was he antagonistic. He was a prejudiced man controlling his prejudices, for the good of *Danion*. He did nothing to hamper their work.

At shift's end one day he told Moyshe, "I'm supposed to take you to Kindervoort's office."

"Oh? Why?"

"He didn't say."

"What about supper?"

"Something will be arranged."

"All right. Let's go."

Kindervoort's office was a place comfy-cozy in nineteenth-century English decor. Lots of dark wood, scores of books. A fireplace would have set it off perfectly.

"Have a seat, Moyshe," Kindervoort suggested. "How's it going out there?"

BenRabi shrugged.

"Dumb question, huh?" He left his chair, came around his desk and sat on its corner. "This isn't really business. Relax." He paused. "No, that's not all the way true. Everything gets to be business, sooner or later. I want to talk about Amy. You willing?"

"Why not?" After all, this was the man he had come running to when things had fallen apart.

"It's personal. I thought you might be touchy."

"I am."

"And honest. I'll be honest too. I want to help because you're my friends. Not close, but friends. And I've got a professional interest, of course. There's going to be more of this kind of trouble. That's bad for *Danion*. I want to find ways to smooth things over."

Nicely rehearsed speech, Moyshe thought. "You want to use me and Amy as guinea pigs?"

"In a way. But it's not just an experiment. You're what counts in the end."

Moyshe fought his reaction to Kindervoort's appearance. He pushed back the anger and resentment this interference stimulated...

Swirling visions of stars and darkness. The image of the gun flaming on a black velvet background. He had never had it so strongly, nor in such detail. Fear replaced anger. What was happening? What did this deadly vision mean to his unconscious mind?

"Moyshe? Are you all right?" Kindervoort bent over him, studying his eyes. His voice was remote.

BenRabi rumbled for an answer. His tongue betrayed him. Ghosts had begun dancing inside his head. He could not focus his attention.

A burning crowbar drove through his right eyesocket.

"Migraine!" he gasped.

It was so sudden. None of the little spots or the geometric figures that were the usual warnings. Just the ghosts, the guns, and that curiously familiar stellar backdrop.

BenRabi groaned. The devil himself had him by the skull, trying to crush it down to pea size.

Kindervoort bounced back around his desk, took something from a drawer, dashed through a door into an adjoining bathroom, returned with pills and water. BenRabi watched with little interest. The pain had become the dominant force in his universe. There was just him and it... And now voices.

He heard them, faint and far away, unintelligible but real, like snatches of conversation caught drifting down a hallway from a distant room. He tried to listen, but the agony made a flaming barrier against concentration.

"Moyshe? Here're some pills. Moyshe? Can't you hear me?"

A hand grabbed benRabi's chin, pulled back. Fingers forced his mouth open. Dry, bitter tablets burned his tongue. Water splashed him. A hand covered his mouth and nose till he had no choice but to swallow. The hand departed. He gasped for air.

He had not screamed. Not yet. Because he could not. The pain was killing him, and he could do nothing but cling to its shooting star. Down it went, down into darkness...

Seconds later he recovered, the pain vanishing as quickly as it had come. With it went the ghosts and voices. But he remained disoriented.

Kindervoort was seated behind his desk again, talking urgently into an intercom. "… exact time you went on minddrive." He glanced at his watch. "Were the comnets open? Thanks." He switched off. His expression was grave.

Moyshe had to have more water. He felt as dry as a Blake City summer. He tried to rise. "Water…"

"Stay there!" Kindervoort snapped. "Don't move. I'll get it." Glass in hand, he rushed into the bathroom.

BenRabi fell back into his chair, shivering both from shock and coolness. He had sweated out a good liter. The painkiller, which hit the system as fast as a nerve poison, worked perfectly but did nothing to ease nervous exhaustion. He would not be able to move for a while.

Several glasses of water and a blanket helped. When he felt human enough to talk again, Kindervoort went on as if nothing had happened. "Moyshe, I think it's important that we work out something between you and Amy. Both on the personal and social level."

"Uhm."

"Will you talk to her?"

"I've been trying for a week and a half."

"All right. Easy. Easy." He thumbed his intercom. "Bill? Send Miss Coleridge in now."

Amy burst through the door. "What happened? I heard?…"

Softly, so Moyshe could not hear, Kindervoort explained. Amy's concern became mixed with dismay. She moved to benRabi. "Are you all right?"

"I'll live. Unfortunately."

"Moyshe. Moyshe. What're we going to do?"

"I'm going to say I'm sorry," he murmured.

The apologies and explanations came easy with the edge off their emotions, though Amy remained sensitive. Her problem, as Moyshe had suspected, had caused her a lot of grief.

Kindervoort thoughtfully absented himself. In an hour or so they concluded a cautious truce.

FOURTEEN: 3047 AD
The Olden Days, Academy

Perchevski stared out the window as the airbus banked into its Geneva approach. Something was happening down by the lake. A cluster of flashing red lights hugged the shore.

"Ladies and gentlemen, this is your pilot. Air Traffic Control has asked me to relay a Security Service warning. There's trouble on the northbound traffic tube. Terrorists have occupied Number Three Station. They could try to retreat through the tubeway or take passenger hostages. The tube is open, but you'll have to use it at your own risk."

Perchevski watched the flashing lights and darting gnat figures of Zone police till the bus dropped too low. Later, as he crossed the tarmac to a waiting hovercar, he heard the shooting. An occasional explosion drowned the titter of light weaponry.

"They're putting up a fight," said the rating leaning against the groundcar. "Sir."

"Sounds like. What do they want?"

The rating shrugged, opened the passenger side door. "I don't think anybody asked, sir. The Zonies don't bother anymore. They just shoot them and get ready for the next bunch." He closed the door, moved to the pilot's side. "Company office, sir?"

"Yes. Who are they? How did they get in?"

"A new mob, sir. Call themselves the Ninth of June. I don't know what it means."

"Neither do I."

"They broke through at Checkpoint Ahrsen yesterday. Usual surprise attack. Another mob hit there the day before and the Zonies didn't get everything put back together fast enough. They always find a way. We had a bunch come in by hot air balloon last year."

Perchevski left the car for the office where he had helped Greta Helsung catch her rainbow. He checked in, said he was returning to Luna Command, and glanced over what they had on the girl. An hour later he was headed for the lakeside launch pits. He drew the same driver. This time the rating regaled him with a saga concerning his conquest of a "pink patch lady." She had loved him so much she had *almost* enlisted.

"Pink patch" people were Old Earthers who worked in the Zone but lived outside. The uniform patch was their entry permit. Each was Kirlian keyed to prevent terrorist use.

Perchevski was back in his lunar apartment before bedtime next evening. He took a pill and put himself out for twelve hours. Old Earth and his mother had been a miserable mistake.

He did not check his calls right away. He did not want to risk finding a summons from the Bureau.

There was none. The only messages were from Max and Greta. Max was missing him. Greta was scared and lonely and amazed by everything.

Perchevski reacted to Greta's call first. He remembered how frightened and lonely he had been when he had come to Academy. Even hating home, he had been dreadfully homesick.

He made a call to Academy Information, learned that Greta had been assigned to a training battalion, but the battalion had not begun training. The rigorous discipline of Academy would not isolate her for weeks. She could have visitors. She would be allowed a weekly visit from her sponsor after she began training.

"Things have changed since my day, Lieutenant," he told the woman handling his call.

"Since mine, too, Commander. We're getting soft."

"Maybe. Seems like a step in the right direction to me. I'll be there this evening. I'd appreciate it if you'd let me surprise her."

"Whatever you say, Commander."

"Thanks for your time, Lieutenant."

He settled back in his bed, stared at the ceiling, and wondered why he was sponsoring a kid he hardly knew. Sponsorship was serious business. His reponsibility under Lunar law equaled that of a parent.

"Will you sponsor?" the man had asked, and he had responded without thinking.

How could he do right by Greta? In his line of work… Maybe Beckhart would move him to a staff post.

"Old buddy, you backed yourself into a corner this time. How do you get into these things?"

Ah, what was the worry? Greta would be locked up in Academy for four years. She would have no chance for anything but training and study. His sponsorship would not amount to anything but quotations in her files. She would reach the age of responsibility before she graduated.

Maybe he knew that unconsciously when he agreed.

He called Max. No answer.

He donned his Commander's uniform and took the high-velocity tube to Academy Station. The tube passed through the core of the moon. Academy was Farside.

Though he still used the Perchevski name, he had abandoned the Missileman's uniform after High Command had announced von Drachau's raid. There seemed little point to the pretense.

The Bureau apparently agreed. No one had called him on it.

The tubeways were the gossip shops of Luna Command. There strangers whiled away the long transits by dissecting the latest in scandal and rumor. It was there that Perchevski first heard the March of Ulant discussed seriously.

Max had talked about it, of course. But Max was a civ. Max had been retailing fourth-hand merchandise. The people he overheard were Planetary Defense Corps general staff officers from worlds far centerward of Sol. They were in Luna Command for a series of high-powered defense strategy seminars.

Cold fear breathed down Perchevski's neck. The *what* might be debatable, but he could no longer deny that something spooky was going on.

He had been seeing the colorful and sometimes odd uniforms of the local forces everywhere he had gone lately. There were even a few from worlds not part of Confederation.

No wonder there were rumors of war.

He checked in with the local office when he arrived. He was wearing the ring, of course, but redundancy of action and mistrust of technology were Bureau axioms. A staff type told a computer terminal where he was, then in boredom resumed watching a holodrama. He caught a bus to Academy's visitors' hotel.

Academy was an almost autonomous fortress-state within the fortress-world of Luna Command. Nearly ten percent of the moon's surface and volume had been set aside for the school, which trained every Service officer and almost half of all enlisted personnel. Academy contained all the staff colleges, war colleges, and headquarters of special warfare schools which kept the Service honed to a fighting edge. At times as many as two million people taught and studied there.

Perchevski had spent eight years in Academy, glimpsing the outside universe only rarely. Passes had been few in his day. Going out usually meant having to take part in some very active training exercise. There had been no time left over for sightseeing.

He was supposed to have graduated as a dedicated, unquestioning Confederation warrior. He supposed even the best systems made mistakes.

He enjoyed his venture into the old, familiar halls, remembering incidents, recalling classmates he had not thought of in years. He was amused by all the bright, freshly scrubbed young faces behind those snappy salutes.

Greta's battalion was quartered not far from the barracks his own had occupied. He spent an hour ambling through school days memories.

It was late when he located the officer of Greta's Training Battalion. The date-letter designation on the door could be interpreted to tell that Greta's was the forty-third officer candidate unit activated in 3047. He whistled softly. They were taking candidates at a wartime rate.

There must be something to the rumors.

Nothing else would explain why Greta had been assigned to an officer training unit almost instantaneously.

A rating was closing the office. "You the officer looking for the Helsung girl?"

"Yes, Chief. Sorry I'm late."

The petty officer muttered something sarcastic.

"That attitude going to relay itself to the middies, Chief?"

"Sorry, sir. It's been a bad day."

"Where can I find her?"

"Alpha Company. Room Twenty-five. We're just starting the battalion, sir. It's one of your remedials, for candidates without a Service background."

"Thanks, Chief. Go ahead and close up. I'll only stay a few minutes."

Perchevski entered the barracks block. Generations of midshipmen had passed through it. The air was heavy with age. And human scent. He found A Corridor and followed it, glancing at the name tags on the cubicle doors. He located HELSUNG, GRETA: HAMBURG, EARTH, paired with JAMES, LESLIE from someplace on Sierra called Token Offering. No one answered his knock.

He followed the noise of a holoset on to the company commons. Some twenty youngsters were watching holo or playing games without enthusiasm. Homesickness thickened the air.

Greta sat in a vinyl-covered armchair. She had heels pulled up against her behind. Her arm embraced her knees. She had an air of infinite sadness, of unspeakable loneliness.

A ten-year-old with a boarding school voice snapped, ""Ten-shut!"

"As you were, people."

Greta hurled herself at him. She flung her arms around his neck. "I didn't think I'd ever see you again."

"Easy, girl. Don't break anything." He felt better about himself suddenly. It was great to have someone glad to see him.

"How come you're here? I thought you were going to see your mother?"

"I did. We were both disappointed."

"Oh. I'm sorry."

"It's all right. I didn't expect much. Come on. Sit down. How's it going? What do you think of the moon?"

"I haven't seen anything yet. Everything's bigger than I thought it would be. What's happening back home?"

"Nothing new. Homesick?"

She shook her head.

"Fibber. I was here too, remember? And I still get homesick. That's why I go back sometimes. Of course, I came up with Neil Armstrong..."

"Don't tease me."

"All right. Tell you what. I talked to your company commander..."

"Old Greasy Hair? I hate him already."

Perchevski laughed. "You'll hate him a lot more before you're done. He's going to be your father, mother, priest, god, and devil. Look, do you want to see the rest of the moon? You won't have a chance after classes start."

"Don't you have something better to do? You've got your job, and your own friends..."

"I'm on vacation. Sort of. And I don't have many friends here."

"I don't want to put you out." A skinny little black girl with pigtailed hair, wearing a ragged woolen smock, was staring at them. "Oh. Leslie. Come here. This is Leslie James, Commander. My roommate."

"Hi, Les. Where is Token Offering? I visited Sierra once, but I don't remember it."

The girl said something into a mouth full of fingers and retreated.

"She's shy," Greta said. "Her parents must be dead. She came from an orphanage."

"We're all orphans, one way or another. Navy is our family."

Greta looked at him oddly. Then, "Can we take her with us if we go?"

"Uhm. You're starting to understand already. I don't know. It might be complicated. I'll ask if you want."

"I think so."

"Okay. I'd better go. It's past visiting hours. I just wanted to see how you were. I'll be back tomorrow."

She squeezed his hand. "Thank you. For everything." Her hands were soft and smooth and warm.

He spent the evening entertaining fantasies he would never pursue.

The inside man never ages. He spends the rest of his life in love with the soft, smooth, warm girls he knew when he was young and just becoming aware of what marvelous creatures females are.

"Where do you want to go, girls?" They were at Academy Station. Perchevski was watching Greta try to people-watch without being offensive. Oddly uniformed folks surrounded them.

"I don't know," Greta replied.

Luna Command was no sightseer's paradise. It had no spectacular ruins or monuments. The real sights were outside, the mountains and craters of the surface.

He took the girls to Tycho Dome and for a ride on one of the surface trains. He treated them to the best restaurants and hotels. Greta's response was gratifying, Leslie's remote.

He ran out of ideas after two days. All but the alien digs, and he had promised those to Max.

Max could take the pressure off. She would have ideas... He took the girls to her shop.

"Hello, Walter," Max said. Her voice was chilly. She stared at Greta. Greta did not notice. She was engrossed in the showcases.

"Hi, Lady. Anything for me?"

"Same old stuff. Is that what you've been doing since you got back?"

"Come on, Max! She's sixteen. Greta, come here. I want you to meet Max. Max, Greta Helsung and her friend Leslie."

Greta was not imperceptive. "Hi, Max. The Commander is my sponsor."

"Your sponsor? You never told me you had a kid, Walter."

"I'm a man of mystery, Love."

"How come she calls you Walter? Your name is Cornelius."

"Because he's a man of mystery, dear," Max replied. "Everybody has a different name for him. He's some kind of spy. I don't think he knows his real name himself."

"Max..."

"Wow! Really?"

"Yes. Really. Max, you talk too much. I came here to see if you still wanted to go to the Farside dig."

Someone entered the shop behind him. Max said hello.

"Hi, tall, blonde, and desirable. Thomas? Is that you? What the hell are you doing here?"

Perchevski turned.

Mouse had come in. He gave Greta an admiring once-over. "That's right. You know Max, don't you? Max, I really want that Manchurian collection, but you're going to have to come down on it. It's just not worth twelve thousand."

"I can see what you want. Hands off. She's your buddy's kid. And I can get fifteen if I send it out to Amonhotep." To Greta she explained, "This is one of your old man's buddies. He's a spy too."

Perchevski shook his head. "She's in a Roman candle mood today, Mouse. I come in to ask her out and she plays mad dog with me. I didn't know you were a collector."

"Lot of things we don't know about each other." That seemed to close the subject.

"Mouse and I were in the same battalion in Academy," Perchevski told Greta.

Mouse gave the girl another admiring look. She moved closer to Perchevski, as if feeling for a protective shadow. Mouse smiled gently and resumed arguing with Max.

Perchevski wondered how he could demonstrate, to her satisfaction, that she was not in competition with inconquerable youth.

"Max, you want to go to the Farside digs or not?"

"When it's convenient."

"Are you really a spy, Commander?"

"I guess you could put it that way, Greta. How about after work, Max?"

"You sure you won't be busy?"

Perchevski closed his eyes, took a long, deep breath, released it. Be patient, he told himself.

"What's your real name?" Greta asked. Mouse watched, his expression unreadable.

"Honey, sometimes I'm not sure myself. Don't worry about it. It doesn't matter. If you need to get in touch, just call the number I gave you. If I can't get back to you, one of my friends will."

"But…"

"Forget it. Subject closed. Max, are you going to the digs or not?"

"You don't have to get snappy, Walter. Yes. I'm coming. What about you, Mouse?"

"Me?"

"Yes. You want to see that new chamber? They think it might shed some light on the Sangaree. There're some primitive murals that might be of human origin. On a Noah's ark theme, with spaceships. Or aren't you the culture type?"

"Sure. Why not?" He looked at Perchevski as if in appeal.

"I don't know, Mouse. Maybe it's the change." Why was Mouse attaching himself? Because of the Sangaree remark? Or because the Old Man wanted somebody to keep an eye on him? After what had happened on The Broken Wings, Beckhart would be wondering about him.

The girls slept during the tube trip. Perchevski and Mouse played chess on Mouse's pocket set. Prodded by Max, Mouse related several anecdotes about Perchevski while saying nothing about himself. Perchevski let him set the limits.

Max did not seem the least interested in his former partner.

Both men loosened up on sips from a flask Max dug out of her jumpsuit. "Emergency rations," she claimed.

"Good thinking," Perchevski told her.

"What is this? A class reunion?" she demanded toward trip's end.

Mouse and Perchevski had begun playing remember when. They were reliving the Great Sunjammer Race of '29, in which they had crewed a ship and had beaten the best starwind yachtsmen in Confederation. That fluke victory was one of the brightest of Perchevski's memories.

He and Mouse had been a team then, almost friends, and for a few days afterward they had been closer than ever before or since.

"Those were the days," Mouse said, ignoring Max. "Wish we could be kids forever. Think we could do it again?"

"Getting too old."

"Nah. I think I'll check it out. Just for the hell of it. Want to try it? If I can find a ship?"

Perchevski laughed. "Better find the time off, first. We're almost there." The capsule had begun decelerating. "I'll wake the girls."

They reached the digs an hour later.

The one-time alien base was being unearthed, studied, and explored at a snail's pace. The xenoarchaeologists had been working for decades, and might be at it for centuries. They sifted every grain of lunar dust, and preserved it. They did not want to miss a thing, even through ignorance.

Thus far the base had revealed more about humanity's past than it had about its builders.

The scientists had concluded that the station had served both scientific and military purposes, and had been occupied continuously for at least ten millennia. It seemed to have been abandoned approximately eleven centuries before its discovery, just as Mankind teetered on the brink of its first tentative step into space.

Perchevski and his companions began with the museum of recovered artifacts, most of which were everyday items comparable to human combs, tableware, worn-out socks, pill bottles, broken furniture, and the like. The aliens had taken their fancy hardware with them.

"Ooh!" Greta said as they approached a group of wax figurines. "They were ugly."

"Notice anything about them, Greta?" Perchevski asked.

"Besides ugly?"

"Yes. Look at how they're dressed. Think. All the legends about little people. Gnomes, dwarves, elves, leprechauns... The kobolds, where you come from." The largest alien figurine stood just a meter tall.

"Yeah. You're right. You know there're still people that believe in them? One time, I guess I was ten, we went on a field trip to the Black Forest. There was this old caretaker, a kind of forest ranger, who told us all these stories about the kobolds in the woods."

Max interjected, "I think it's more interesting that they resemble the spacemen of the UFO era."

Everyone looked at her. "Oh, it's not my idea. I just liked it. It was on the educational channel one time. In the old days people used to see what they called flying saucers. Sometimes they claimed that space people talked to them. They described them like this. But nobody ever believed them."

"Where are they now?" Leslie asked.

"Nobody knows," Perchevski replied. "They just disappeared. Nobody's found any other traces of them, either. Ulant got into space before we did, and they never ran into them."

"What if they're still watching?" Mouse asked.

Perchevski gave him a funny look.

"Spooky idea, isn't it? Let's look at that new chamber. Max says they found some stuff there that isn't just cafeteria or rec room equipment."

Maybe not. Perchevski could not guess what it might have been. The chamber was large and well-preserved, with most of its furnishings intact and in place. "Parallel function ought to result in parallel structure," he said. "Meaning you ought to be able to figure what this stuff is." All he recognized were the faded mural walls, which looked somewhat Minoan. He would have bet his fortune they had been done by human artists. Those he could see seemed to tell some sort of quest story.

"It's a solarium," Greta said. "Without sun."

"A hydroponics farm?"

"No. That's not right. Hydroponics is different."

"What?"

"What I mean is, it's almost like the Desert House at the State Botanical Gardens in Berlin. See how the beds are laid out? And those racks up there would hold the lights that make plants think they're getting sunshine."

Mouse laughed. "By Jove, I think the lady has something." He indicated a small sign which proposed a similar hypothesis. It also suggested that the painters of the murals might have been humans who had become proto-Sangaree.

Mouse suddenly gasped and seized his left hand in his right.

Perchevski nearly screamed at the sharp agony surrounding his call ring.

"What's the matter?" Max and Greta demanded.

"Oh, hell," Perchevski intoned. "Here we go again."

"Let up, you bastards," Mouse snarled. "We got the message. We're coming, for Christ's sake. Business, Max. We've been called in. And I mean in a hurry. Thomas?"

"I'll kill him. Just when... Max... I'm sorry."

"What's going on?" she asked again.

"We have to report in. Right now. Could you take the girls back to barracks?"

"Business?" She sounded excited.

"Yeah. The bastards. Mouse, they said no more team jobs."

Mouse shrugged.

"I'll get them home," Max promised.

Perchevski kissed her, turned to Greta. "I've got to run out on you, Honey. I'm sorry. I really am."

"Thomas, come on. The Old Man means it."

"Wait a minute, damn it! I don't know how long I'll be gone, Greta. If you need something, call my number. Or get ahold of Max. Okay, Max?"

"Sure." Max did not sound enthusiastic.

"Thomas!"

He waved a hand, kissed Max again, then Greta, and trotted off after Mouse. Greta called a sad, "Good-bye, Commander."

He was angry. He was ready to skin Beckhart with a butter knife.

The chance never came. He and Mouse were seized by Mission Prep the instant they hit Bureau territory.

The training was intense and merciless, and the explanations impossibly far between. It went on around the clock, waking and sleeping, and after a few weeks Perchevski was so tired and disoriented that he was no longer sure who he was. Tiny, unextinguishable sparks of anger were all that kept him going.

Education passed him to Psych. Psych eventually passed him

to Medical. For a week every opening of his eyes meant he was fresh off another operating table. Then Education took another go at him. While he recovered he had to read. And when he slept computers pressure-injected information directly into his brain.

Dragons in the night. Golden Chinese dragons. Starfishers… What the hell was it all about? Who was Moyshe benRabi? What was becoming of Cornelius Perchevski?

Sometimes he screamed and fought them, but they were as stubborn as entropy. They kept right on rebuilding their new man.

This was the most intensive, extensive prep he had ever undergone.

He saw Mouse just twice during the whole prep period. They shared the intense hypno-teaching sessions briefing them about Starfishers, but did not intersect again till they met in their master's office. Perchevski thought they were prepping for different missions. Till the Admiral got hold of them personally.

"Boys," Beckhart said, "you've just gone through hell. And I did it to you. I'm not proud of it. It hurt me as much as it hurt you. I don't like operating this way. You'll just have to take my word that it's necessary. And I know what you think about that, Tommy. I don't blame you. But give me the benefit of the doubt, and try to trust me when I tell you that it's imperative that we bring the Starfishers into Confederation as soon as possible."

Such was the opening barrage in a one-way discussion lasting more than three hours. Beckhart talked endlessly, and never answered even one of the questions Perchevski thought pertinent.

He once protested, "You promised no more team jobs."

"And I meant it when I said it, Tommy. But this is the most hurried hurry-up job we've ever had. The CNI told me to put my best men in. She picked you. My God, Tommy, it's only for a couple of weeks. You can't put up with Mouse that long?"

"It's the principle…"

Beckhart ignored him, veering instead into another track.

Almost before he knew what was happening Perchevski found himself aboard a warship bound for the nether end of The Arm.

For a world that was, galactically, only a stone's throw from The Broken Wings.

He did not like that. It seemed to be tempting fate too much.

There wasn't a thing he *did* like about this mission.

They hadn't even let him say his good-byes. Bureau thugs had surrounded him from the moment he had departed Beckhart's office...

"Hey, Moyshe," Mouse said cheerfully, within an hour of their going aboard, "Let's go up to the wardroom and play some chess."

FIFTEEN: 3048 AD
Operation Dragon, *Danion*

Danion became as comfortable as an old, well-worn shoe.

"Fact is, it's getting downright dull," Mouse complained toward the end of the third month.

"What?" benRabi demanded. "All those ball games, and you up to your ears in women, and you're bored?"

"You got it, partner. Like the man in the joke said, women are fine, but what do you do the other twenty-three hours of the day?"

Amy made a remark that Moyshe did not catch.

"If that's how you feel," Mouse replied, laughing, "you can carry your own damned books."

They were moving her into Moyshe's cabin. BenRabi was not overwhelmed by the idea. Nor was he sure how it had come about. It had just sort of fenced him in, pushed by Amy and Mouse till the move actually began and he still had not said "No!"

He preferred living alone. Sharing struck him as synonymous with imposition. Amy's mere presence foreordained increased demands… At least he would have someone around when the headaches came.

Mouse and Amy kept bickering. Mouse was teasing, but Amy sounded serious. She did not like Mouse much.

BenRabi's migraines came several times a week now. He was scared. The voices and visions… He thought it might be a tumor, but the Seiner doctors would not take him seriously. They gave him pain pills and told him not to worry.

He had been on continuous medication the last ten days. He was pale, dehydrated, weak, and shaky.

Amy seemed to be the only one who cared, and she would not say why.

His old downdeep fear that he was going mad seemed ever more creditable.

This is a hell of a time to take a live-in lover, he thought, dumping an armload of clothing. The relationship was paraplegic.

The inexplicable recurring memory of Alyce did not help. It frightened and disoriented him.

There was no reason for that old, dead affair to obsess him.

It was just another symptom of whatever was happening to him. But it was damned scary.

On The Broken Wings he had, almost, been the tough, hard character he had been portraying. Now, less than a year later, he was a spineless, whimpering… Disgusted, he tried to kick a chair across the cabin. It did not move. All shipboard furniture was bolted down.

He resumed work in grim silence.

"Moyshe, I need your help," Mouse said a month after the move, voice sounding a plaintive note.

"What? How? I'll do whatever I can." He glanced over his shoulder to make sure Amy remained in the women's head. He was surprised. This tone did not fit his partner at all.

"Figure out a way to keep me from killing her."

BenRabi followed Mouse's gaze. It was fixed on the Sangaree woman like the cross hairs of an assassin's rifle scope.

"She's working on me, Moyshe. She's got me working on myself. I've been having trouble sleeping. I just lay there thinking up ways… Thinking about her being right down the passage. It's because of the mess on Blackworld. I can't get it out of my head. And I thought I had it under control."

"You too? What the hell did Beckhart do to us?"

Amazing, Mouse's finally owning up to a connection with the Shadowline War. He must be under real stress.

"Self-discipline, Mouse. That's the only answer I've got. And maybe the notion that you ought to save yourself for a bigger target. She's not worth getting burned over."

"She's the queen in the game. And the stakes are as big as they can get, Moyshe. Watch her. I've never seen anybody so sure they had a winning hand. She's got a royal flush in spades look."

"You're mixing metaphors."

"Metaphors be damned, Moyshe. I need help."

Jesus, benRabi thought. *Here I am halfway to the psycho ward and my partner is crying for me to keep him out. Are we going to have one nut stand guard over the cracks in the other's noggin?*

"Let's take it to Kindervoort, then."

"Oh, no. This stays in the family. Jarl doesn't get anything free. How's your head doing?"

"The docs keep saying there's nothing wrong. It don't sound right. I mean, how come I hurt so goddamned much? But maybe it's true. For a while I thought it was a tumor and they were just jollying me so I wouldn't panic. But the scans didn't show anything when I finally got them to let me see them. Now I think something external is causing it."

"Allergy?"

"No. I can't explain yet. It's just barely a suspicion so far."

That suspicion did not leaf out, blossom, and bear fruit for months.

Time lumbered forward. Mouse worked himself into the shipwide chess finals. BenRabi had a falling out with the collector crowd, among whom he had been a brief, bright star. They were older, more prejudiced people, and unable to tolerate his alienness indefinitely. He trudged onward in his laborious relationship with Amy.

He tried to make it work. He sincerely believed he was giving it an honest go, and for a while the curious Alyce memories and attendant mental oddities withdrew, but he never saw any long-term hope.

He even abandoned his writing in order to give her more time.

"I just don't feel like writing," he lied. "It isn't me anymore."

She protested, but with such restraint that he began to resent her presence during moments when he could have written.

Turn around twice and there went another month into the file cabinets of time. And here was Mouse with another. "Moyshe, I think I need help."

"Stay out of her way."

"Not the Sangaree woman this time, Moyshe. Another one."

"What else?"

"Carrie just gave me the word. That Sally I was going with… She's peegee."

"Come on. You're shitting me. People don't get pregnant unless… Oh, my."

"Oh, my, yes. Unless they want to."

Moyshe fought a grin.

"You laugh and I'll kick your head in."

"Me? Laugh? I'm sorry. It's just that… What do you want me to do?"

"Shee-it, Moyshe. I don't know. Talk to me. I've never been up this tree before."

"What is it? She figure you'd do the honorable thing?" *Why are you doing this to me, Mouse? I had a handle on the Alyce thing.*

"That's the name of the game. That's the way they do things here. And the way they lay their little traps. Straight from Century One."

"No law says you've got to give her what she wants, though. Kiss her good-bye." That was how he had failed Alyce, so long ago. He had not found the strength to say no until it was too late.

"I don't like to hurt anybody's feelings."

"That's the chance she took, isn't it?" How come it was so easy to say, but so hard to do? "I don't see how anybody could believe in a marriage that started out that way anyway. Go on. Tell her to kiss off."

"Easier said than done, Moyshe."

"I know. Advice is that way. Here's some more, while we're at it. Take your own precautions so it doesn't happen again."

"That much I figured out for myself." Mouse went away. He returned within the hour, shaking his head. "She couldn't believe that landsmen don't give a damn if a kid's parents are married or not. But I think I finally got through to her."

For a while Mouse's social calendar was less crowded. But only for a while. The ladies seemed incapable of remaining away.

"Tell me something, Amy," benRabi said one afternoon. "Why are we here?"

She started giving him the standard story.

"That's not true. *Danion* didn't really need us. Certainly not a thousand of us. Even with only two hundred we'll finish up six months early. Your own Damage Control people wouldn't have taken much longer. So what's really going on?"

She would not tell him. She even refused to speculate. He suspected, from her expression, that she might not know, that she was beginning to ask herself the questions that were bothering him.

His came of a long line of thinking sparked by snippets of information and flashes of intuition that had begun accumulating on Carson's.

"Correct me if you can fault this hypothesis," he told Mouse when Amy was out of hearing. "We're guinea pigs in a coexistence experiment. They've got something big and dangerous going and they thought they could hire outside help to get through it. I'd guess they expect heavy fighting. Our job descriptions all deal with damage control. But the experiment was a failure. No takers."

"I wouldn't know, Moyshe. You've got your head working. Who were they going to fight? Not us."

"Sharks?"

"Maybe. But it doesn't add up. Still, I'm not much good at puzzles. How's your head doing?"

"Real good. Why?"

"I thought so. You're more like the old Moyshe lately." They completed the last scheduled repair three weeks later. From then on there was little to do.

One day a long-faced Amy announced, "They just told me. Starting Monday you'll be assigned to Damage Control. To the emergency ready room at D.C. South. I'll take you over and introduce you."

"Breaking up the team, eh?" Mouse asked. "Where are you going?"

"Back to Security." She did not sound pleased.

BenRabi felt a guilty elation. Though he loved Amy, he did not like having her around all the time. He felt smothered.

The damage control assignment was a crushing bore. "A fireman in a steel city would have more to do," Mouse complained. A few days later, he cornered benRabi in order to update him on his own snooping.

"Our fleet commander looks like a maverick. He won't bow down to Gruber of Gruber's Fleet as the head honcho Starfisher. He wants to do things his own way. The other fleets treat this one like an idiot cousin."

"That why the Old Man targeted Payne's Fleet?"

"No. He just jumped on a chance to get somebody onto a harvestship. You were right about the experiment, by the way. It was something Gruber put Payne up to. I get the impression that now he's using the failure as an excuse to go haring off on some adventure of his own as soon as we're done harvesting."

"Speaking of which. Amy says it's the best they've ever had. They're going to hold their auction after we leave."

"Kindervoort still on you about crossing over?"

"He mentions it sometimes. Came to the cabin last week." Did Mouse suspect that he found the offer tempting?

Sports season became crazier than ever as playoff time approached. For Moyshe it was all bewildering color and madness. Mouse, of course, was right in the thick of it. Football was his latest passion. He could quote records and statistics by the hour. BenRabi studied the game just so he could carry on a conversation.

Their lives, increasingly, became frosting, sugar-bits having nothing to do with their assignments. They had come here to find starfish. Despite a thousand doubts and distractions, benRabi kept his wavering cross hair sighted near his programmed target. He even resumed wrestling with *Jerusalem* so he could keep his invisible notes.

Sharing quarters with an agent for the other side constantly hampered him. He was not so naïve as to believe that Amy had been struck deaf and blind by love.

He had come aboard thinking starfish were a wonderful concept, a miraculous hook on which to hang modern myths and legends. They had been one with the lost planet Osiris and the fabulous weapons of Stars' End. Now he knew that the hydrogen streams teemed with "life." The fairy magic was gone, but still the fantastic fish were something to play with during his long hours of waiting for an emergency that never arose.

The starfish, the leviathans of the airless deep, were more fields of force and the balances between them than they were creatures of matter. The longbeards of the breed could be three hundred kilometers long and a million years old. They might occupy thousands of cubic kilometers, yet have fewer atoms in them than a human adult. In them atoms and molecules functioned primarily as points upon which forces anchored. Here, there, a pinpoint hawking hole left over from the big bang formed the core of an invisible organ.

The fabric of space and time were the creature's bone and sinew. He could manipulate them within himself. In essence, he built himself a secondary universe within the primary, and within that homemade pocket reality existed as tangibly as did men in their own reality. The part of a starfish that could be detected was but a fraction of the whole beast. He also existed in hyperspace, null space, and on levels mankind had not yet reached.

Those beasts of the big night were living fusion furnaces. They fed on hydrogen, and enjoyed an occasional spice of other elements in the fusion chain. At first Moyshe had wondered why they did not gather where matter was more dense, as in the neighborhood of a protostar.

Amy told him that the field stresses around stellar masses could rip the creatures apart.

A starfish's stomach contained a fire as violent as that at the heart of a sun. Not only did fusion take place there, but matter annihilation as well when the beast browsed on anti-hydrogen with that part of him coexisting in a counter-universe.

BenRabi did not speculate on the physics. He was a field man. A supernova seemed kindergarten stuff by comparison. He simply noted his thoughts in invisible ink and hoped the Bureau's tame physicists could make something of them.

"Mouse, I've run into a philosophical problem," he said one morning. "About the fish."

"You've lost me already, Moyshe."

"I've gotten onto something that's turning my thinking inside out."

"Which is?"

"That this isn't your usual man/cattle relationship. It's a partnership—if the Fishers aren't the cows. The fish are intelligent. Probably more intelligent than we are." He looked around. No one was listening. "They have what they call a mindtech section in Ops Sector. Somehow, they communicate with the starfish. Mind to mind."

"Where'd you get that?"

"Around. Keeping my ears open. Adding things up."

"So the ugly old psi theory raises its head again. Out here. You know what the Old Man's scientists will say about that?"

"They'll have to loosen up those stiff necks. But what I think is interesting is the research possibilities."

"Research?"

"Historical research. The fish have been in contact with other races. And some of them are over a million years old. That's a lot of remembering, I'm thinking."

Like oceans, the hydrogen streams supported a complete ecology, including the predatory "shark," the starfish's natural enemy. There were a dozen species. Even the biggest and most dangerous was much smaller than an adult starfish. However, like man and wolves, several of the species hunted in cooperative packs. They could even pursue their prey through hyperspace.

Packs shadowed all the great herds. They struck when a fish straggled. Sometimes, when driven by hunger, they tried to cut individual fish from the herd. And occasionally, when their numbers reached a certain critical mass, a whole pack went berserk and threw itself at the herd.

The starfish were not helpless. They could burp up balls of gut fire and sling them around like granddaddy nuclear bombs. But sharks were fast and the burping was slow. A starfish under attack seldom had a chance for more than one defensive attempt.

He had to count on the help of his herdmates, who might be under attack themselves. Thus inadequate, the starfish sometimes needed allies to survive.

When the earliest Seiners had located their first starfish herd the shark packs had been expanding rapidly. That first herd had been threatened with extinction.

Its fish had touched the minds of those early Seiners, had found in them a hope, and so had contacted them and had made a bargain. They would produce ambergris in quantity in exchange for human protection.

"There're times when I think they're trying to touch me," ben-Rabi told Mouse, after rehearsing what history he had learned.

"What makes you think that?" Mouse seemed excited by the idea.

"Probably just my imagination." He was reluctant to tell Mouse that he sometimes dreamed of vast, swimming spatial panoramas, oddly alive with things never seen by human eyes. Dragons flew there, and played, with a ponderousness unmatched even in Old Earth's vanished whales. Each time he dreamed the dream, he wakened with a screaming migraine.

"So those first Fishers armed themselves," he said, resuming his history lesson. "The fish taught them to detect the sharks. The herd slowly recovered."

But the sharks, in their slow fashion, reasoned. They learned to associate casualties with the hard things shepherding their prey. In the middle thirties they had begun getting harvestships as well as herds, forcing the Seiners to defend themselves before they protected their allies.

This past year they had begun attacking the ships first, and cooperating between packs of different species.

Their numbers were still expanding. Soon, the Seiners feared, they would be numerous enough to attack and destroy whole harvestfleets.

No ships had yet been lost, but the attack on *Danion* had demonstrated the reality of the peril.

The Starfishers believed themselves at war, and feared it was a war they could not win. They were too few and too weakly armed.

"Packs are migrating here from deeper in the galaxy," Moyshe concluded. "I suppose because of a depleted food supply there."

"That's it?" Mouse asked.

"What'd you expect? It's hard to get anything out of Amy. She may be sleeping with me but she doesn't forget that I'm the other old enemy, the landsman. About the only other thing is that they're desperate for more and better weapons. They might have something cooking there. Any time I mention weapons, Amy changes the subject fast."

In fact, she usually left the cabin. That scared him. Something big was going on and she did not want to risk giving him a hint.

Her behavior confirmed the feeling he had had from the beginning. This was no ordinary harvest.

Danion had been under drive for weeks. Moyshe's suspicions had become stronger. Harvestships seldom went hyper. The fish did not like it.

Were the beasts following the fleet?

Nobody was talking. Even the friendliest Seiners had little to say anymore.

The year was winding down. He had learned a lot, but still nothing concrete, nothing of genuine advantage to the Bureau and Confederation. Was the mission going to end up a wild goose chase?

Playing spy-vs.-spy in the bedroom with Amy had become agonizing. Yet he had to pursue his tradecraft. He had to try to learn, and he did not dare relax.

He could not forget the Sangaree woman. She was still there, and still very much involved in her own mission.

Whatever her game was, it was in its final moves. She had resumed pushing Mouse, hard, confident of her strength.

The drives had been dead a week. *Danion* had reached her destination. Whole new sections of the ship had been closed to landsmen. The Seiners who came and went there were more closed-mouthed than ever. Some, whom Moyshe considered friends, would barely acknowledge his greetings. Whatever they were doing, they wanted no hint to get back landside.

Work schedules went to shift-and-a-half. There were no exceptions. BenRabi and Mouse just spent that much more time being bored.

"Whatever it is, it's dangerous," Mouse said. "They're all scared green."

"The shark packs are collecting. Like ten times thicker than they've ever seen."

"I watched one of the Service Ship crews come in this morning. They rotated with an alternate crew."

"Fighting?"

"Just exhausted, I think. I didn't see any stretchers. But Kindervoort's thugs ran me off before I could find out anything."

Despite Kindervoort they gleaned their bits of information. "They're in a race against time," benRabi told Mouse. "I heard one guy say they wouldn't get a chance to gamble if the sharks hit aggressive mass before they finish their experiments."

"What did he mean? Are they working on some new weapon?"

BenRabi shrugged. "I didn't ask. But I sure wouldn't mind knowing what they're risking my life for."

One evening, after a workday spent within taunting distance of the Sangaree woman, benRabi and Mouse tried to relax over a chessboard.

"You're shook up again," Mouse observed while staring at his pieces. "What's up? Trouble with Amy?"

"That's part of it. I've only seen her twice all week. She just comes in long enough to shower and change."

"So? She's not sitting on the only one in the universe. The little redhead, Penny something, from New Earth…"

"She's young enough to be my kid, Mouse. Only a couple of years older than Greta."

Mouse flung his hands up in mock exasperation. "What's that got to do with it? She's willing, isn't she?"

"Maybe. But I think I'm more a father image…"

"So indulge in a little incest."

"It doesn't matter anyway. Sex isn't the problem."

"What? It's always a problem. One way or another." Mouse chuckled. He chuckled again as he ambushed Moyshe's queen.

Moyshe could not keep his mind on his game. The *want* had returned, mildly, along with that damned thing with the gun. "What *is* the problem, then?"

"The way people are treating us? I guess. They're so scared they won't have anything to do with us."

"Check. Check there too. Part of it's the Sangaree woman, Moyshe. She's telling stories on us again. Trying to isolate us. I wonder why? One move to mate."

They batted possibilities around. Moyshe so loathed the one that occurred to him that he refused to mention it right away.

His game grew increasingly poor. He became irritable. The *I want* grew stronger, louder, mocking him, telling him that he was on the threshold of its fulfillment and was too blind to see it.

"I can't hold off much longer," Mouse said, taking a pawn with a savage grab. "Next time she gouges me, or the next, I'll bend her, and damned be the consequences."

"Please don't. We're almost home. We've only got five weeks to go."

Mouse slaughtered a knight. "You think we should let her set us up?"

BenRabi glanced at Mouse's emotionless face, back to the disaster already developing on the chessboard. "I yield." The more he reflected, the more he was sure he knew what Marya was planning. He stood abruptly, scattering chessmen. "We may have to."

"Have to what?"

"Bend her. For our own good. I know what she's doing. We ignored the obvious. Suppose she has the same kind of tracer we did? They've got the technology. And suppose she has control and didn't turn it on till after the Seiners stopped worrying about things like that?"

"Got you. Let's not bend her. Let's just chop the tracer out." Mouse returned his chessmen to their box with loving care, then recovered a wicked homemade plastic knife from beneath his mattress. "Let's go."

BenRabi thought of a dozen reasons for putting it off, but could not articulate a one. It was time Marya was put out of the game. She was too dangerous.

They were halfway to her cabin when he stopped, struck by a sudden thought. "Mouse, what if she's expecting us?"

"Doesn't seem likely."

"You can't overlook anything in this business."

"That's true. Let me think a minute."

For months they had known that the Seiners sometimes listened in on them. When they did not want to be overheard they carefully lipread one another, never verbalizing anything that might excite an eavesdropper.

"I think I made a mistake bringing this up in your cabin."

"Yeah. Maybe. But it's too late to cry. If she bugged us, she bugged us."

"What're you going to do?"

"I'm thinking. I don't got a whole lot of use for Pyrrhic victories, you know."

They continued talking quietly, ten meters from Marya's door.

Three Seiners on a flying scooter squealed round a corner and skidded to a stop at Marya's door. They wore Security patches. One moved toward Mouse and benRabi, hand on his weapon, then stood easy. They tried to look like curious bystanders. The other Security men eyed the door.

"Looks like we get it done for us, Mouse."

"They're not thinking!" Mouse growled. BenRabi's heart pounded out a flamenco. These guys were too sure of themselves.

They overrode the door closure. A pair of explosions greeted them. One man fell in the doorway. The other flung himself inside.

The one facing Mouse and benRabi whirled, charged into the cabin too. His face had gone grey.

They heard grunts and a cry of pain. "Homemade gunpowder weapons!" benRabi gasped. "Nice welcome she had for us."

Mouse looked up and down the passageway. "Come on. Before we draw a crowd."

BenRabi did not know what Mouse planned, but he followed. Mouse went in the door low, scooping the weapon from the hand of the dying Seiner. BenRabi scrambled after him, seizing another fallen handgun.

The Sangaree woman had her back to the door. She was struggling with the last Security man. Her left hand darted past his
guard, smashing his windpipe. He gagged. She followed up with
a bone-breaking blow over his heart.

BenRabi's grunt of sympathy warned her of enemies to her
rear.

"Slowly," Mouse said as she started for the Seiner's weapon.
"I'd hate to shoot."

For once she had no instantaneous retort. Mouse's tone made
it clear there was nothing he would hate less than killing her.
Emotional pain twisted her face when she turned. Once again,
from her viewpoint, they had out-maneuvered her—and this
time might be fatal.

Her agony turned into a strained smile after a moment. "You're
too late." The smile broadened. It became anticipatory. "They're
on their way by now."

"Moyshe, get that man in here and close the door. How bad
is he?"

"He's gone."

"Better be nice," Marya said as benRabi forced the door shut.
She had the sense to keep her voice neutral. To survive, to enjoy
her victory, she had to overcome the obstacle she had made
of Mouse. "They'll be here soon. You won't want them mad at
you."

"This one's gone too," benRabi said. "The other one might make
it. Marya, don't think the Seiners will hand over a harvestfleet
because a few raidships turn up."

She smiled that gunmetal smile.

He remembered ruined merchantmen left in the wake of
Sangaree raiders. They would come with enough gunpower.
There would be no survivors.

An alarm began hooting. It was a forlorn call to arms.

"General quarters, Mouse. She's for real." The borrowed
weapon seemed to swell painfully in his hand. A part of him
was telling him it was time he finished what he had started on
The Broken Wings.

SIXTEEN: 3049 AD
Operation Dragon, Combat

Time telescoped, then coiled around itself like some mad snake trying to crush itself. It detached Marya's battlefield cabin from the macro-universe, establishing an independent timeline. Ten seconds became an eternal instant.

BenRabi was afraid.

Something clicked inside Mouse. He slipped into assassin's mind. BenRabi vacillated between answering the alarm and staying to restrain the organic killing machine.

Danion shivered. Moyshe recognized the feel of service ships launching.

"I'm going on station, Mouse. Keep her here till Jarl's people come. And keep her alive."

Mouse nodded mechanically. He was easily guided while in assassin's mind—if Psych had keyed him to accept your direction. He would be upset later. He wanted to show the woman the death of a thousand cuts, or something equally grisly.

He was on his way back to the real universe already. "Take the guns, Moyshe. Hide them."

"What about?…"

"This." He tapped the plastic knife thrust through a tool loop on his jumpsuit.

"All right." BenRabi collected the weapons. He hid them in Mouse's cabin, then headed for Damage Control South.

"What's up?" he asked one of his teammates when he arrived.

"Sangaree raidships. They say there's at least fifty of them. That's scary."

"In more ways than one."

"What do you mean?"

"That their show is being put on by a consortium. No one Family has that kind of muscle. The last time they put that many ships together was for the Helga's World thing during the Shadowline War."

The Seiner regarded benRabi with a puzzled fearful frown. Moyshe was talking foreign history.

Moyshe found his fellow landsmen in a low-grade panic. They had no faith in Seiner arms. And they were sure the Starfishers would fight. He did not understand till he heard the Seiners themselves second-guessing Payne.

Fleet Commander Payne had refused to negotiate or back down. He had told the Sangaree that he would fight to the last harvestship.

"What're we fighting *about?*" Moyshe asked plaintively.

His Seiner companions refused to enlighten him.

He felt that touch of panic himself. He never had wanted to die with his boots on. Not since he had given up boyhood daydreams. He had no interest in dying at all. Not for several thousand years.

Time moved with the haste of pouring treacle. He knew the Sangaree ships were maneuvering in the darkness outside. Outgunned service ships were moving to meet them. The death dance had begun.

Moyshe stood facing the dark gate with all the unanswerable questions still banging around in his mind. The nature of his want remained the biggest, closely followed by the meaning of the gun thing.

He started worrying about Amy. Where was she? Would she be safe? "Stupid question," he muttered. Of course she was not safe. Nobody was safe today.

Then he saw her standing at the tool crib. What was she doing here? She spotted him, started his way.

"Where's Mouse?" she asked.

He explained quickly.

"Good," she said when he finished. She tried to remain cool, but a tear formed in the corner of one eye. She brushed at it irritably. She had caught some of the groundside uninvolvement disease from him, he thought. Why else would a Seiner hide her emotions? Three men had died. It was a sad affair.

She said, "I'll call Jarl. He may not have sent anyone else down."

Moyshe resumed his seat, stared at the deck tensely, counting rivets and welds. When would the Sangaree missiles arrive?

The attack, when it came, was not Sangaree. The dull-witted sharks, confused and distressed by the sudden appearance of so many more ships, reached emotional critical mass. They attacked in all directions.

Scraps of news filtered in from Operations Sector. Some were good, some bad. The Sangaree were having a hard time. But the sharks attacking the harvestfleet were concentrating on *Danion.*

In the sea of nothing the service ships were killing, and sometimes being killed by, sharks. The Sangaree vainly fought an enemy invisible to their equipment while, foolishly, continuing to try for a position of vantage against the harvestfleet. There was a wan hope in that, Moyshe thought. The sharks might take care of them. But, then, who would take care of the sharks?

Danion shivered continuously. All her weaponry was in action, firing on Sangaree and sharks alike. BenRabi grimaced as he wondered just what the monster ship mounted.

He waited with his team in the heart of the great mobile, he smelling their fear and they his. Amy quivered like a frightened rabbit in the crook of his arm. Alarms screamed each time the sharks penetrated the defenses, but D.C. South received no emergency calls.

Courage brewed beneath the fear. There was no tension between landsman and Seiner now. They were united in defiance of an unprejudiced death.

Danion rocked. Sirens raked their wicked nails over a million blackboards. Officers shouted into the confusion. A damage-control team piled aboard an electric truck and hurtled off to aid technicians in the stricken sector. Behind them the mood gradually turned grim as the fear, unable to sustain itself indefinitely, faded into a lower key, an abiding dread. Each technician sat quietly alone with his or her thoughts.

The damage reports began arriving. Nearly ten percent of *Danion*'s population were either dead or cut off from the main life-support systems. More trucks left. Survivors had to be brought out before the emergency systems failed.

And there Moyshe sat, doing nothing, awaiting his dying turn.

Somewhere in the big nothing the Sangaree raidmaster decided he had had enough. His fleet took hyper, bequeathing the Starfishers his share of ghostly foes.

"Suits," said the blank-faced Fisher directing D.C. ops when the news arrived. He foresaw the end.

They drew spacesuits from the emergency lockers. BenRabi donned his while thinking that this was the first time he had worn one seriously. Always before it had been for training or fun.

He wondered why Mouse had not yet shown. Was he in the sector cut off? He asked Amy.

"No. There's no damage there yet. Jarl probably hasn't had a chance to do anything. Our people should all be manning weapons."

Danion screamed, whirled beneath them. Moyshe fell. His suit servos hummed and forced him to his feet. The gravity misbehaved. He floated into the air, then came down hard. The lights weakened, died, returned as emergency power entered the lines.

A shark had hit *Danion*'s main power and drives.

Somebody was yelling at him. Amy. "What?" He was too upset to listen closely, heard only that his team was going out. He jumped at the truck as it started rolling. Seiner hands dragged him aboard.

Twenty minutes later, in an odd part of the ship devoted to fusion plant, his team captain set him to securing broken piping systems. Whole passageways had been ripped apart. Gaps opened on the night. Sometimes he saw it, starless, as he worked, but thought nothing of it. He was too busy.

Hours later, when the pipes no longer bled and he had time for sloth, he noticed a vacuum-ruined corpse tangled in a mass of wiring, dark against an outer glow. That gave him pause. Space. It was what he was not supposed to see, so of course he had to look. He walked to the hole, saw nothing. He pushed the corpse aside, leaned out. Still nothing. No stars, no constellations, no Milky Way. Nothing but a tangle of harvestship limned by a sourceless glow.

He stood there, frozen in disbelief, for he knew not how long. No stars. Where were they that there were no stars?

The harvestship rotated slowly. Something gradually appeared beyond tubing, spars, and folded silver sails—the source of the glow. He recognized it, but did not want to believe it. It was the galaxy, edge on, seen from beyond its rim. His premonitions returned to haunt him. What, outside the galaxy, was near enough to be reached by ship?

Far away, another harvestship coruscated under shark attack. *Danion* had shuddered to several while he worked, but none had been bad. There was an explosion aboard the other vessel. Gases spewed from her broken hull. But his eyes fled her, hurrying on to the coin-sized brightness rising in the direction of rotation.

It was a planet. Self-illuminating, no sun. There was only one such place...

Stars' End.

Certain destruction for all who went near.

What were the Seiners doing? Were they mad? Suicidal?

Something broke, something blossomed across the face of the galaxy, a hundred times brighter, a fire like that of an exploding star. A harvestship was burning in a flame only a multidimensional shark could have ignited. They were growing more cunning, were spraying antimatter gases that totally devoured. In a corner of his mind a little voice asked, as a Fisher would, if that vessel's death had served the fleet. Were sharks dying there too?

His gaze returned to Stars' End. All his myths were hemming him in. He did not doubt that the Sangaree would return. It was not their style to back down when the stakes were high, and there was more on the line now than a source of ambergris.

He knew why the Seiners had come here. As did all who sought Stars' End, they wanted the fortress world's fabulous weapons. For centuries opportunists had tried to master the planet. Whoever possessed its timeless might became dictator to The Arm. No modern defense could withstand the power of Stars' End weaponry. Nor could sharks. The weapons were the salvation for which Payne had dared hope.

What a faint hope! BenRabi knew there was no way to penetrate the planet's defenses. Battle fleets had failed.

A hand touched his shoulder. A helmet met his. A voice came by conduction. "We're pulling out. *Danion*'s been hit inboard of us. We don't want to get trapped here." In those words Moyshe imagined great sadness, but little of the fear he felt himself.

They managed to reach D.C. South again only by trekking several kilometers afoot through regions of ship that looked like they had been mauled by naval weaponry. Moyshe found it hard to believe that the wrecking had been done by a creature he could not see.

A room had been prepared for them to relax in, with snacks and drinks, and secure enough so they dared shed their suits.

Mouse was there, wounded and bleeding.

"Mouse! What the hell!..."

"I should've bent her straight off, Moyshe. She got to me. Tricked me. Now she's into it somewhere."

It was a big and confused ship. She could disappear easily. "How?" Moyshe examined Mouse's left arm. It was angled. Mouse had gotten a tourniquet on somehow.

"Thing like a hatchet." Mouse's face was drawn and bloodless, but he did not protest benRabi's rough hands.

"She must've caught you napping. That don't sound like you."

"Yeah. We were playing chess..."

"Chess? For Christ's sake..."

"She's pretty good. For a woman. Nailed me when I was moving in for a mate."

BenRabi shook his head. "Are you for real?"

He could picture it. An overconfident Mouse suggesting a game to kill time, getting too deep into alternate moves to react quickly. Stupid, but in character. "How many times have I told you it was going to get you into trouble someday?"

"God damn, Moyshe, don't mother me. Not now. Do something about the arm, eh? Nobody around here is interested. I could lose it. And these clowns don't do regeneration surgery."

"Amy? Where's Amy Coleridge?" benRabi asked. He found her. "You seen Mouse? He needs a doctor bad."

"I saw him come in. There's one on the way. The woman?"

"Yeah." What was Marya doing now?

This was the price of not having let Mouse have his way on The Broken Wings. On his hands was the blood of a friend; in his mind a nagging gunmetal smile. Whatever feeling he might have had for her, or she for him, they were of enemy tribes. That was the overriding rule. In the end, neither could give quarter.

"I'll take care of it, Mouse," he whispered to his friend. "You keep Amy busy." He rose. "Keep an eye on him, will you, love? I'll be back in a couple minutes."

She asked no questions, probably assuming he was off to the toilet.

From the tool crib he drew an old Takadi Model VI laser cutting torch. It was a light-duty one-handed tool meant for sheet metal trimming. The crib attendant asked no questions.

He slipped out of D.C. and into an empty office nearby. It took just minutes to make the modifications he had been taught in a Bureau school. He created an unwieldy lasegun. Then he stole a scooter and took off.

He had tried to think like the woman while modifying the torch. He presumed that she would not know the attacks were shark and not her own people's. She would do something to neutralize the ship without damaging it. Her specialty dealt with atmosphere…

She would head for Central Blowers. She could take out Operations if she could cut its oxygen supply.

He hurtled through passageways, impatiently trying to remember the way to the blower rooms. Fate seemed determined to stall him. Damage compelled long detours. He had to wait on emergency traffic. People kept stopping him to tell him to get a suit on. The scooter, low on power, slowed to a crawl. He had to walk a kilometer before he found another unattended.

But he eventually reached his destination and instantly knew that he had guessed right. Dead men guarded the closed blower room door from within. Their weapons, if they had been armed, were gone. Moyshe glanced at the thing in his hand. Would it work?

The blower room was vast. It served only *Danion*'s core, but still was a wild jungle of massed machinery and ducting. A lot of air needed moving and scrubbing…

She was in there somewhere, trying to kill them.

Half an hour departed with antelope fleetness. He wandered among the brobdingnagian machines and found nothing. *Danion* kept shivering but the battle had become so old that it no longer caught his attention. An overpowering fatalism had set in now, a feeling that he was completely powerless in the greater situation.

But, damn! it was a long skirmish.

Weariness preoccupied him. He had been through twenty hard, emotionally draining hours.

He finally located the huge ring of consoles from which *Danion*'s core oxygen levels and humidities were controlled.

He crawled, he climbed, he attained himself a perch on a high catwalk from which most of the controls were visible. He saw only empty seats where a dozen technicians should have been stationed. Corpses lolled lifelessly in two more. A body lay like a broken doll on the aluminum grate decking.

She had been here. What was she doing now?

The question answered itself. She appeared as if spontaneously generated, moving among the boards, selecting cutoffs.

BenRabi aimed his makeshift weapons.

"Marya… Maria…" Her names ripped themselves from him against his will. She had been closer to him, in some hidden part of him, than he had realized.

Her head jerked up, turning, startled. Her eyes were narrow and searching. That mocking smile exploded across her face. "Moyshe. What are you doing here?" She hunted him with jerkily moving eyes, her hand hovering near a holstered, captured weapon. She was afraid. And she wanted to shoot.

"You're trying to kill us," he croaked.

What a stupid thing to say. Of course she was. Why was he waiting? *Pull the trigger, pull the trigger*, he screamed at himself.

He had done it a million times in imagination. All those images of the gun... *Go! Go!*

He couldn't. It was real this time. It was not some insane, inexplicable daydream oozing from the nether pits of his mind. Had the gun thing ever had anything to do with real weapons?

She stepped over a dead Seiner. "Moyshe, how can you say that? Not you. You'd be repatriated."

Repatriated to Hell, maybe. Her lie was a kilometer tall. After The Broken Wings and von Drachau's raid? She was going to have his guts on her breakfast toast if he did not do something.

She crossed his aim repeatedly, but he just could not end it. It had seemed so easy when he had been angry. It was easy for Mouse... wasn't it? Sweat beaded on his forehead as he tried to force his trigger.

His aim fell.

The movement gave him away. Her smile gave way to clashing-sabers laughter. Her weapon leapt into her hand. Her hand rose.

He reacted. Her shot reddened metal where he had crouched. But he was moving, across an open space. His finger was frozen no more, though he fired wild, scoring a section of console. He dove into the shelter of a huge machine. Disinterested, it went on grumbling to itself. Like a lot of people, it would do nothing till it was hurt, and then it would just sit there and scream.

Her shouts mocked him. He did not catch her words, but they did not matter. She was taunting him, trying to get him to give himself away again. Beams licked here and there, probing his cover, making metal run like tongues of candlewax.

He was scared. He had swum too deep this time. He had taken the dive he had feared since his assignment to Beckhart.

In an instant of insane gallows humor he told himself that death would certainly end his psychological woes.

But both he and the woman were too confident of his inability, his uncertainty, his lack of commitment. Something within him cracked. Something hatched from an egg of darkness lying in his deeps. He suddenly knew that there was something he could believe in, something worth fighting for. It had been trying to break through from the beginning.

He grinned, then laughed at the ludicrous irony of life. His Grail. He had found it here on the marches of Hell, as he was about to die. This ship, these Seiner people...

In marveling stupidity, he stepped into the open. The woman was so startled she hesitated. He did not. He shot first. His hand was steady, his aim flawless. Just as they had taught him.

The madness of the moment faded. He felt as empty as he had on the day he had entered the Blake City spaceport. Had he found anything after all? Or had his gun-need just thrown up a light-show of justification?

He was standing over her when Kindervoort's people arrived. He did not know how long he had been there. The battle had died away while he waited. And he had reversed all the switches she had thrown, though he did not remember doing so. Operations was getting its desperately needed oxygen.

He was crying when they found him. He had wondered about that for a long time. Mouse sometimes shed tears afterward, as if the new corpse were that of a favorite brother. He supposed Mouse spent his stored emotion then, while it was safe, while no one could grab a handle on his soul.

Someone pried the torch from his bent rod fingers.

"Moyshe?" Amy asked. "Are you all right?"

He seized her, held her. She was a warm fire in a cold, dark, and lonely cavern. She let him cling for a second, then pulled away, retaining a grip on his arm. She seemed a little distant, a little frightened. And who wouldn't be, after what he had done? "Come on. You've got to talk to Jarl."

He nodded. Yes. Kindervoort would want to know all about it. Old Doctor Deathshead would poke and prod and try to pry open the lid of his soul. Even on a battle day Kindervoort would want to keep an eye on the blood of his ship. That was all people were to *Danion*. The harvestship was the real living thing here. The folks inside were just specialized cells.

He let Amy lead him away, but looked back at Marya as he went. They were taking pictures and nattering into recorders. Medics were piling bodies onto stretchers. Techs were weeping over the damaged console and impatiently trying to cajole readouts on atmospheric quality... But he had eyes only for Marya.

Marya. She was dead now. He could ease up and let her be more than just "the Sangaree woman."

He did not know why or how, but he must have loved her in some odd, psychotic way. Or maybe he was in love with the death she had symbolized. But, now that she was lying there, sprawled inelegantly, brokenly, he felt a little freer. And a little sadder.

Kindervoort's office was hectic. People came and went hastily, crowding its outer reaches. The chaos was probably typical of every office aboard, Moyshe thought. There would be plenty of work for everyone.

Kindervoort pushed through the crowd. "Moyshe. Amy. Come on in the office." He broke trail. Settling behind his desk, he said, "Thank God for this lull. I was in-suit for eleven hours. The damned things drive me crazy. Give me claustrophobia. You all right now, Moyshe? You look a little pale."

BenRabi sat with his elbows on his knees, staring into infinity. He shrugged.

"For a long time you had me worried, Moyshe," Kindervoort said. "You seemed so solitary, so introspective, so ineffectual. Not exactly up to advance billing. I don't know what I expected Beckhart's top man to be, but you weren't it. Not till today. Then you acted when you had to. Intuitively, quickly, correctly, efficiently. The way I was told to expect. And in character. All on your own. Except maybe you told Mouse?"

Kindervoort had steepled his fingers in front of his mouth. He seemed to be thinking out loud. "Now tell me what happened. An unedited version."

Moyshe started talking. It helped. He began at the beginning and told the whole story, presuming Jarl had enough details to catch any major deletions. He tried to be objective.

Kindervoort nodded, occasionally doodled, once made a call for corroboration. He asked Moyshe to go over several things twice. It was a brief and gentle holiday compared to a Bureau debriefing. He had Amy call to make sure Mouse was getting medical attention.

BenRabi left out nothing but the hiding of the weapons.

When he concluded, Kindervoort asked, "Did today change anything for you? You ready to cross over now?"

Moyshe considered it. Hard. He wanted to be part of what he had found here. But he could not. Not on Kindervoort's terms. "No, Jarl. I can't."

Amy was disappointed. He expected her to be. The signs were unmistakable. She had plans. Bells and white satin, a regular Archaicist extravaganza.

"Why'd you go after Gonzalez, then? We would've gotten her eventually. Maybe too late to have saved Ops, though," he conceded.

BenRabi could not bring himself to answer truthfully. Landsmen did not avenge friends. They had no friends to avenge. And he did not want them to know that a prime rule of the Bureau was that you let no blow against one of its people slide. "That's why. It meant my neck too." Briefly, he sketched what had happened on The Broken Wings.

"I wish you'd done it for us... If you change your mind... I really want you on my team, Moyshe."

"Not on your terms."

Kindervoort looked perplexed. He started to say something, but was interrupted by a comm buzzer. He pressed a button, said, "Kindervoort, Security." He stared at Moyshe, frowning.

"LeClare, Contact," a tiny voice said. "You got a landsman named... let's see... benRabi, Moyshe benRabi, down there?"

"Right. He's here with me now."

"Good. Been trying to track him down all over. He the one with the headaches?"

"The same."

"Has he been Warner tested, do you know?"

"No. He's landside."

"But he's a marginal?"

"I'd guess a strong full. Looks to me like repeated and intense spontaneous contact reaction."

Moyshe began to feel like a sample on a microscope slide.

"Good. I'm sending a man to pick him up. Priority Alpha. The Old Man's okay. The paperwork will come down later. Off."

"Off," Kindervoort said, puzzled. He leaned back, studied Moyshe speculatively, finally said, "Well. Things change. Desperate times, I guess. I just hope they know what they're doing. Moyshe, when you're finished in Contact I want you to get plenty of rest. Amy, see that he does. Then report back here."

Moyshe looked from one to the other. Both seemed shaken, disturbed.

What the hell was going on? That comm exchange made no sense at all, but it had gotten these two as antsy as a cat in heat. What was a Warner test? Why were his migraines so important? He studied Amy. His thoughts drifted back to the attack he had suffered after being switched on. She had become as nervous then.

He had tried a dozen times to discover why she thought his migraines important. She would not tell him.

They were important to *him*, heaven knew. They had become one of the central features of his life. He had had scores since coming aboard. So many that he had become conditioned to recognize the slightest warning symptom. He gulped his medication instantly.

For a while, though, he had not been bothered much. Till *Danion* had come here. He had been eating the pills like candy the past few days, at regular intervals, not waiting for symptoms to begin. What did it mean?

"Well," Jarl said, "I've got a ton of work. Have to sort things out, count the bodies, inform the next of kin. Amy, turn him over to Contact, then get some sleep. This break probably won't last."

She took benRabi's hand, guided him to the door. Why was she so quiet? Because of Marya?

As he was about to close the door behind him, Kindervoort called, "Moyshe? Thanks."

SEVENTEEN: 3049 AD
Operation Dragon, Mindteching

The man who came for Moyshe, when he arrived meteorically on a fast orange scooter, wore a jumper of a style Moyshe had never before seen. It was black, trimmed with silver, instead of being the off-white of the technical groups. It was an Operations group uniform.

The man looked and smelled as if he had not changed for a week.

"Trying to find a man name of…" He checked a card. "BenRabi. Moyshe benRabi. What kind of name is that?"

"A literary allusion," Amy replied. "This's him here."

"Right. Teddy Larkin, Contact Support. Who're you?" He was brusque. And tired. He appeared to be on the verge of collapse. Moyshe felt sympathetic. He was on his last legs himself.

"Amaranthina Amaryllis Isolte Galadriel de Coleridge y Gutierez. Security," she snapped.

"Oh. All right, let's go, benRabi." He headed for his scooter.

Moyshe did not move. He was fighting his temper. Larkin's rudeness might be excused, intellectually, because he was tired, but emotionally Moyshe could not let it slide. He had the feeling that Larkin was this way all the time.

Larkin reached his vehicle, noticed that Moyshe was not tagging along dutifully. "Come on, grub. Get your ass…"

BenRabi was there. And Teddy was yon, seated on hard steel deck plating wondering what had hit him.

There was no forgiving his remark. "Grub" was the Seiner's ultimate epithet for landsmen. BenRabi moved in. He was ready to bounce Larkin all over the passageway.

Amy's touch stopped him. "Go gentle, you ape," she snarled at Larkin. "Or yours will be the second big mouth he's shut today."

Larkin took it as a wisecrack, started toward Moyshe.

BenRabi bounced him off the bulkhead and floor a couple of times.

"I meant what I said," Amy told Larkin. Her badge was showing now, literally. "How was your air supply this afternoon?"

"Eh?" Larkin's eyes widened. His face grew pale.

"Yeah. You see what I mean," Amy told him.

Moyshe slowly relaxed. "Have the covers turned down when I get home, Love," he said, blowing a kiss. He did it to irritate Larkin. Would you want your sister to marry one? "I'm going to sleep for a week." He settled himself on the scooter's passenger seat. "Ready when you are, Teddy."

He had to hang on for his life. The scooter seemed designed for racing. Its driver was a madman who did not know how to let up on the go-pedal.

"What's the hurry?"

"I get to get me some sleep when I deliver you."

A big airtight door closed behind them the instant they entered Operations Sector. Sealed in, Moyshe thought. An instant of panic flashed by. Nervous, he studied his surroundings. Ops seemed quieter, more remote, less frenzied than his home sector. It looked less touched by battle. There was no confusion. People seemed more aloof, more calm, less harried. He supposed they had to be. They had to think *Danion* past defeat. The fighting may have stopped, but it was not finished.

Larkin braked to a frightening, squealing stop that almost threw Moyshe off the scooter. Larkin led him into a large room filled with complex electronics. "Contact," Larkin muttered by way of explanation.

The battle had reached this place. Acrid smoke hung thick here. It still curled up from one instrument bank. Ozone underlay the stench. Casualties awaiting ambulances rested along one wall. There were at least a dozen stretchers there. But the hull had remained sound. There were no suits in evidence.

Larkin led Moyshe to the oldest man he had yet seen aboard *Danion*. "BenRabi," he said, and instantly disappeared.

Moyshe examined his surroundings while waiting for the old man to acknowledge his presence. The vast room looked like a crossbreed of ship's bridge and lighter passenger compartment. The walls were banked with data processing equipment, consoles, and screens whose displays he could not fathom. Seiners in black, seated shoulder to shoulder, manipulated, observed, and muttered into tiny mikes. The wide floor of the room was occupied by corn-rows of couches on which more Seiners lay, their heads enveloped in huge plastic helmets which twinkled with little telltale lights. Beside each couch stood a motionless pair of Seiners. One studied the helmet lights, the other a small, blockish machine which looked uncomfortably like a diagnostic computer. A constant pavane of repairmen moved among the couches, apparently examining the empties for defects.

BenRabi finally spied something familiar. It was a spatial display globe that lurked blackly in a far corner. Centered in it were ten golden footballs apparently representing harvestships. He supposed the quick, darting golden needles represented service ships. They were maneuvering against scarlet things which vaguely resembled Terran sharks. The tiny golden dragons at the far periphery, then, should represent distant starfish. Stars' End would be the deeper darkness biting a chunk from the display's side. He saw nothing that could be interpreted as Sangaree. He hoped they would stay gone, though it was not their style and he did not expect it.

"Mr. benRabi?" the old man said.

"Why dragons?"

"Image from our minds. You'll see."

"I don't understand."

Instead of responding, the old man plunged into a prepared speech. "Nobody explained this to you, did they? Well, our drives are dead, except for minddrive. The sharks can't kill that till they get to us here, or till we stop getting power from the fish. But we're in trouble, Mr. benRabi. We do have minddrive, but the sharks mindburned most of my techs." He indicated the nearest stretcher. A girl barely out of creche smiled in vacant madness. "I've lost so many I'm out of standbys. I'm drafting marginal sensitives from the crew. You're subject to migraine, aren't you?"

Moyshe nodded, confused. Here they came with the headaches again.

He had suspected for several months now... But the implications were too staggering. He did not want to believe. The psi business had been discredited.

Maybe if he remembered that hard enough this man and place would go away.

"We want you to go into rapport with a fish."

"No!" Panic smote him. He did not entirely understand his response.

A niggling little demon named Loyalty, to whom he seldom listened, urged him to surrender for the sake of information. Beckhart would reward him with a shovel full of medals.

He thought of sudden, terrible headaches, and of frightening, haunting dreams. He recalled his fear that he had made involuntary contact with the starfish. "I couldn't."

"Why not?"

"I don't know how."

"You don't need to. The techs will put you in. The fish will do all the work. All you do is serve as a channel."

"But I'm tired. I've been up for..."

"Tell me a story. So has everybody else." He gestured impatiently. A couple of technicians, hovering nearby, approached. "Clara, put Mr. benRabi in Number Forty-three." Both techs nodded. "There's nothing to be afraid of, Mr. benRabi."

Moyshe wanted to protest being pushed around, but lacked the will. The technicians pressed him into a couch. He surrendered. Undoubtedly he had been through worse.

The technician whom the old man had called Clara reminded him of the professional mother of his childhood. She was grey-haired, cherry-faced, and chattered soothingly while strapping his arms to those of the couch. She placed his fingers on grip-switches before she started on his legs.

Her partner was a dark-haired, quiet youth who efficiently prepared Moyshe's head for the helmet. He began by rubbing Moyshe's scalp with an unscented paste, then he covered benRabi's short hair with a thing like a fine wire hairnet. Moyshe's skin protested a thousand little tingles that quickly faded.

I'm taking this too passively, he thought. "Why are you strapping me down?" he demanded.

"So you can't hurt yourself."

"What?"

"Take it easy. There's nothing to be afraid of. It's just a precaution," the woman replied. She smiled gently.

Damn, he thought. *Better be two shovels full of medals.*

"Lift your head, please," the younger Seiner said. Moyshe did. The helmet devoured his head. He was blind.

His fear redoubled. A green ogre with dirty claws shoved nasty hands into his guts, grabbed, yanked. His heart began playing a theme for battle drums. Words came echoing through his mind, Czyzewski's, from his poem "The Old God": "… who sang the darkful deep, and dragons in the sky." Had Czyzewski had starfish in mind?

Moyshe felt his body growing wet with fear-sweat. Maybe the contact wouldn't work. Maybe his mind wouldn't be invaded. That had to be the root of his terror. He did not want anything looking inside his head, where the madness lay behind the most fragile of barriers.

It had taken him all year to get it under control… Guns, dragons, headaches, improbable, obsessive memories of Alyce, continuous instability… He did not dare go under. His balance was too delicate.

Guns! Did the image of the gun have anything to do with the Stars' End weaponry? Was it some twisted symbol his mind had created for a part of the mission that Psych had not wanted him to remember?

Somewhere, a voice. "We're ready, Mr. benRabi." The old woman. It was an ancient trick for calming a man. It worked, a little. "Please depress your right side switch one click."

He did. He lost all sensation. He floated. He saw, smelled, felt nothing. He was alone with his tortured mind.

"That's not bad, is it?" She used the voice of the professional mother this time. His cunning, frightened mind made it that of the woman of his youth. He remembered how she had comforted him when he had been afraid.

"When you're ready, depress your right switch another click, then release it. To withdraw you have to pull *up* on your left switch."

His hand seemed to act on its own. Down went the switch.

The dreams he had been having returned: space swimming, the galaxy wrong in color, Stars' End strangely misty yet bright. Things moved around him. He remembered the situation tank. This was like being bodiless at the heart of the display. The service ships were glimmering needles, the harvestships glowing tangles of wire. The sharks were reddish torpedoes in the direction of the galaxy. Far away, the starfish looked like golden Chinese dragons. They were drifting toward him.

Moyshe's fear faded as though a hand had erased it from the blackboard of his mind. Only an all-encompassing wonder remained.

Gently, warm, friendly as a loving mother, a voice trickled into his mind. "I do it. Starfish, Chub." There was a wind-chimes tinkle of something like laughter. "Watch. I show me."

A small dragon rose from the approaching herd, did a ponderous forward roll. Shortly, "Oh, my! Old Ones don't like. Dangerous. This no time for fun. But we winning, new man-friend. Sharks afraid, confused. Too many man-ship. Running now, some. Many destroyed. Big feast for scavenger things."

The creature's joy was infectious, and Moyshe supposed he had cause—if the sharks were indeed abandoning herd and harvestfleet.

Funny. His conscious mind was not questioning, just accepting.

His fear remained, down deep, but the night creature held it at bay, infecting him with its own excitement. When did the power thing start? he wondered. It had already, the starfish told him. He did not feel anything other than this creature Chub exploring the ways of his mind like a kid on holiday exploring a resort hotel.

"Shark battle won, mind battle won," the starfish said after a while, when Moyshe finally had himself under control. "But another fight coming, Moyshe man-friend. Bad one, maybe."

"What?" And he realized, for the first time, that he really was talking with his mind.

"Ships-that-kill, evil ones, return."

"Sangaree. How do you know?"

"No way to show, tell. Is. They come, hyper now. Your people prepare."

BenRabi did not want to be out here during combat. He felt exposed, easy prey. Panic began to well up.

The starfish's control did not slacken. He soon forgot the danger, became engrossed in the wonders around him, the rippling movements of retreating sharks, the ponderous approach of dragons, the maneuvers of the shimmering service ships as their weary crews prepared for another battle. The galaxy hung over everything like a ragged tear in the night, vast in its extension. How much more magnificent would it be if it could be seen without the interference of the dust that obscured the packed suns at its core? Nearby, Stars' End waited, a quiet but furious god of war as yet unconcerned with the goings-on around it. Moyshe hoped no one aroused its wrath.

"Coming now," his dragon told him. Spots appeared against the galaxy as Sangaree raidships dropped hyper. Down in his backbrain, behind his ears, Moyshe felt a gentle tickle. "More power," Chub told him.

The raidships radiated from their drop zone in lines, like the tentacles of a squid. They soon formed a bowl with its open side facing the harvestfleet. It was an obvious preliminary to englobement.

The distant, decimated shark packs milled uncertainly. They withdrew a little farther. They were not yet wholly defeated.

A ball of light flared among the Sangaree. A lucky mine had scored. But it made little difference. The power and numbers remained theirs.

Only a handful of service ships remained combat-worthy. Even the halest of the harvestships had lost some main power and drive capacity to shark attack. Minddrive and auxiliary power were insufficient for high-stress combat maneuvering.

BenRabi sensed something changing. He cast about, finally saw the great silver sails that had been taken in before the earlier fighting spreading between *Danion*'s arms and spars. The ship looked so ragged, so injured, so vulnerable... A blizzard of debris drifted about her, held by her minuscule natural gravity.

The Sangaree maneuvered closer but held off attacking.

"Trying to talk First Man-friend into surrender," Chub to ben-Rabi. "Creatures of ships-that-kill want herd without fight."

"Payne won't give up," he thought back.

"Is true, Moyshe man-friend."

The starfish drifted closer. They were almost upon the Sangaree. They meant to join the battle this time, though cautiously. Their enemies still watched from afar, looking for another chance to savage fleet and herd.

"Fight soon, Moyshe man-friend."

The slow, stately dance of enmity ended. The negotiations had broken down. The Sangaree struck fast and hard, firing on the service ships to show their determination. The service ships dodged. Suddenly, there were missiles everywhere, streaking around like hurrying wasps. Beam fire from the harvestships wove gorgeous patterns of death.

And Moyshe became depressed. He had done his Navy fleet time. He could see the untippable balance written in the patterns. There was no hope of victory.

Chub chuckled into his consciousness. "You see only part of pattern, Moyshe man-friend."

In the far distance a starfish crept close to a raidship. The vessel's weapons could destroy the dragon in an instant—but the ship stopped attacking. It simply drifted, a lifeless machine.

"We do mind thing," Moyshe heard. "Like Stars' End, with much power. We stop ships-that-kill like human eyeblink, so fast, if no guns, no drive field to fear."

A second raidship fell silent, then a third and a fourth. Moyshe felt less pessimistic. The raidships would be locked into an overcommand directed by a master computer aboard the raidmaster's vessel. That master computer would be burning up its superconductors trying to adjust fire fields to accommodate the losses. If it became the least hesitant, the least unsure of its options...

A too-cautious starfish burped a ball of gut-fire. The micro-sun rolled through space sedately, devoured another raidship.

"Bad, Moyshe man-friend. Old Ones angry. Will give away unsuspected attack."

The Sangaree hemisphere closed steadily. Its diameter rapidly dwindled. The harvestships threw everything they had, fire heavier than anything benRabi had ever witnessed, yet were barely able to neutralize the incoming. Offensive capacity seemed to have been lost.

The starfish mindburned another raidship, and proved Chub and the Old Ones right. The fireball had given them away. Moyshe felt the deep sadness of his dragon as one of the herd perished beneath Sangaree guns.

The starfish threw a barrage of fireballs before beating a hasty retreat. Sangaree missiles broke up most of them.

The globe closed around the harvestfleet. It tightened like a squeezing fist. A desperate ship's commander, piloting a three-quarters dead service ship, knocked a small hole in the globe by ramming a raidship and blowing his drives.

"They'll know they were in a fight," Moyshe thought. There was no response from Chub.

The Sangaree stepped up the attack. Their ships began piling up toward Stars' End. Moyshe suddenly intuited their strategy. "They're going to push us into the sharks!"

Again there was no response from his dragon, unless it were that wind-chime tinkle he caught on the extreme edge of his sensitivity.

The Sangaree seemed to have managed some equipment adjustments during their absence. They appeared to have no trouble detecting the sharks now. And, since detecting the starfish attack, they were having no trouble keeping the dragons at bay.

Chub returned to his mind suddenly. "It works well, Moyshe man-friend. Be patient. Will have little time to chat. Is hard to think thoughts in commanders of ships-that-kill, and in machines-that-think. Sangaree minds twisted. Different than man-minds." The dragon faded away.

What was this? he asked himself. Were the fish trying to control the Sangaree?

The raidships massed thickly, then pushed hard. The sharks grew agitated, as if dimly aware that they were about to be drawn into the inferno. The starfish began drifting their way, as if to cover the fleet's retreat.

"Be ready, Moyshe man-friend!" It was a sudden bellow, and all the warning he received.

The trickle in the root of his brain suddenly became a flaming torrent. It hurt! God, did it hurt! Searing, the power boiled through him, into whatever *Danion* used to control and convert it, and out to the silvery sails. Moyshe followed the flow for an instant, then became lost in an ocean of pain.

The harvestship began moving *toward* the massed raidships, all weapons firing, not aiming, simply trying to erect an irresistible wall of destruction. The compacted Sangaree were unable to bring all their firepower to bear. They wavered, wavered.

A raidship blew up. It left a momentary hole in the fire pattern. Another vessel began to come apart.

Service ships were doing the same. One harvestship ceased firing. Her auxiliary power was exhausted. Sangaree missiles began picking her apart.

BenRabi felt that infinite sadness again.

The enemy drifted backward, not really retreating, just being pushed inexorably. It could not last, but the harvestfleet's ferocity, for the moment, was greater than the raidfleet's.

Afar, the starfish suddenly struck at the sharks, who scattered in dismay. The strike was pure bluff on the dragons' part. A determined shark attack would have destroyed the herd in minutes.

Something screamed across benRabi's mind, a mad voice babbling, shrieking fear and incoherencies. Its power was such that it inundated his pain. He made no sense of the mind-touch, other than warning and terror.

Phantoms, grotesqueries from the most insane medieval imagination, gathered in space around him. Things that might have been gargoyles and gorgons, Boschian nightmares writhing, all fangs and talons and fire, became more real than the battleships. Every one of them shrieked the message, "Go away or die!"

I've gone completely insane, he thought. *My mind has snapped under contact pressure. They can't be real.* He screamed.

Then the warm feeling came, soothing, gently calming his terror, pushing the madness away. His dragon told him, "We succeed, Moyshe man-friend. Maybe win." Then, darkly, "Monsters are Stars' End sending. Fear and visions are Stars' End mind-thing. Planet machine is mad. Mad machine uses madness weapons. Soon, other weapons.

"Look, Moyshe man-friend!"

Shielded by Chub's touch, Moyshe turned his attention to a Stars' End grown huge with their approach. The Sangaree were silhouetted against the glowing planetary disk. The face of the world had become diseased behind them. It was spotted blackly in a hundred thousand places.

The disk was receding. The harvestfleet was on the run, scattering as fast as it could. Moyshe suspected that, had any been able, the harvestships would have gone hyper. That could not be accomplished on minddrive.

The Sangaree could not jump out while locked into their master battle-computer. Breaking lock and getting up influence took time.

Two thousand kilometers closer to the fortress world's weapons, they were trying. With the desperation of the condemned they were breaking lock, scattering, throwing out defensive missiles, trying to get up influence.

They did not have time. The mad world's weapons reached them first.

"Close mind!" Chub shrieked. "Get out! Not need power now. Save mind!"

How? He couldn't remember. It became another nightmare, of the sort where all efforts to elude pursuit were vain.

Feeling returned to his left hand. Another hand rested upon it, pulling upward. The reality of the Contact Room returned.

He could feel his helmet, the couch beneath him—and a tremendous sense of loss. He missed his dragon already, and in missing Chub he understood Starfishers a little better. Maybe the contact was one reason they stayed so far from the worlds of men. The fish-Fisher thing was a unique experiential frontier.

Perhaps only one in a thousand Fishers would ever experience contact, but that one could share the vision with his blind brethren... He had suffered a range of emotions out there. Only one thing had been missing while Chub was in his mind. The ordinary, everyday insecurity which so shaped human life.

He was drowning in his own sweat. And he was shivering cold, as if his body temperature had dropped while he was linked. The room surrounding him was silent. Where were his technicians? Was he alone? No. Someone had helped him get out.

The thoughts, reflections, fears flashed by in scant seconds. Then:

His head exploded in a thundering migraine, the most sudden and terrible of his experience. It obliterated all conscious control and thought. He screamed. He fought the straps that held him, the helmet that stole his vision. He became pure trapped animal.

Danion shuddered, staggered, staggered. Vaguely, through the agony, he heard screams. Loose objects rattled around. Gravity surged and faded. Mind monsters momentarily broke through the pain, taunting him with visions of Hell.

The Stars' End weapons had found the Sangaree. The fringes of their fury had brushed the harvestfleet like the cold breeze of the passing wings of death. And he was pinned here, helpless, in agony.

Slowly, slowly, the breeze faded. The screams died with it—all but his own. Excited chatter surrounded him. He could distinguish no words. His head was tearing itself apart. Once, when he was a kid, it had been almost this bad. He had nearly killed himself smashing his head against a wall.

Someone finally noticed him. His helmet came off. A needle stung his arm. The pain began fading.

The room was nearly dark, so weak were the lights. Gravity had been reduced to half normal. *Danion* was rationing power.

The faces crossing his field of vision seemed unconcerned with *Danion*'s condition. They were exuberant. There was laughter.

Little jokes flew.

"We've won!" motherly Clara told him. "Stars' End killed them."

Not all, Moyshe thought, though he said nothing. One or two had made hyper in time.

The Seiners had just moved up the Sangaree vendetta list, perhaps surpassing Jupp von Drachau.

"But we lost four harvestships," the younger half of his tech team told him. "Four harvestships." He was having a hard time believing that.

It was a victory day, all right, but one which left the Seiners little to celebrate.

Blessed darkness enfolded Moyshe. He fell into the blissful sleep of the needle, a sleep untroubled by fearful dreams.

EIGHTEEN: 3049 AD
Operation Dragon, the Change

He ignored the shoulder-shaking as long as he could. Finally, sleep-slurred, he muttered, "Wha'd'ya wan'?"

"Get up, Moyshe. Time to go to woik. There's a million things to do."

So. Amy, he thought. Altogether too businesslike for a girl who thought she should be a wife. He opened an eye, checked the time.

"Five hours? What the hell kind of rest is that?" he grumbled. "How the hell did I get here? I was in Contact."

"It's been eleven hours. The clock's unplugged. To save power. They brought you down on a stretcher. I thought you'd been mind-burned…" She threw herself on top of him, clinging with desperation. "Moyshe, I was so scared…"

"All right. All right. I survived," he grumbled. He still was not accustomed to the Seiner habit of showing emotion.

She reached under the sheet, tickled him. "Come on, Grump. There're things to do."

He threw his arms around her and rolled her over, his mouth seeking hers.

"Moyshe!"

He smothered her protest with a kiss. "It's been a week, lady."

"I know. But…"

"But me no buts, woman. The hump-backed crocodiles of entropy are gnawing at the underbellies of our allotted spans. I'm not going to waste an opportunity on tinkering with a piece of pipe."

"Moyshe! What kind of talk is that?"

"Shut up."

"Yes, Boss."

They dressed hurriedly afterward. Amy decided on a fresh coverall.

"Now, what's the hurry?" Moyshe demanded.

"You've got to get back to work. Moyshe… We really are desperate this time. We're in a decaying orbit around Stars' End. The mindsails went in the spillover from whatever killed the Sangaree. We'll hit the boundary in two days unless we get the drives working."

"Boundary?"

"Limit of approach. Stars' End starts shooting if a ship passes it."

"I wondered why we're alive."

"Only the Sangaree violated it. The machine is very literal. Anyway. We're due on shift in three hours, and Jarl needs you to take some tests first."

"Can't they wait?"

"He said today."

"Might as well. I'm awake now. Where's Mouse?"

"Hospital block. He's doing okay."

Hospital block was fifteen kilometers away. Maybe more if there were detours. Moyshe knew he had to move fast. "We'll go there first."

"Why?"

"To see Mouse."

"But the tests!"

"Damn the tests. I want to see Mouse. You coming?"

"Not anymore. Hey! Wait!"

They ran to a scooter, laughingly fought for the controls. Moyshe made a point of winning. He did not trust her to take him where he wanted to go.

He whipped down the passageway, scattering cursing pedestrians. The wind in his face exhilarated him—till he remembered what had happened. Memories of what he had done kept him quiet till he reached the hospital block.

Bluff and bluster got him past nurses who believed they were running a monastery.

They wandered the ward where Mouse was supposed to be confined, unable to find him.

Feminine laughter suddenly rippled through the passageway. "What do you think?" Moyshe asked.

"Wouldn't bet against it," Amy replied. Her good cheer had not faded.

Moyshe followed the laughter to a small private room where he found Mouse making friends with his nurse. BenRabi began to wonder why he had come. It did not look as if Mouse needed him. Then he understood. He had not come for any good, businesslike reason. He just wanted to see how Mouse was. And that was silly. Landsmen did not behave that way.

Mouse was fine, needless to say.

"What're you doing in here?" Moyshe asked, embarrassed because he was interrupting. "There's work to do."

Mouse grinned, winked. "Moyshe, everybody gets a vacation. Besides, I had to meet Vickie here. Darling, say hello to my friend Moyshe."

"Hello to my friend Moyshe."

"Isn't she something? Been trying to find out if those long lean legs are as fine as they promise to be. Those work outfits just don't do a thing for a woman."

"How are you, Mouse?" benRabi asked.

"Like the man said before they closed the coffin, as well as can be expected under the circumstances." He whipped his top sheet back. His arm and shoulder were heavily bandaged and in a partial cast. "They'll have me back on light duty in a couple of days. Unless I can blow in that dainty ear there and get somebody to keep me here."

Vickie giggled.

"Well, good. I just wanted to check. Sorry I interrupted. Behave."

"Don't I always?" Mouse chuckled. "Hey, Moyshe, go by my cabin and make sure nobody's run off with the silverware."

"All right."

"See you in a couple days."

"Yeah." BenRabi withdrew, Amy on his heels. "Damn!" he told her. "I feel silly."

"What? Why?"

He shook his head. He could not explain. Not to her. A Seiner would never understand what he meant when he said he and Mouse had passed a point of no return and become genuine friends. Amy did not have the background to comprehend what that could mean to a landsman.

She was worried. "Thinking about what Jarl is going to say when we show up late?" he asked.

"Uhm." She remained thoughtful as they stalked the sterile white corridors.

"What're the tests for?"

"I don't know. Just some tests."

He caught a whiff of untruth. He was not supposed to learn their purpose. He always hated that kind of test, though people were always taking them back home: IQ, emotional stability, prejudicial index, social responsiveness, survival index, environmental response, flexibility, adaptability, the government's euphemistically labeled Random Sample Report...

Bureau agents suffered bombardment with them during briefing and debriefing. They even had a test to test one's resistance to testing. His was strong. He did not like having people look inside him. He did too damned much of that himself.

"Wouldn't be the famous Warner test, would it?"

She did not respond. He tried a couple of different tacks, could not get a rise out of her, so gave up.

They had to make a detour returning to the scooter. Their planned path was blocked with casualties just in from one of the dead harvestships.

"It's bad, Moyshe," Amy said looking down that long hallway of stretchers. "They've been bringing people in since the shooting stopped. They may never get them all out of the wrecks. They're falling in toward Stars' End too."

"Where are they going to put them? We'll end up having to sleep standing up."

"We'll find something."

"Reminds me of my senior year midshipman cruise," he said. "There were war scares that summer too. The Shadowline War and the Sangaree. And somebody had found a McGraw world. The fleet was tied up. Academy contracted our shipboard astrogation training to private carriers."

Memories. That had been the summer he had ended it with Alyce...

"Tell me about it."

"Eh? Why?"

"Because I don't know anything about you. You never talk about yourself. I want to know who you are."

"Well, I got the worst billet on the list. Some people didn't like me. It was a raggedy-ass Freehauler on the Rim Run from Tregorgarth to The Big Rock Candy Mountain to Blackworld, then Carson's, Sierra, and The Broken Wings. Broomstick all the way, with crazy passengers. The Freehaulers carry some real weirdos. Between The Broken Wings and Carson's, coming back, we got jumped by McGraws. My first taste of action."

After he had been silent a few seconds, she asked, "What happened?"

"It was a complete surprise. McGraws don't usually bother Freehaulers, but Navy was pushing them hard and we were carrying weapons for Gneaus Storm..." Why was he telling her this? It was none of her business. Still... Talking kept his mind off the upcoming tests.

"Go on, Moyshe."

He did not doubt that details of the incident were in Kindervoort's files.

"Tinker's Dam—that was the ship—had a cranky drive. Just a hair out of synch. The Freehaulers couldn't afford to tune it till after the run. So the McGraws couldn't phase in and pull us into normspace. They tried putting a warning shot across our nose. The drive did one of its tricks, phased in with theirs, and dragged us both into the explosion. The McGraw was destroyed. Tinker's Dam was hurt pretty bad, but we kept one section airtight. I was trapped there with this crazy family from some First Expansion world. They hated everybody, and Old Earthers and aliens especially. And it was up to me and a Ulantonid radioman to find out where we were and call for help. Took three weeks to rig a transmitter, and three more months before anybody caught our signal. It was miserable. There I was, nineteen years old, scared to death, and all that on me... Hey! Where are we?"

Chagrined, Amy replied, "I was listening. I guess we took a wrong turn. We'll have to go back."

Back they went till she found a passage that would take them in the right direction. It led through a women's intensive-care ward. The casualties were out where the harried nurses could examine them at a glance. There were at least three hundred women crammed into a ward meant for fifty. "It's really bad, isn't it?"

"They're moving the walking wounded into the residential blocks."

Moyshe stopped suddenly, stricken. The face of the final patient, confined to a burn tank, was one he had not expected to see again. "Marya!"

She was alive, and inside her tank, amid the jungle of tubes, she was aware. She met his gaze, tried to communicate her hatred. Her I.V. monitor fed her a little nembutol.

"Moyshe? What's the matter?"

He pointed.

"You didn't know?"

"No. I thought she was dead."

"She would have died if we hadn't gotten her here so quick."

"But..."

"You used the torch from too far away."

"I see."

She dropped the subject, realizing he wanted done with it.

He should have realized that Marya would not go easily.

Did she have a partner? The answer was critical. His life might depend on it.

And if he survived here, Marya would come after him landside. He was winning the battles, but the war remained in doubt.

He did not look forward to their next encounter.

"What's the rush, suddenly?" Amy asked. He was almost running.

Kindervoort was not pleased with his being late, but he shuffled Moyshe into a testing room without remonstrance. "This's benRabi."

Psych types took over. Moyshe suffered through the old parade of idiot questions. Since childhood he had been trying to beat them with random answers—which was why his test sessions always lasted so long. The computers needed a big sample to pin him down.

When the psychs were done they turned him over to regular medical types who gave him a thorough physical. They were in love with his head. He told the life story of his migraine three times, and endured dozens of shallow and area skull scans.

They also wanted to know all about his instel implant.

He developed a sudden muteness. Bureau activities were beyond discussion.

Just when he was about to scream they turned him loose. The chief examiner apologized profusely for taking so long. There was not a hint of sincerity in his tone. Both he and Moyshe knew the time factor was Moyshe's fault.

Moyshe was told to get a good night's rest before going back to work.

He hoped they had not learned anything, but suspected that they had. Profile tests were hard to beat.

Time slipped away quickly, almost as swiftly as it did in the mad, hectic culture groundside. Moyshe returned to Damage Control. His working hours were gruesome.

Somehow, they got the drives functioning and pushed *Danion* into a stable orbit. Then the real work began. Everyone not engaged in rescue work, or in keeping the ship alive, began preparing her for a hyper fly to the Yards.

Moyshe's work was less demanding than he expected. *Danion* had suffered more damage to personnel than to plant, had been hurt more by shark attack than by Sangaree fire.

He heard rumors claiming half the harvestship's people had perished, or had been made as good as dead by mindburn. His acquaintances had been lucky. He knew no one who had been a victim. But every day, in the course of work, he encountered new faces, and missed a lot of old ones.

Every time he wakened Moyshe was amazed to find himself still alive. The battle of Stars' End was over and won, but winning had left the harvestfleet on the brink of disaster. New problems arose as fast as old ones were conquered.

And the sharks had not given up. They stalked the fleet and herd still, their numbers growing daily. In a week, or a month, they would strike again.

The fleet was in a race against time. It had to make the Yards before the sharks reached critical...

Time fled swiftly when sudden death lurked behind the veil of time, and every day passing brought Moyshe closer to an hour he dreaded, the moment when he would have to return to Carson's and his old life.

He did not want to leave.

The *I want* had not sipped at the blood of his soul since the battle, nor had he had visions of imaginary guns. He seemed to have undergone a spontaneous remission of his mental diseases. In that way the weeks were close to tranquil. His problems became more direct and personal.

He had found what he needed, a combination of things to do with belonging: a woman, a useful occupation, and a place in a society that considered him something more than a bundle of statistics to be manipulated. He could not yet quite understand what had happened, or why, but he knew he belonged here. Even if he was not yet wholly accepted.

This was what he had been seeking when he had abandoned Old Earth. Navy had given him some of it, but not enough. This was the real thing.

He had come home.

But how could he stay? There were prior demands on his loyalties. He simply could not accept Kindervoort's terms. He could not betray the Bureau.

Should he see Jarl and try to arrange something?... He vacillated. He swung this way and that. He decided and changed his mind a hundred times a day.

What about Mouse? What would he think? What would he

do and say?

And all the while, like a recording mechanism, he kept making his notes for the Bureau. Sometimes he worried about getting them off the ship, but that did not much matter. Writing them down fixed them in his backbrain, from which the Psychs could dredge them with narcohypnosis.

Assuming he went home.

Assuming he wanted them recovered. He had not wanted this mission back when, and wanted it even less now. By carrying it out he might destroy something that had become dear.

He was in a proper mood for concluding *Jerusalem*. And he had found just the quote for summation:

> *The world was all revenge and thou hadst said:*
> *"It is a seething sea!" Earth had no room*
> *For walking, air was ambushed by the spears,*
> *The stars began to fray, and time and earth*
> *Washed hands in mischief...*
> —*Firdausi* (Abul Kasim Mansur)

All *Jerusalem*'s characters had perished while trying to seize their hearts' desires. *Farewell, old companions*, he thought.

So much for that. It had been a pretentious trial of modern literature anyway. He did not like the thing anymore. Only his suicidal mood had let him finish quickly, rather than with the intimate detail he had planned originally. Sometimes he felt so like his own creations, denied anything but a deadly end...

Ten days remained on his contract when he received the second summons from Contact. Jarl Kindervoort relayed it personally.

"I'd really rather not do any more mindteching, Jarl," he said. "I'm not trained for it, and I'm perfectly happy where I'm at."

"I'd rather you didn't myself." Kindervoort seemed caught in a baffled daze. "You know too goddamned much already. But orders are orders, and these came from the top."

A chill breeze swept Moyshe's cabin. He knew too much... Would they let him go? If they did... Kindervoort was capable of arranging a deep-space accident that would silence the returning landsmen.

Would Jarl's superiors authorize an incident? Starfishers were feisty, but did not go out of their way to provoke Confederation.

"What's going on, Jarl?"

"I don't know. And I don't like it. They've shut me out. They want you reassigned to Contact. That's all I know. I'm just a messenger boy. Grab yourself a scooter and go. Here's your pass."

"But I don't want to…"

"You're still under contract. You agreed to perform whatever duties were assigned."

"Damn. All right. Right now?"

"Right now."

Moyshe reached Contact a half hour later. He found the same old man in charge. "You'll be working with Hans and Clara again, Mr. benRabi. Strictly basic contact exercises. I don't know which fish your rapport will be. They decide that for themselves."

"Why am I here? There's no point in this. I'm leaving the end of next week."

The man acted deaf. "You'll probably link with several fish during the coming week. They like to get different perspectives on a mind before they decide on a permanent partner. Hans. Clara. Mr. benRabi is here. Go ahead with the basic program."

"Now wait a goddamned minute…"

The old man walked away, pursuing a black-uniformed electrician whose repair work did not please him.

"Good morning, Moyshe," Clara said. "Good to have you back. How have you been?"

And the youth, Hans, said, "We'll be your regular support team. They've given us Number Fifty-one…"

"Who the hell does that guy think he is? When I speak to somebody I expect them to answer."

"Take it easy," Hans suggested. "He does that to everybody. You'll get used to him."

"He's a dreadful boss," Clara said. "Just dreadful. But we won't have him much longer. They're booting him upstairs. Why don't you show Moyshe our station, Hans. I'll get us all some coffee."

"What do *you* think is going on?" benRabi asked Hans. He sat on the end of the Contact couch. "I've got no business being here."

Hans shrugged. "I haven't the faintest. They just told us you'd be our new mindtech, that we should start breaking you in. Clara thought you'd decided to stay. Didn't you?"

"What's that?" Clara asked.

"Say that Mr. benRabi decided to stay with *Danion*."

"Yes. Hasn't he?" She handed Moyshe a cup of coffee. "Black?"

"That's fine. No, I'm not staying."

"I don't understand." She seemed confused.

"Neither do I. I tried to tell them somebody screwed up. Nobody would listen. You know how things go. When their minds are made up..."

"I'd better check," Clara said. "There's no point going ahead if it's all a mixup."

"Do that."

She returned fifteen minutes later looking more puzzled than ever. "They said go ahead."

"Dammit, why?"

"I don't know, Moyshe. That's what they told me."

"It just doesn't make sense."

"Thought you were a soldier," Hans said. "Thought you were used to taking orders you didn't understand."

"I knew they made sense to the man who gave them..."

Hans smiled.

Made sense to the man who gave them. He barely heard Clara when she said, "We'd better get started. We're behind schedule."

So Beckhartism existed here too. He must have that look of the born pawn.

Try as he might, he could see no way the Seiners could profit from training him as a mindtech. Not if he was going back.

"Ready, Moyshe. Same drill as the other day. It shouldn't bother you this time. We won't be drawing power. Just go out and float. Try to open to the fish and get the feel."

Hans slipped the helmet over benRabi's head. Clara's voice came through, warm and gentle.

"Remember, one click down on the right for TSD, Moyshe.

Two for Contact. Up on the left to come back. Go when you're ready."

He pushed the right-hand switch without knowing why.

The womblike comfort of total sensory deprivation enveloped him. He let it take him, carrying off the aches and fears of reality. He ran through a mantra several times, trying to take his mind into the same nirvana his flesh occupied.

This was nice. A man could lower his guard here, could relax his vigil against the universe. Nothing could reach him...

Wrong. His hindbrain, the ancient brain that had crawled out of the sea of Old Earth a billion years ago, could not tolerate an extended absence of stimuli. It became claustrophobic.

"You're staying in TSD too long, Moyshe," Clara said from a thousand kilometers away. "That's not good for your mind."

He depressed the switch again.

Weirdly distorted and colored space formed around him.

He was falling toward a milky scar some cruel god had scratched on the face of darkness. Logic told him it was the galaxy, that it looked both solid and fuzzy because his brain was trying to translate something seen in hyper into conventionalized images.

What *was* he seeing? Tachyon scatter? Gravitation? The frenzied dance of the gluons that cement all matter? The scar was most intense toward the galactic core, which would have been concealed by dust clouds in norm space.

Long pink streaks, like the fire of ruby lasers, winked past him, arrowing to a point of convergence centered on the heart of the galaxy. A barrage of golden tracers skipped along inside the circle of pink lines. Sharks and starfish skipping along with the harvestfleet?

He extended his attention till he detected several egg-shapes of St. Elmo's fire, with cometary tails, that had to be harvestships in hyper transit. He searched, but could find no trace of Stars' End. The fortress world had been left behind. The Seiner gamble had failed. That episode had ended. Payne's Fleet was running for the Yards...

"Hello, Moyshe man-friend."

BenRabi felt a rush of elation as he recognized Chub. It became a feeling of, "I'm home! This is where I belong."

"You came back, Moyshe man-friend."

"Yes. I didn't think I would. You survived the battle. I'm glad." The starfish's mental fingers slithered into his mind, bringing comfort. He did not resist.

A feel of laughter accompanied, "Me too, Moyshe man-friend. You came to learn to be linker?"

"I guess."

"Good. I teach. Me, starfish Chub, best teacher ever. Make you best linker of all time. Show Old Ones. We begin. You study universe around, try to see, tell me what you see."

Moyshe did as he was told.

"No. No. See everything at once. Forget eyes. Forget senses of flesh entire, let universe soak in, be one. Forget self. Forget everything. Just be, like center of universe."

It was the prime lesson he had to learn, and the most difficult one for the beginning mindtech. He tried valiantly, hour after hour, but it was like forcing sleep. The more effort he invested, the more remote his goal became.

He heard a faint voice calling. "Moyshe? Moyshe? Time to come out now."

He did not want to go. This being outside, this being free, this made everything he had endured worthwhile. At Stars' End death had been leaning over his shoulder. Here, unthreatened, he found himself closer to heaven than anything else he could imagine. It was almost a religious experience, like a first space-walk EVA, or a first orgasm.

Reluctantly, he commanded his left hand to lift.

All the aches and pains of mortal flesh crept back into his consciousness, and for an instant he understood those people who sought the false nirvana promised by drugs and religion.

Something stung his arm as the helmet slid off his head.

"Just a precaution," Clara told him. "You shouldn't have much of a contact reaction, but we never know for sure."

The agonies of the flesh receded. His incipient migraine died unborn. "That was something," he said. "I didn't want to come back."

"You've got the true linker touch, then," Hans told him. "They never want to go and they never want to come back."

"Eat big and get a lot of sleep," Clara said. "Contact takes more out of you than you think."

He shared three more extended sessions with Chub, and they became solid friends—within the limits of two such alien backgrounds.

His fifth training link brought him in touch with a creature calling itself a Judge of the Old Ones. The Judge was nothing like Chub. It was completely and truly alien. It entered his mind as coldly as a serpent, digging, exploring, till he felt like a bug under a microscope. It made no effort to teach him, nor did it chat, nor conceal its task of determining if he was fit to link with starfish. Moyshe was glad to break that contact, real-world pains notwithstanding.

He went into contact with the Old Ones twice more, and each was as chill and phlegmatic as the Judge. These were the passionless creatures Czyzewski must have had in mind when he had penned "The Old God." Their minds were exactly what benRabi imagined a god's to be.

Then there were two glorious, rollicking, fun days with Chub, who had been appointed his "permanent" link. Irreverent, Chub made the most libelous observations about the Old Ones Moyshe had encountered. BenRabi countered by trying to teach the starfish the concept of humor.

And then it was over. The dream came to an end.

"Good-bye, Moyshe man-friend," Chub said, setting benRabi's mind to echoing sadness. "I will think of you often, stranger than any man-friend."

"I'll remember you, too, Chub," Moyshe promised. "Try to catch me when I reach out in my dreams." He ripped upward on his exit switch.

Clara and Hans thought he was in pain and tried to give him a second pain shot, but he pushed them away. He let the tears flow. Then he hugged Clara. "Good-bye." He took Hans's hand. "I'm going to miss you both."

They stood and watched as, slump-shouldered, he shuffled out of Contact for the last time.

NINETEEN: 3049 AD
The Homecoming

The days were gone. And with them most of the hours. He was down to his last few and still he had not contacted Kindervoort, still he had not found the courage to seize what he wanted. While he had slept *Danion* had dropped hyper preparatory to launching a service ship.

The starfish and sharks would be orbiting the remnants of the harvestfleet. Chub would be out there watching for the little steel needle that would take him away forever.

He lay in his bunk and remembered story time at the creche where he had lived as a small child. All those tales had had heroes who had never been indecisive, never been terribly afraid. But they had all come from a remote and probably unreal past.

There was little room for the self-assured Mouse types in this kaleidoscopic modern universe. Nowadays timidity was pro-survival.

He often wondered if Mouse was genuinely as cool as he appeared. He *had* to be bothered by something beside takeoffs and landings.

In two hours the service ship would leave for Carson's. What could he do? What *should* he do? He knew what he wanted, knew what Amy wanted, but still he teetered between the new commitment and the old. To betray Bureau secrets for personal gain, he felt, would constitute a self-betrayal.

It looked like he had picked up a bunch of new haunts to replace the ones he had conquered. The new ones at least made more sense.

His remaining time dwindled to an hour. His things were packed. He prowled his cabin like a beast caged, unable to remain still. And Amy sat on her bed, motionless, alternately sulking and subjecting him to verbal assaults. He had to get out, had to get away...

He went looking for his partner. Maybe Mouse could help. Paranoia had its merits.

They had seen little of one another after benRabi had begun mindtech training.

Mouse answered his door with pleased surprise. First thing he said was, "I was just going to look for you." His one hand was shaking. "Want to play a game while we're waiting?"

"All right." They could help each other. A game or two might relax them both.

"How's Amy taking it?"

"Like a trouper. A storm trooper." Mouse was awfully excited. His shakes were not always confined to his bad hand. Moyshe paid no attention. The usual pre-fly jitters, he thought.

"Did you hear what I found?" Mouse bubbled. "Been after it for years. I finally got it off one of our own people, a guy who carried it for luck." He displayed an ancient bronze coin with a hole in the middle. BenRabi judged it to be at least two thousand years old, Oriental, in good condition, but comparatively common. Certainly nothing special. Mouse's excitement began to puzzle him.

"Nice, I guess. Amy's really taking it worse than I expected." He glanced at the coin again, because Mouse kept shoving it in front of him. "You sure it isn't fake?"

"She'll get over it. They always do if you've loved them right. No, it's not fake." Mouse seemed disappointed about something. "You take white."

BenRabi tried to broach his problems over his almost ritualistic opening. "Mouse, I want to stay here."

Mouse looked at him strangely, as if with mixed emotions, as if he had been expecting this but hoping for something else. He fingered his coin nervously, replied. "Let's talk about it after the game. How about a drink? You look like you could stand to unwind."

A man about to undergo high acceleration and temporary weightlessness should not imbibe, but benRabi agreed. He needed something. Mouse went to a cabinet, got a bottle of something pre-mixed. While he hunted glasses, benRabi examined the cabin. Almost everything that was Mouse was gone, all the memorabilia that for a time had made the place his home. Everything but the ubiquitous chess set.

A glass broke. Mouse cursed, gathered the pieces, cursed again as he cut himself. "Why the hell aren't these things made out of plastic?"

"I wish you wouldn't use your bad hand." Then benRabi saw why he was. With his good hand Mouse was smearing something gooey over Security's bug. He then brought the drinks, resumed the game.

It was a slow one. Mouse was off his usual confident form. He had to study every move carefully. He kept fingering his coin as if he wanted to wear it out before boarding the service ship. BenRabi downed his drink, and several more, began to relax, to turn off the troubled part of his mind. He got involved in the game. For once he was holding his own. Mouse, despite his studiousness, remained remote, disturbed, and inattentive.

Mouse suddenly unleashed a series of rapid moves. BenRabi's queen went, and then, "Checkmate!"

The alcohol no longer helped. The defeat, so small a thing but so inevitable, suddenly became an analog of benRabi's whole life. His depression deepened.

A moment later, while fumbling the pieces into their box with his bad hand, Mouse said, "I kept this out so we could play on the way home. But now you say you want to stay."

"Yes. This is what I've been looking for…"

"I was afraid of that." Mouse turned. His fumbling had not been without purpose. His good hand clutched a Fisher weapon salvaged from Marya's cabin.

"You should've figured, Moyshe. You should've run to Kinder-voort." Mouse was playing the game to its end. "Wheels within wheels, you know. We're still working for Beckhart. I can't just leave you."

Maybe he had known, down deep, he thought. Maybe he had come here so Mouse could make his decision for him.

"Psych programed you to cross over. So you could get where I couldn't. They might even have known about Stars' End. That's what that gun thing makes me think of."

Moyshe glanced at the coin turning in Mouse's bad hand. Strange that he had never mentioned wanting one of that type. Maybe it was a hypnotic key. Maybe it had opened the full mission to Mouse's memory.

"It was meant long term from the beginning, Moyshe. We need ambergris for the fleet. All of it. For the war."

"War? What war? Nobody takes the Ulantonid rearmament business serious. You told me it was manure yourself."

Mouse shrugged. "You were a remote data-collector. One of my missions was to be your keeper. Most of the rest was window-dressing and obfuscation."

Though it was a club-footed effort, Mouse was trying to do more than just explain. He did not like what he was doing. He was trying to convince himself.

Yes. They had grown too close. Far too close. They cared.

"We're friends, Moyshe. So let's fly gentle, eh?"

Yes, gentle. As in chess, he was outskilled here. He was the half of the team trained and programed for the "soft" work. Mouse always handled the "hard." Friendship or no, Mouse would bend him if he did not cooperate. Mouse was the perfect agent. He let nothing stand in the way of getting his job done.

BenRabi searched his partner's face. He saw the pain there. *Maybe*, he thought, *Mouse doesn't want to go back either*. But Mouse's nature would leave him less choice... It would be stupid to push him. He tended to overreact under stress.

BenRabi's shoulders slumped. He surrendered. Back to being a chip in the stream.

A dread voice rang through *Danion*, godlike, calling all depart-ing landsmen to Departure Station for payoff and checkout.

Mouse pocketed his weapon, said, "Sorry, Moyshe."

"I understand." But he did not, not really.

Mouse nodded to the door. "Let's go."

They went. Moyshe gave him no trouble, even when the opportunity arose. He had given up completely.

No home at all, he thought. *Guess I'll never have one. I'll just go on being a chip in a universe like those Sierran flood rivers. I'm back where I started.*

He stared at the lock that would open on the service ship. One long step through and he would come out in the terminal on Carson's. How much would things have changed during their absence? Greta would have grown...

Greta. "Mouse, I forgot to get something for Greta. I've been gone a whole damned year... I got to bring her something."

"Mr. benRabi?" A man pushed through the crowd, some of benRabi's belongings in hand. "You left some of your things."

Moyshe recognized him. He was one of Kindervoort's people. Had they found his notes? "Mike, do I have time to get a souvenir for my daughter?"

Still talking about Moyshe's forgetfulness, Mike stepped between benRabi and Mouse. Landsmen milled around them, talking excitedly of home, rushing to the paymaster when their names were called. BenRabi paid no attention. He was fascinated by the sudden despair on Mouse's face.

"The weapon, please?" Mike said.

Several men surrounded them now. Kindervoort himself was approaching, having just left a nearby office.

Mouse surrendered the gun meekly, consternation becoming a weak smile.

"Told Beckhart it wouldn't work," he said loudly. "But he never listens to the man in the field..."

There was a stir. Shouts. Screams. Mouse hit benRabi with a flying tackle. Mike grunted, twisted, came down atop them, an expression of incredible surprise fixed on the unburned half of his face. The shouting redoubled. People tried to run. A handgun flashed again. Security men tried to reach the source of fire.

"Wheels within wheels," Mouse said into benRabi's ear, his voice coldly calm. Kindervoort, kneeling beside them, looked at him questioningly. "This was mine," Mouse told him. "I figured he'd have a fail-safer in."

Fail-safer. That was a trade name for a man hyped and programed to do everybody in if a mission went bust. Fail-safers seldom knew what they were. Usually they were innocents dragged in off a street somewhere and run through the Psych mill. Even after assassinating agents about to defect or to be captured they seldom knew what they had done, why, or for whom.

BenRabi had never considered himself, Mouse, and this mission that critical.

"Sorry, Moyshe. I didn't think I should tell you. Made it look better, you believing."

Is he telling the truth? Moyshe wondered. *Or is he playing the ends against the middle? Is he just bending with the breeze, hoping to keep his skin?*

"We had to spot him before we could cross over, and this was the only place to do it. It's too late for him now. He can't hunt us down." Mouse shrugged, then smiled. So did benRabi.

He chose to believe. He did not want to stay here alone.

That was why he had had so much trouble deciding. Amy was not enough. Chub was not enough. The Seiner culture itself was insufficient. He had needed that one extra, Mouse, his heartline to the past.

Kindervoort's men returned. "You get him?" Mouse asked.

"Somebody did. He was dead when we got there. Looks like a nerve poison."

Kindervoort regarded them oddly, appraisingly. "Fail-safer for a fail-safer? Your Admiral is bizarre, but I've never heard of that before."

Unusual? Moyshe thought. *It's unprecedented. It doesn't make sense.* But what the hell? It was over now. He was home free.

Home, after all, and with a good woman— Amy was running toward him, through the crowd, pale with worry—and a friend. Life, it seemed, had finally taken a happy turn.

"Are you ready now?" Amy asked anxiously, after having made sure he was unharmed.

"Ready? For what?"

"To cross over, stupid. Are you, darling?" She seemed afraid his stiff-neckedness would persist.

It did. "Seems like I don't have much choice. But I won't talk."

"Talk?" Kindervoort asked. "What do you mean? About what?"

"About the Bureau. About its policies, its goals, its mission, things I might know that you'd want to know. I won't tell you. The man who was Commander Thomas Aquinas McClennon is dead. Everything he knew died with him. Don't try to call him back from the grave."

"That's what's been bothering you?" Kindervoort asked. "Moyshe, Moyshe, why didn't you say so? I wondered what the hell was stopping you. It was so obvious you wanted to come over. There never have been any conditions. Never. I'm sorry you got that impression. Hell, anything I want to know you don't—otherwise Beckhart never would have risked you."

BenRabi considered. It made some sense. But there were things he could tell... The hell with it. He would take the chance. He put an arm around Amy, pulled her close to him. "Thanks, Jarl. Mouse. Oh. Say, Jarl. Is there time for me to get a real Starfisher souvenir for my daughter?"

"Daughter?" Kindervoort and Amy said together.

"What daughter?" Amy demanded. "You said you weren't ever married."

"I wasn't. She's not really my daughter. A girl I met on Old Earth. I sponsored her. That's sort of like adopting a kid... She doesn't know where I'm at or what I'm doing or anything."

"Find something quick," Kindervoort said. "The service ship is going to space in twenty minutes."

"Hey, Moyshe," Mouse said. "Throw this in." He offered the coin with the hole in the center. "Tell her to mail it to the Admiral."

"A little personal message, eh?"

"You might say."

"Come on, Amy. Give me an idea."

"How come you never told me about this girl? What's her name anyway?"

Mouse watched them go, smiling wanly. That was not going to be a classic love match. But it did not have to be. It only had to last a few months more.

His mission was complete. But a Bureau man did not leave his comrades behind. And a Storm never abandoned a friend.

GLEN COOK

THE BESTSELLING AUTHOR OF *THE BLACK COMPANY*
DELIVERS CLASSIC NOVEL OF MILLITARY SF

"ONE OF THE BEST EVOCATIONS OF
LIFE IN CLOSE QUARTERS ONBOARD A
SPACESHIP... THE DAS BOOT OF SF."
— JEFF VANDERMEER, *SF SITE*

PASSAGE
AT ARMS

ISBN 978-1-59780-119-5, Mass Market Paperback; $7.99

The ongoing war between Humanity and the Ulant is a battle of attrition that humanity is unfortunately losing. However, humans have the advantage of trans-hyperdrive technology, which allows their Climber fleet, under very narrow and strenuous conditions, to pass through space almost undetectable. *Passage at Arms* tells the intimate, detailed, and harrowing story of a Climber crew and its captain during a critical juncture of the war. Cook combines speculative technology with a canny and realistic portrait of men at war and the stresses they face in combat. *Passage at Arms* is (or should be!) one of the classic novels of military science fiction.

Jacket illustration by John Berkey.

Night Shade Books Is an Independent Publisher of Quality SF, Fantasy and Horror

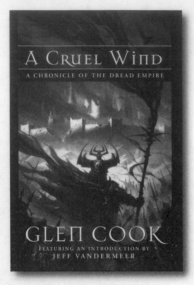

ISBN 978-1-59780-104-1
Trade Paperback; $16.95

Before The Black Company... before The Garrett Files... Before The Instrumentalities of the Night... There was The Dread Empire. Glen Cook's first foray in fantasy world-building was the enormously influential Dread Empire series. This series has been incredibly hard to find, and has never had a hardcover release, until now. Night Shade Books is proud to publish three omnibus volumes that cover the three main sub-series of the Dread Empire, with a fourth volume of Dread Empire short fiction to follow.

The first volume in the series, *A Cruel Wind,* collects the first three Dread Empire novels: *A Shadow of All Night Falling, October's Baby,* and *All Darkness Met,* and contains an introduction by Jeff VanderMeer.

The second volume in the series, *A Fortress in Shadow,* collects the two volumes that make up the prequel series to The Dread Empire. *The Fire in His Hands* and *With Mercy Toward None* were written and published after the first three books, but the war in the east chronicled herein precede the events in *A Cruel Wind.* This second volume features an introduction by Steven Erikson

Cover illustration by Raymond Swanland.

ISBN 978-1-59780-100-3
Trade Paperback; $15.95

Find these Night Shade titles and many others online at http://www.nightshadebooks.com or wherever books are sold.

Night Shade Books Is an Independent Publisher of Quality SF, Fantasy and Horror

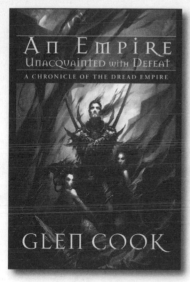

ISBN 978-1-59780-188-1
Trade Paperback; $14.95

The third volume in the Dread Empire series, *An Empire Unacquainted with Defeat*, collects all of Glen Cook's short fiction set in the vast world of the Dread Empire, from "The Nights of Dreadful Silence," featuring the first appearance of Bragi Ragnarson, Mocker, and Haroun bin Yousif, to the culture-clashing novella "Soldier of an Empire Unacquainted with Defeat"; from "Silverheels," Cook's first published work of fiction, to "Hell's Forge," a haunting tale of cursed pirates and strange lands, appearing here for the first time.

ISBN 978-1-59780-150-8
Trade Paperback $14.95

Lost and alone in the woods, hounded by the Dead Captains, Gathrid takes refuge in a vast cavern. There he discovers an ancient sword—Daubendiek, the Great Sword of Suchara, the fabled weapon once wielded by the legendary tragic hero of an ancient age, Tureck Aarant. Daubendiek, a restless and thirsty blade, promises Gathrid the ability to claim his vengeance. But as he begins to take that vengeance, Gathrid starts to understand the terrible price that the sword will exact of him. Enemies soon become allies and strange bedfellows abound as the prophesies of an age swirl into chaos.

Find these Night Shade titles and many others online at http://www.nightshadebooks.com or wherever books are sold.

Night Shade Books Is an Independent Publisher of Quality SF, Fantasy and Horror

ISBN 978-1-59780-062-4
Trade Paperback $14.95

Years ago, the last desperate hopes of Earth were crushed as corporate Orbital blocs ruling from on high devastated the planet's face. Today, the autocratic Orbitals indulge in decadent luxury far above the mudboys, dirtgirls, zonedancers, and buttonheads who live out violent lives of electronic distraction and dependence amid the flooded, ruined cities and teeming slums of a balkanized America.

But there are heroes: those who would stand against the hegemony of the Orbital powers. From Walter Jon Williams comes *Hardwired*, the hard-hitting, seminal classic that feels as prescient today as when it was first published. Like a steel-guitar-fueled *Damnation Alley*, as directed by Sam Peckinpah, *Hardwired* demonstrates how Williams's singular vision helped define the cyberpunk genre.

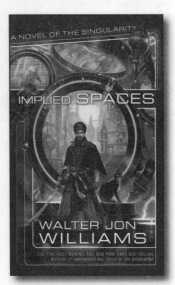

ISBN 978-1-59780-151-5
Mass Market Paperback; $7.99

Aristide, a semi-retired computer scientist turned swordsman, is a scholar of the implied spaces, seeking meaning amid the accidents of architecture in a universe where reality itself has been sculpted and designed by superhuman machine intelligence. While exploring the pre-technological world Midgarth, one of four dozen pocket universes created within a series of vast, orbital matrioshka computer arrays, Aristide uncovers a fiendish plot threatening to set off a nightmare scenario, perhaps even bringing about the ultimate Existential Crisis: the end of civilization itself.

Find these Night Shade titles and many others online at http://www.nightshadebooks.com or wherever books are sold.

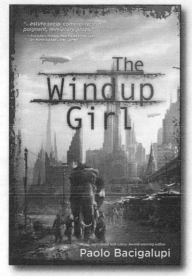

Night Shade Books Is an Independent Publisher of Quality SF, Fantasy and Horror

ISBN 978-1-59780-174-4
Trade Hardcover; $24.95

Nasim Golestani, a young Iranian scientist living in exile in the United States, hopes to work on the Human Connectome Project—which aims to construct a detailed map of the wiring of the human brain. When government funding for the project is cancelled and a chance comes for Nasim to return to her homeland, she chooses to head back to Iran. Fifteen years later, Nasim is in charge of the virtual world known as Zendegi, used by millions of people for entertainment and business. When Zendegi comes under threat from powerful competitors, Nasim draws on her old skills, and data from the now-completed Human Connectome Project, to embark on a program to create more lifelike virtual characters and give the company an unbeatable edge ...but Zendegi is about to become a battlefield.

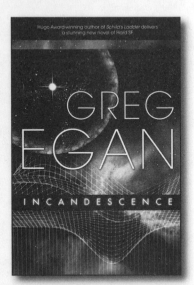

ISBN 978-1-59780-129-4
Trade Paperback; $14.95

Are you a child of DNA?

Composed of innumerable beings from a wide variety of races, human and otherwise, the vast meta-civilization known as the Amalgam spans nearly the entire galaxy—except for the bright, hot center. There dwell the Aloof, silent residents of the galactic core, who for millions of years have deflected all attempts at communication and contact. But when Rakesh encounters a traveler who claims to have been contacted by the Aloof and shown a meteor bearing traces of DNA, he cannot turn down the opportunity to explore uncharted space in search of a lost world.

Find these Night Shade titles and many others online at http://www.nightshadebooks.com or wherever books are sold.

Night Shade Books Is an Independent Publisher of Quality SF, Fantasy and Horror

An eclipse is a rare and unusual event, when the world is transformed and the sky becomes a dark, eldritch thing. It's a time when anything could happen, when any kind of story just might be true…

In the spirit of classic science fiction anthologies such as *Universe, Orbit,* and *Starlight,* master anthologist Jonathan Strahan (*The Best Science Fiction and Fantasy of the Year Volume One, Two,* and *Three*) presents the non-themed genre anthology *Eclipse: New Science Fiction and Fantasy.* Here you will find stories where strange and wonderful things happen—where reality is eclipsed by something magical and new.

With stories from the likes of Andy Duncan, Garth Nix, Peter S. Beagle, Maureen F. McHugh, Jeffrey Ford, Terry Dowling, Eileen Gunn, Gwyneth Jones, Ysabeau Wilce, Kathleen Ann Goonan, Margo Lanagan, Ellen Klages, Bruce Sterling, Karl Schroeder, Stephen Baxter, Ken Scholes, Paul Cornell, Nancy Kress, Daryl Gregory, Ted Chiang, David Moles, Richard Parks, Tony Daniel, Alastair Reynolds, Karen Joy Fowler, Pat Cadigan, Nnedi Okorafor, Elizabeth Bear, Nicola Griffith, Daniel Abraham, Paul Di Filippo, Jane Yolen, Adam Stemple, Molly Gloss, Caitlín R. Kiernan, and Ellen Kushner, shouldn't *Eclipse: New Science Fiction and Fantasy* deserve a marked spot on your reading calendar?

Find these Night Shade titles and many others online at http://www.nightshadebooks.com or wherever books are sold.

Glen Cook is the author of dozens of novels of fantasy and science fiction, including *The Black Company*, *The Garret Files*, Instrumentalities of the Night, and the Dread Empire series. Cook was born in 1944 in New York City. He attended the Clarion Writers' Workshop in 1970, where he met his wife, Carol. "Unlike most writers, I have not had strange jobs like chicken plucking and swamping out health bars. Only full-time employer I've ever had is General Motors." He currently makes his home in St. Louis, Missouri.